SOMETHING FISHY

Enjoy the Book

Tom Schmitt

Something Fishy Copyright © 2019 Lois Schmitt

Hardcover ISBN 13: 978-1-64599-194-6
Paperback ISBN 13: 978-1-948338-79-0
E-book ISBN 13: 978-1-948338-80-6
Kindle ISBN 13: 978-1-948338-81-3

Editor: Cynthia Brackett-Vincent
Cover design by Christopher and Deirdre Wait
Cover illustrations © Getty Images

Published by:

Encircle Publications
PO Box 187
Farmington, ME 04938

info@encirclepub.com
http://encirclepub.com

SOMETHING FISHY

A Kristy Farrell Mystery

LOIS SCHMITT

Encircle Publications
Farmington, Maine, U.S.A.

CHAPTER ONE

"Something bad happened to Sam. I know it."

Katie Chandler's sea-green eyes filled with tears. A sea lion trainer at the Clam Cove Aquarium, Katie had been my daughter's college roommate.

"Maybe Sam worked late and forgot to call," I said.

Katie shook her head, her chestnut hair flying in the bay breeze. "No. He hasn't answered my texts or phone calls. I stopped by his house this morning, too. No one's home."

Silence. I tried thinking of something helpful, or at least hopeful, to say.

"I called the police, Mrs. Farrell. The officer said being stood up for a dinner date isn't enough for a missing persons case—that maybe it was Sam's way of breaking up."

I shifted my gaze to the whitecaps on the bay while Katie's statement sank into my brain. Perhaps the officer was right. I knew from my daughter Abby that the relationship between Katie Chandler and Samuel Wong had hit a rough patch.

The conflict: Katie, who served as executor of her late grandmother's will, was donating six million dollars of this money to the aquarium's expansion project, which included the acquisition of twenty acres of adjacent land. I wasn't sure of the will's exact terms, but I remembered Katie had leeway in determining how much money to distribute among several charities, including the aquarium.

Meanwhile, Sam worked as legal counsel to multi-millionaire developer Lucien Moray, who wanted to buy the bay-front property for luxury condominiums. What started off as friendly bantering between

1

Katie and Sam had escalated into explosive arguments that had become increasingly personal.

But Katie and Sam weren't the only ones embroiled in this controversy. The community at large had become like the Hatfields and McCoys. Environmentalists wanted the property to go to the aquarium where it would be used for breeding grounds, a marine animal rehabilitation center, and a research camp for marine scientists. Local business owners sided with Moray, hoping high-end condo owners would bolster the area's economy, especially after summer tourist season. I was writing an article on this for *Animal Advocate Magazine*. That's why I was at the aquarium today.

Katie continued. "No matter what happened between us, Sam would never stand me up. He's my fiancé, not someone I picked up a few hours ago at a bar. Besides, Sam came around to my point of view. He's had it with Lucien Moray. He hadn't told anyone but me yet, but he is quitting his job at the end of the month."

"I've an interview later today with Moray," I said. "I'll check around and see what I can find out. Someone in Moray's office may know Sam's whereabouts."

"What if no one does?"

"Let's take it one step at a time." I glanced at my watch, then pushed myself off the rock where I'd been sitting, a task that would have been easier if I were ten years younger and twenty pounds lighter. "Speaking of interviews, my appointment with your aquarium director is in ten minutes, so I better head inside. I'll call you tonight."

Katie sighed. "Thanks. I should get back to my sea lions, too. We've a show at eleven." She rose and stretched her small wiry body. "After the show, I'll stop at Sam's house again."

Katie, shoulders slumped, wandered off in the direction of the outdoor sea lion amphitheater. I stood for a moment, inhaling the salt air while watching a seagull dive into the bay and zoom back to the sky with a fish in its mouth. As the autumn wind sent a sudden chill down my spine, I wrapped my arms around my body, thinking back to when Katie and my Abby attended college. Abby had inherited my fiery Greek disposition and often acted impulsively, out of emotion, but Katie had always been levelheaded, never someone to jump to conclusions. What if Sam is really in trouble? The thought nagged at me as I trekked up the sandy beach and stepped into the building that housed the indoor exhibits.

After maneuvering through the crowd gathered in front of the octopus tank, I veered down the administration wing, finally coming to a door marked DIRECTOR. I glanced again at my watch. Right on time. I knocked.

"Enter," a booming voice responded.

I stood face to face with the director. It was more like face to chest. I was five feet tall and this man towered over me by at least a foot and a half.

"Commander Conrad West," he said, extending his arm and firmly grasping my hand. He stood ramrod straight, probably a throwback from his military training. A former naval commander—the youngest African American to be appointed a commander in the navy's history— he had started his career as a medical corpsman. He had been director of the Clam Cove Aquarium since his retirement from the navy last year.

He walked behind his desk, positioned himself in a large swivel chair, and motioned me to sit. As I suppressed the urge to playfully salute, he went straight to the point. "I understand you're writing about the land acquisition. Have you seen our expansion plans?"

"Yes, and they are impressive. But how will the aquarium come up with the money to buy this land? You're competing with the bottomless pockets of Lucien Moray."

Commander West leaned forward, his hands clasped in front, as if praying that what he was about to say would come true. "The current property owner, Stuart Holland, is a business man who's not about to forgo a profit. But he's also an active conservationist and lifelong resident of this area who would like to see the land used in an environmentally friendly manner. He's kept it vacant until recent financial losses forced him to put it up for sale."

The commander leaned back. "There'll be no bidding war. He agreed to sell the property to the aquarium for ten million dollars. The land is worth more, but Stuart wants it to go to us, so he set a price he feels we can reach. If we can raise the money by next summer, the land is ours."

"Ten million is a high goal."

He nodded. "Katie has promised us six million from Alicia Wilcox Chandler's estate. We also have one million in reserve that we accumulated during the past few years. Of course, we're still three million short, but our new development officer is planning an aggressive fundraising campaign with—"

A loud knock on the door interrupted the conversation.

Commander West scowled. "Enter."

A plump woman with a bad case of acne barged into the room. She wore jeans and a light blue shirt with an aquarium patch on the upper left pocket identifying her as Madge.

"Commander," she said, slightly out of breath. "We have a problem. The sea lion show is in ten minutes, and Katie just ran out."

"What do you mean she ran out?"

The woman shrugged. "She took a call on her cell phone, then flew out of the amphitheater."

"Didn't she say anything?" The scowl hadn't left his face.

The woman paused, furrowing her eyebrows as if deep in thought. "Oh, yeah. But I don't know if it had to do with why she left."

"What did she say?" He appeared to be talking through gritted teeth.

"She said two fishermen found a body in the inlet."

4

CHAPTER TWO

M y stomach flip flopped, but Commander West stayed on course. "Give Katie until exactly five minutes past eleven," the commander ordered Madge. "If she doesn't come back by then, cancel the show. Announce that our sea lion trainer had an emergency and provide everyone in the audience with free passes to our 3-D movie on piranhas. That should satisfy all."

"Sure." Madge wiped her nose.

"And when Katie returns, I want to see her immediately."

"What if she returns in time for the show? You still want to see her immediately?"

The commander gritted his teeth again. "No," he said, perhaps a little too loudly. "Let her do the show. Have her see me once she finishes."

Madge nodded.

"That's all for now. You're dismissed."

"Yes, sir." Madge left.

Commander West turned his attention to me. "Let's see. Before we were interrupted, I was about to describe our new fundraising effort."

Perhaps it was his military training that enabled Commander West to get right back to business, but my mind was on the body in the inlet. Was it Sam Wong?

"You should meet our new development officer, Bradford Monroe," the commander continued. "I'm sure we could arrange for you to attend the cocktail party this Saturday which will launch our fundraising campaign. It's being held at Alicia Wilcox Chandler's old house."

That house now belonged to her granddaughter, Katie Chandler.

As if reading my mind, he added, "Katie is gracious and generous enough to let us use the place for our fundraiser."

My interview continued another twenty minutes. When finished, Commander West handed me his business card which listed both his office and cell phone numbers.

"Call me, if you think of more questions," he said as I exited.

I dashed out of the building into the parking lot where I hopped into my car. Autumn leaves whirled in the wind as I sped along a tree-lined portion of the main road. Minutes later, the sun disappeared, enveloping the landscape in grayness. A storm was brewing.

I made it to the inlet before the rain. Police vehicles as well as Katie's Vespa were parked along the side of the road. Directly down the embankment about two dozen people gathered outside yellow police tape. Spread across the sand inside the taped off area was a body. Tasting bile, a rush of dread flooded through me.

After regaining my composure, I scanned the scene, spotting a familiar figure standing aside the crowd, head down as if staring at her shoes.

"Katie," I called, making my way down the slope.

"Oh, Mrs. Farrell." She raised her head and began sobbing.

I ran down the incline toward her, the wind gusts propelling me forward. "I'm so sorry." I said, throwing my arms around her body and hugging her tightly. "It's Sam, isn't it?"

Katie shook her head. "It's not Sam."

"What?" I jumped back. "Well, then… Do you know—"

"It's a close friend of mine. Jack Patterson. He was one of the fish keepers at the aquarium." Katie took a deep breath. "Jack grew up here just like me. We've known each other since kindergarten. His family owns a horse farm up the road."

"Did he drown?"

"That's what the police think, but we won't know for sure until the autopsy. There's a bump on his head, so the theory is he fell off the dock and hit a rock. But I don't believe it." She turned toward the water and frowned. "This was no accident."

CHAPTER THREE

"If not an accident, then what?"

"I don't know." Katie shrugged. "But he had no reason to be here. This dock is owned by the Clam Cove Sailing and Yacht club, and the only people permitted in the area are members and their guests."

"Could he have been visiting someone?"

"Then wouldn't that person have noticed if he fell in the water? The normal reaction would be to help or at least seek help."

"Unless the person Jack was visiting was responsible for his death."

Katie nodded. "Right."

I frowned. "What do you think happened?"

"My theory. I think he got into a fight and was pushed. Jack had a temper."

"But why would he be here in the first place?"

Katie shrugged. "No clue."

"One more question. Could the body have floated in from somewhere else?"

"Jack was found wedged between the dock and a boat. It would be nearly impossible for a body to float into that position."

I heard a ping. Katie glanced at her phone. "My staff is texting me." She paused. "I don't feel up to it, but I need to go back to the aquarium. Knowing Commander West, he'll insist we go on as though nothing happened. I've missed the eleven o'clock sea lion show, so I'd better be there for the next performance." She wiped a tear from her eye.

I didn't mention she would probably be called to task by Commander West for running out on the earlier performance. I hoped when he discovered her reason for leaving, he'd be understanding.

7

Then again, she was donating six million dollars from her grandmother's estate to the aquarium. How tough could he be?

As we began our trudge up the embankment, Katie said, "Don't you have an appointment with Lucien Moray?"

"In fifteen minutes. That's where I'm headed now."

"You'll ask if anyone there has seen Sam?"

I nodded. "Absolutely."

"This is a terrible thing to say, but I'm relieved the body wasn't Sam's."

"I understand."

"Still, it was such a shock, and I feel awful. Jack was a great guy. I can't believe he's dead. Only five nights ago, Sam and I had dinner with him."

I stopped to catch my breath. "Katie, were Sam and Jack close?"

She shook her head. "Not at all. The only time they saw each other was if I was there. I was the connection."

"If Jack worked at the aquarium, didn't anyone miss him today?"

"No. Jack had yesterday and today off."

"Any particular reason?"

"That's his regular schedule. He works Tuesday through Saturday." She paused. "I don't think Jack was in the water for long."

"Why not?"

"Part of his body would have been eaten."

I shuddered and remained silent as the image of flesh-eating fish and crustaceans flashed through my brain.

Upon reaching the top of the embankment, Katie hopped on her Vespa and pulled her helmet out of the basket. "And good luck with your interview, Mrs. Farrell. Before you get to see Moray, you'll need to deal with Mama Grizzly."

"Mama Grizzly?"

"Moray's administrative assistant. Helen Eubanks. Sam says everyone calls her Mama Grizzly. She's tough and sees herself as Moray's protector, like a mama bear with her cubs."

"Don't worry. I've dealt with difficult people before." I hugged Katie. She fastened her helmet and sped off. I stood for a moment, my eyes focused down the embankment. Drops of rain began falling from the sky as the body of Jack Patterson was loaded into the medical examiner's van.

Above the building's front door were the words *Moray Industries* in big bold letters. The charcoal clouds had exploded, and I'd left my umbrella home, so I darted from the parking lot into the building, shaking off excess water before approaching the main desk. A receptionist ushered me into the executive suite where I found myself facing Moray's administrative assistant-Mama Grizzly-pecking at her computer keyboard. Helen Eubanks appeared to be in her mid-forties with short frosted hair, rimless spectacles, and an expression that looked as if she'd just eaten prunes.

"Hi, I'm Kristy Farrell from *Animal Advocate Magazine*. I've an appointment with Lucien Moray."

Without looking up, she nodded, barely acknowledging me as she continued pecking. "Mr. Moray is on a phone call. Have a seat, and I'll let you know when he's ready."

I noticed a small cameo hanging from a gold chain around her neck. It was similar to one I'd inherited from my grandmother. Thinking a compliment might break the ice, I spoke up. "Your necklace is lovely."

"Thank you, but please have a seat."

After plunking down on a black leather couch, I decided to try another approach. "I met one of your employees a while back," I lied. "Sam Wong. I thought I'd stop and say hello to him later. Is he in today?"

Mama Grizzly shot me a look that would cause a wolf to retreat. "I don't know if he's here. I work for Mr. Moray not Sam Wong."

I smiled and decided to shut my mouth. I wasn't going to get anything out of Mama Grizzly. Hopefully, I'd have better luck with her boss.

After ten minutes, I was ushered into Moray's private office. All décor contributed to one theme—a tribute to the multi-millionaire developer. The right wall was plastered with plaques from community and charitable groups honoring Moray for his service to their organizations. The left wall featured photos of Moray with the rich and famous. I spotted a former New York State Governor and United States Senator as well as a popular game show host.

Moray rose from his desk to greet me. He was dressed casually in khakis and a forest green golf shirt. Two decades ago, he had served in the special forces, and today, with his shaven head, black goatee, and husky build, he looked every bit the part.

He must have noticed me staring at his brag wall because he said, "Not bad for a boy from Brooklyn. I wasn't born rich. I've earned every penny. Along the way, I've helped people."

"I can see that from all your awards."

"I'm not talking about the plaques." He sat back down. "Sure, I've served on boards of several charities, but I've also assisted the community by creating jobs with my land developments, which my new condo project will do again."

Great segue. I grinned.

"But what about the environment?" I asked as I sank into a black leather chair and pulled out my pen and pad. The aquarium wants the land to be used for—"

"I know." He held up his hands. "If I succeed in buying the property, I intend to donate one of the twenty acres to the aquarium, so they can do a small expansion, perhaps ensure breeding grounds for the piping plover."

I suppressed a smile. Piping plover had been found nesting on that land this spring. As an endangered species, federal law required the area be protected. Moray wouldn't be permitted to build in this section even if he owned the property. Deciding to ignore this point for the present time, I asked, "That's generous, but one acre will severely limit the aquarium's plans. What can they do with one acre?"

"In this economy, we all need to compromise, something I find most environmentalists are unwilling to do." He leaned forward, spreading out his hands. "The environmental community in Clam Cove can't even come to agreement on this land issue. Not all want it to go to the aquarium. Take Ruby Diamond."

"Ruby Diamond?"

He shook his head. "Ruby heads a group called Friends of the Fish. They oppose not only my resort but the aquarium's project, too. Her group says any interference by humans, no matter how well intentioned, is unnatural and wrong. They want the acres to remain just as they are."

Commander West had not mentioned Ruby Diamond or her

organization. Friends of the Fish would provide a twist to my story. I scribbled notes as fast as Lucien Moray talked.

"Ruby lives on the beach in a small cottage with a pottery studio in front," said Moray. "Interesting how it's okay for her to own beach front property, isn't it?"

We talked for another fifteen minutes. While rising to leave, I asked, "Is Sam Wong here? We have a mutual friend and I want to say hello."

"I don't believe he's in today."

"Do you know where he is?" Perhaps I was too blunt, but, hey, the interview was finished, and in the worse case scenario, Moray would say it was none of my business.

Moray smiled. "Micromanaging is not my style. All my people have their assignments. I don't require them to account for every minute of the day."

Bottom line: He didn't know Sam Wong's whereabouts, or if he did, he wasn't telling me.

On the way out, I asked Mama Grizzly if I could use the restroom. She sighed as if this request placed a great burden upon her, but she handed me a key and told me to turn left and go to the end of the corridor.

I really didn't need to use the facilities, but I wanted an excuse to wander down the hall. I hoped Sam Wong's office would be along the way, and I was in luck. Half way down, I spotted a door with a sign that read SAMUEL WONG, ATTORNEY.

After making sure I was alone in the hallway, I tried the door. It was unlocked. I opened it slowly and peeked inside.

The walls were bare. The only furniture consisted of a desk, one chair, and an empty book case. There were no photos, personal mementos, or computers.

The room looked as if no one worked here.

CHAPTER FOUR

"I wonder if Sam Wong's disappearance and Jack Patterson's death are related?" Abby asked after biting into her third slice of pizza and wiping the cheese off her chin. A size six, my daughter consumed as much food as a longshoreman, but she exercised like an Olympic contender.

Abby, who rented a beach house with her lawyer boyfriend, was eating a late dinner at my home since Jason was working extra hours on a case for his firm. My husband, Matt, a veterinarian, was meeting with his accountant tonight, something he was doing with more and more frequency.

"But Katie said there's no connection between Sam and Jack," I argued. "They hardly knew each other."

"Nothing makes sense." Abby paused. "I talked to Katie before coming here. She's so depressed."

I nodded while chewing my pizza. "I called Katie earlier to let her know that both Lucien Moray and his administrative assistant claim to know nothing about Sam's whereabouts."

"What are you going to do?" Katie stared at me with her molasses colored eyes. "Are you going to investigate Jack's death and Sam's disappearance?"

"I haven't decided. I don't know Jack, so there's no reason to get involved. I hesitated. "But I might nosy around a bit—just in case it involves the aquarium. And I will try to help Katie find her fiancé."

"Good. Let me know what I can do to help."

I grinned. Since Abby helped me solve the murder this summer of a local zoo director, she viewed herself as Watson to my Sherlock Holmes.

"How well do you know Sam?" I asked.

Abby shrugged. "Not that well. Usually, when Katie and I were together, he was working. I was with him a few times, when Jason and I went out with Sam and Katie to dinner or a movie."

"Has Katie contacted Sam's family about his disappearance? Friends?"

"Most of his family still lives in China. His closest relative is his cousin Ray in Connecticut. They usually call each other at least once a week, but Ray hasn't heard from him. Katie talked to Sam's friends, too, but no one knows a thing."

I broke my pizza crust in two and slipped one half to Brandy, my eight year old collie, and the other half to Archie, my one hundred pound mixed breed, who resembled a small, black bear. They had been waiting patiently at my feet. Abby, a veterinarian—she worked at her father's veterinary hospital—didn't believe in feeding the dogs from the table. She shot me a look but said nothing. I knew she wanted to keep the conversation focused on Katie.

"I'll touch base with Katie again tomorrow. She may know more than she realizes," I said. "And I'm attending a community meeting later tomorrow evening on the land acquisition. Moray's key people will be there. Maybe I can find out something from them about Sam."

I began cleaning up. Abby stretched her five-foot body and reached for the aluminum foil from the top cabinet. She had inherited her height genes from me. "Can I take some pizza home?" she asked. "Jason may be hungry when he gets out of work."

"Jason is always hungry. I'm sure his law firm will send out for food, but you can have a slice. I want to save the others for your father. He said he'd grab a bite, but sometimes he gets so preoccupied he forgets to eat."

"You're right." Abby frowned. "He's worried about finances."

I nodded in agreement. A Health and Wellness Center for Companion Animals had opened only a few blocks from Matt's veterinary hospital. It featured herbal remedies, chiropractic adjustments, massages, and water therapy, along with traditional veterinary medicine. We were all concerned about the impact on Matt's business.

My mind had switched from Katie Chandler, Sam Wong, and Jack Patterson to my husband and his veterinary hospital. This was his life's work, and he had recently taken a large loan to update his facility. But I didn't have long to ponder this problem as I was jostled out of my thoughts when the doorbell rang.

As the two dogs charged out from under the table, Archie bumped his head, lost his footing, slipped on the tile floor, and crashed into the garbage can. Turning his head in my direction with a goofy grin on his face, he scrambled to his feet and joined Brandy by the kitchen door where the two stood at full alert, barking.

Abby and I exchanged wary glances.

"Are you expecting someone?" my daughter asked.

"No." I rose from my chair and headed toward the door with trepidation. Rarely would someone drop by at night without first calling.

I glanced out the side window, then quickly pulled open the door. There she stood. A woman in her early seventies but who, at first glance, appeared at least fifteen years younger, with blonde hair worn in an elegant twist, creamy skin perfectly made-up, and dressed in camel colored pants and a chocolate cashmere sweater. She toted a designer suitcase.

"Hello, Kristy."

I blinked, not believing my eyes. "Mom?"

CHAPTER FIVE

I hugged my mother, then stepped back. My mouth was open, but nothing was coming out.

"Are you just going to stand there, Kristy, or do you plan to let me in?"

I moved aside, and Mary Frances O'Hara Vanikos paraded into the room. My mother, a widow for nearly a decade, lived in Florida. She visited us on a schedule that hadn't wavered once during the past ten years—Christmas through New Years and the last two weeks in April. Why was she here now?

"Grandma." Abby rose and hugged my mother while the dogs barked and wagged their tails.

"You look terrific, Abby. Are you still living with that lawyer? What's his name again? Jason? When is he going to make an honest woman of you?" I cringed. Abby grinned.

"We're doing fine, Grandma."

My mother spun around. "You look pretty good, too, Kristy. Although I liked your old hair style better. Did you put on a few pounds?"

Before I could sputter a reply, Abby asked, "What brings you here?"

"I've a surprise." She winked. Never a good sign. "I'll tell you later. But first I should get settled since I'll be here for about a month. I probably should have called."

She had called three days ago and said nothing about this visit.

"I want to use the bathroom to freshen up. I'll unpack later. Kristy, why don't you pour us some wine. Then we can sit down, have a nice chat, and I'll tell you what this is all about.

Wine sounded like an excellent idea.

15

Minutes later, we were sitting around the kitchen table, wine glasses filled to the brim.

"Mom, what's going on? You never visit in the fall."

"I'm meeting a friend."

"A friend?" I gulped some wine.

"I met him this spring. His name is Paul Andre. Isn't that a wonderful name. He lives in Florida, but he's in New York on business. He'll be here for most of October, so I decided to come up and spend time with him. Since you're not too far from the city, I thought I'd combine visiting him with visiting you. I'd like you to meet him."

"He sounds like a close friend," Abby said.

My mother grinned. "He's more. Paul's my fiancé."

"Fiancé!" I choked on my wine and coughed.

"It's not official yet. But that's why I'm here. He's buying a ring." Turning her head toward Abby, she winked. "Paul's got all sorts of connections in the diamond district."

"How long have you known him?" I asked, after the coughing ceased.

"It's not the length of time, dear. It's the depth of feeling. Besides, I'm not Abby's age. I don't have lots of extra years for prelims."

Prelims? "Where did you meet Paul?"

"Florida."

"I meant how did you meet him? Through friends? Did he move into your condo development?"

"I met him at an art gallery opening. You'll like him. He's handsome, sophisticated—"

"What does he do for a living?"

She paused, furrowing her brows. "He calls himself a venture capitalist. Paul doesn't talk much about business. Says it would bore me. But he's well off." She grinned. "Drives a convertible. We toot all around Florida with the top down."

The dogs barked as headlights flooded the driveway adjacent to the kitchen window. A few seconds later, Matt strolled through the door.

"I'm home," my husband said, announcing the obvious. His somber expression told me things hadn't gone well with his accountant.

"Hello, Matt," my mother called.

"Mom's visiting for… a few days," I said. I'd tell him how long later. "She's engaged."

"That's nice." His tone was the same as if I had told him I bought a new pair of shoes. He ran his hand through his thinning sandy hair. "I'm going to work for a while in my study."

"Is everything okay?" I asked.

"Yeah, it will be fine. I just need time to think." He wandered toward his study without saying good-night.

"What's with Matt?" My mother frowned. "He didn't ask why I was here or about my engagement."

Abby and I exchanged glances. "He had a long day, Grandma." Abby rose from her chair and stretched her arms. "So have I. It's time for me to go home."

"I'm tired, too," my mother said, "and I have to unpack. I think I'll call it a night."

After Abby left and my mother headed to her room, I settled back down at the table with another glass of wine.

As I sipped my drink, dozens of thoughts squirreled through my mind. Katie's friend died today. Her fiancé was missing. My mother was engaged to a man she appeared to know little about. And what was the news from Matt's accountant?

I swallowed what remained of my wine, washed my glass, and trudged up the stairs to bed with Archie and Brandy at my heels. I was bone tired and tomorrow was another day.

* * * * *

"These bagels smell heavenly," my mother said stepping into my kitchen the next morning. I'd risen early and picked up bagels, still warm from the oven, from the local bagel shop.

The dogs positioned themselves on either side of my mom. She wasn't a food sharer, but they could hope for crumbs.

"I'm sorry I can't spend the day with you," I said as I handed her a mug of coffee. "But I've got to work all day, and I'm busy tonight, too. I'm attending a village hall meeting this evening in Clam Cove."

"I figured you'd be busy, so I'm going shopping today. I rented a car. Tonight, I'm having dinner in the city with my Paul."

"By the way, when will we meet him?"

"I'm glad you mentioned that. I invited him here for Wednesday. Thought you might throw a little dinner party."

Wednesday? Today was Tuesday. "That doesn't give me much time."

"Keep it small. You, Matt, Abby, and her boyfriend. Oh, let's also invite your brother and that wife of his."

"Barbara," I said. My mother never referred to my brother's wife by her name.

"Whatever. I think you should—"

My cell phone rang. Glancing at caller ID, I saw it was Katie. I held up my hand. "I need to take this call."

"Sam still hasn't returned," Katie said, her voice quaking as she spoke. "I called the police again, but they don't seem concerned. Mrs. Farrell, what else can I do?"

"I have an interview with the aquarium's development officer, Bradford Monroe, later this afternoon. Why don't I stop by the sea lion amphitheater when I'm finished. It will be about four-thirty. We can put our heads together and see if we can come up with a plan to find Sam."

She agreed. I asked her if there was any news about Jack Patterson's death, and she said no. When I hung up, my mother picked up our conversation from when we had been interrupted.

"So Kristy, what will you make for dinner with Paul?"

"A phone call to a caterer."

CHAPTER SIX

Running late, I sped off to the *Animal Advocate* office, located in a two-story building in one of Long Island's downtown business district. The first story housed a law firm and insurance agency. *Animal Advocate* occupied the second floor.

The magazine had been here since its inception five years ago. Last month, it was bought out by a large publishing conglomerate. Although all staff, including its editor-in-chief, Olivia Johnson, had been kept on, we were all walking on eggs. The new publishing house had a reputation for cost cutting, most of which involved eliminating jobs.

Once settled inside my cubicle, I switched on my computer, hit the keyboard, and began researching Stuart Holland, current owner of the twenty acres of land that the aquarium hoped to purchase.

I discovered that in the late 1800s, when eastern Long Island was considered the boondocks, Stuart Holland's great grandfather moved here and bought the land for a song. Originally, the family owned more than half of what is now Clam Cove, but over the years, they sold most of it until all that remained was twenty bay front acres.

When Stuart Holland inherited the land, he put a stop to selling off more property. During his heyday, he had been active in several Long Island environmental groups that focused on keeping the water unpolluted and protecting marine life. Unfortunately, when the family's once-lucrative hardware business went belly up five years ago, the then seventy-one year old Stuart sold his home and moved in with his daughter and her family in North Carolina.

I remembered Katie telling me that Stuart's offspring pressured him to put the twenty acres up for sale, but Stuart didn't agree until a year ago when he stipulated the aquarium be given first opportunity to buy. The deadline was June thirtieth of next year. If they could come up with the money, it was theirs. If not, it was up for grabs.

He probably realized that once he was gone his heirs would sell it anyway, I thought. At least now he had some control regarding who bought it.

Next, I researched the aquarium's new development officer, Bradford Monroe. I wanted to learn as much as possible before my interview with him later today. His first fundraising job was for a small museum in Chicago where he started off as an aide and ended up as assistant development officer. After that, he served as director of development for the Throckbrush Academy, a small prep school for boys in Pennsylvania. I checked the sites for both the museum and the Throckbrush Academy, finally satisfied that I was armed with plenty of background data.

Lastly, I checked if there was any news on Jack Patterson's murder. I found a small blurb stating the autopsy was expected to be completed tomorrow.

I was about to shut down my computer and head to my next appointment when an idea flashed through my mind. I hit the keyboard and searched for Paul Andre. I was curious about the man my mother planned to marry, but to my surprise, there was nothing about him online.

"I guess it's not that unusual for his generation," I mumbled.

"What's not unusual?" A voice interrupted my thoughts. Clara Schultheis, office snoop and administrative assistant to the editor, stepped into my cubicle.

"What's not unusual?" she repeated, while staring at me over her half moon glasses.

"People in their seventies who aren't on the web. No social media presence."

"But many are computer savvy, and many more want to be. Do you know that Olivia volunteers once a week as a computer teacher at a senior center?"

"Her students would be afraid not to learn." I grinned as I envisioned our editor, Olivia Johnson, as a teacher. "Olivia sizes up people like a fox in a chicken pen. Whenever I'm called in to see her, I feel like a third grader being summoned to the principal's office."

"So," Clara said, peering over my desk and attempting to read my notes upside down. "What have you been up to?"

"Research for my article." I began logging out. "By the way, where is Olivia today? Her office is dark."

Clara winced. "Manhattan. A budget meeting at corporate headquarters."

"Uh, oh."

"You said it. Know what I was doing this morning? Inventory. Counting paper clips and pens. Can you believe that I actually have to prepare a report on this?"

"Not a good sign. After rationing rubber bands, does eliminating jobs come next?" I switched off my computer and rose from my chair. "Hopefully, nothing will happen soon. But keep me posted. I have no doubt you'll be among the first to know." With Clara trailing me, I left my cubicle. She returned to her desk, and I went out the door.

As I drove to the aquarium, I sighed. Ever since watching *Superman* as a kid, I wanted to be Lois Lane but wound up teaching high school English for more than two decades. A few years ago, when I heard about an opening for a feature writer at *Animal Advocate Magazine,* I decided to go for it. Someone else got the position, but I was offered an editorial assistant spot with a future promotion held as the dangling carrot.

This past summer, I caught the carrot. I was promoted to feature writer. Now it appeared my new position might be snatched away, because of corporate downsizing. I loved this job. And with the loans on Matt's veterinary business, I couldn't afford to be unemployed.

CHAPTER SEVEN

"Will you join me in a cup of espresso?" Bradford Monroe asked as he rose from his chair to greet me. He had the build of a runner, and his tanned complexion led me to believe he spent lots of time outdoors. According to my research he was thirty-five years old.

"Thanks. I'd love a cup." Sharing a cup of coffee with the person I was interviewing usually created a relaxed atmosphere, allowing conversation to flow freely. Besides, I was a coffee addict.

Displayed on the back wall of Bradford's office were more than a dozen awards, most of which were for athletic contests. According to these citations, Bradford had been a swimming champion, sailboat racer, marathon runner, college track star, and a successful participant in a recent triathlon. Just looking at these commendations made me tired.

"My espresso machine is state of the art. Cost nearly seven hundred dollars." As he handed a cup to me, I noted the watch on his arm, recognizing it as a brand that sold for more than ten grand. Bradford Monroe apparently liked expensive things.

He sat down and leaned back in his chair. "So, you want to hear about our fundraising campaign."

"I'm interested in how you plan to raise enough money for the land acquisition. I know the aquarium has one million dollars in reserve and that six million dollars comes from Alicia Wilcox-Chandler's estate, but you still need to come up with—"

"Three million. I'm aware. It's a high goal but I can reach it. I've been fundraising for more than a decade. My last position was at the Throckbrush Academy where I saved the school from bankruptcy."

I smiled. My research had shown that during his time at Throckbrush, the nearly bankrupt academy had become solvent. But that was because of five million dollars bequeathed to the school by a wealthy alumnus. Although the alumnus passed away during Bradford's tenure at the academy, the will was written five years before Bradford was employed by Throckbrush.

Deciding to let this go for the present time, I asked, "Specifically, how do you plan to raise this three million? The aquarium's past development campaigns only realized modest amounts." I glanced down at my notes. "I believe it took five years to raise the one million you have in—"

"Because those past campaigns were poorly run. Mine won't be."

"What will you do differently?"

"First, I'm initiating a facility naming project. Sponsorships. For a one hundred thousand dollar donation, you can have an exhibit named after you."

"One hundred thousand dollars is a lot of money."

"Not for some of our wealthy supporters. Think of it. Parker's Penguin Rookery or Saperstein's Seal Sanctuary. People love seeing their name in lights."

"In lights?"

He waved his hand dismissively. "Figure of speech. I'm also coordinating four major fundraising events—a golf tournament, car raffle, arts and antique auction, and a kick-off cocktail party. The cocktail party is this Saturday." He winked. "Tickets are twenty-five hundred dollars, but I think I can get you in."

"Commander West invited me yesterday."

"Good. While you're there, you can talk to our supporters and hear why they feel the land acquisition is so important to the future of the aquarium."

As I scribbled notes, he continued. "We also have our email and snail mail campaign for the little people."

"Little people?"

"Yes." He pushed a wisp of his dark blond hair away from this forehead. "Those individuals who want to support our cause but can only afford to give small amounts—fifty dollars, one hundred dollars— you get my drift. There are so many of those *little* donors that it adds up."

Bradford and I talked until I gathered the facts and figures I needed for my story. Rising up to leave, I said, "By the way, I'm sorry about Jack Patterson."

Bradford stared at me blankly.

"Jack Patterson," I repeated. "The man whose body was found in the inlet. He was one of your fish keepers."

"Of course. I didn't recognize the name immediately. I don't have much contact with aquarium staff outside of top administration."

"Have the police determined if his death was an accident?"

"I've no idea." He glanced at his watch and came around to the front of his desk. "I'm afraid I have to leave for a meeting in town. I'll walk out with you."

As we headed down the corridor, we passed an exhibit featuring sea life from the Great Barrier Reef. I was momentarily distracted, gazing at the brightly colored fish and pastel coral behind the glass walls.

"You're lucky," I said. "You get to stroll by this all the time. It's so relaxing."

"Relaxing. I don't have time for relaxing."

"If I worked at the aquarium, I'd spend a few minutes here everyday." I pointed to a jellyfish, floating through the water, its tentacles resembling delicate strings of lace. "What a peaceful scene."

"Peaceful? Deadly is more like it. That's the box jellyfish. It's one of the most lethal creatures in the world. If you were stung by one of those tentacles…" He paused. "You'd be dead."

* * * * *

Outside the building, Bradford and I went our separate ways. I wandered to the sea lion exhibit to talk with Katie. Since the four o'clock show had just finished, throngs of visitors were leaving the amphitheater. Feeling a little like a lemming swimming upstream, I maneuvered through the departing crowds into the arena. Katie was still on stage, two sea lions on either side. A moat separated her from the seating area. Several sea lions were in the water.

"Katie," I called.

"Come on up, Mrs. Farrell." Katie unlatched a gate on a small bridge that spanned the furthest corner of the moat. I made my way across the bridge, noting a large sign that read, EMPLOYEES ONLY.

"You're sure this is okay?"

"I promise I won't tell the insurance company." Katie motioned toward the two sea lions. "Meet Bea and Barney. Bea, high five Mrs. Farrell." The sea lion stood on her haunches, raised her right flipper, and we high-fived. Barney clapped his flippers and barked, a sound similar to throaty burps.

"I don't know what I'd do without these two. They're all that's keeping me going now." Katie grabbed two small fish from a pail and palmed one to Bea and one to Barney.

"I'm worried sick about Sam, Mrs. Farrell." She shook her head. "I can't stop thinking about Jack's death either. I wish they'd hurry up with his autopsy."

"They only discovered Jack's body yesterday. These things take time."

"Speaking of time, it's almost three days since my Sam disappeared."

A thought flashed through my mind. "When you stopped at Sam's house yesterday, did you go inside and look around?"

"I have a key, so I went inside to see if he had returned and was sick in bed or if he had hurt himself." Katie furrowed her brow. "But I didn't look around. What for?"

"I'm not sure, but maybe there are clues as to his disappearance. Something missing. Or something there that shouldn't be."

"I did check his mail, but it was only bills." Katie glanced at her watch. "I'm due a break now. Why don't we drive over and see what we can find?

* * * * *

Sam Wong rented a house by the bay, about a ten minute drive from Clam Cove. We whizzed by homes ranging from small beach bungalows to mini mansions before reaching Sam's sprawling contemporary ranch.

Katie unlatched the front door and we stepped into a huge living room with sliding glass doors opening unto a wooden deck overlooking the water.

"Katie, when you checked to see if Sam was home, did you switch on the lights?"

"No. I left everything the way it was. Why?"

"The lamp by the sofa is on. That's an indication Sam left at night."

Katie nodded. "What should we do first?"

"Let's check if anything is out of place. Where's the bedroom?"

"Down that hall. Second door on the left. You go there. I'll search the living room and his study."

I made my way to the bedroom. Clothes lay strewn across an unmade bed, making me wonder if Sam left in a hurry.

Or he may just be a slob. But judging by the neat appearance of the living room, I didn't think this was the case.

I rummaged through Sam's dresser drawers and found nothing out of the ordinary. But the way his clothes were neatly folded and put away confirmed my suspicions that the mess atop the bed was unusual.

Next, I looked in his closet, checking pants and jacket pockets for crumbled notes that might provide a clue. I came up empty.

I moved to the master bath. Sam's toothbrush and shaving equipment were in plain sight. Not a good sign. If he went away of his own free will, those items should be with him. Still, he might have a separate overnight bag packed and ready to go.

I swung open the door to the medicine cabinet, immediately noticing an open box of prescription allergy capsules. Autumn on Long Island was accompanied by a high pollen count. If Sam had allergies he would need these pills.

Unless he was traveling to a climate where pollen allergies were uncommon.

Finally, I made my way to the kitchen and pulled open the refrigerator door. The only foods represented were diet soda, ketchup, and mustard. The garbage can was filled to the brim. On top was a half eaten pastrami on rye stuffed in a bag from a local deli. Judging by the smell, that meal must have been several days ago.

"Sam was the most factitious person I knew," Katie said as she snaked around the kitchen island to join me. Her face was ashen. "He would never let garbage overflow."

"It appears he left here in a hurry," I said.

We continued looking in the kitchen cabinets and drawers.

"Oh, no," Katie cried out. "His cell phone and charger are here."

I took a deep breath. No one, especially of his generation, would leave willingly without their cell.

"Does he have a home phone?" I asked, aware that many folks didn't bother with a land line, opting to save money by using only their cell.

"Yes, he does. It's in the study. The cell reception on this part of the beach is pretty bad, so to contact him when he's home, you need to use the land line. I've been calling both his cell and home phone."

"Let's see if there are any messages."

We headed to the study and played back the voice mail. The last four calls, all from Katie, had gone unanswered. But when I heard the call preceding Katie's first message, my blood froze.

"Sam, this is Lucien. We've got problems. I need to see you immediately. Meet me at—"

CLICK. "I'm here, Lucien." CLICK.

CHAPTER EIGHT

"That was Sam." Katie balled her hands into tight fists. "Moray's responsible for Sam's disappearance."

"We don't know that."

"But it was the last call Sam answered. They obviously met someplace. After that, Sam vanished."

My mind wandered back to my conversation with Moray. He claimed not to know Sam's whereabouts. Did Sam disappear before rendezvousing with Moray? Or maybe they met and something happened afterwards? Instinct told me Lucien Moray knew more than he was saying.

"I'm going to Moray's office now to confront him," Katie said.

"Bad idea. You won't get in to see him. But there's a community meeting tonight at Village Hall on the land acquisition and—"

"I know." Katie nodded. "I'll be there. Proponents for the aquarium expansion will be out in force."

"So will Moray and his people. That's when we can find out more."

Katie agreed. Since she needed to feed the sea lions before tonight's meeting, I dropped her back at the aquarium then drove into town. Main street, lined with trees and dotted with boutiques, restaurants, and historic buildings looked like a Norman Rockwell painting. After wolfing down a slice of pizza and diet cola at the only fast food establishment I could find, I headed up the block to Village Hall, a large clapboard building dating back to the late nineteenth century.

Following the signs for the community room, I made my way down a narrow winding corridor with hospital-green walls. Although the meeting wouldn't start for another thirty minutes, crowds had begun gathering.

I'd seen happier faces in my dentist's office. A few voices were raised in argument and about a dozen attendees sported signs reading: SUPPORT THE ENVIRONMENT—SAY YES TO THE AQUARIUM, and the opposing CREATE JOBS—PEOPLE BEFORE FISH.

Lucien Moray dominated the center of the room. He was deep in conversation with a large woman—both height and girth—who sported tortoise shell glasses and frizzy gray hair. She wore an ankle length floral designed skirt topped with an orange tee-shirt. Sandals and chunky silver jewelry completed the outfit.

"Sorry, Ruby. It's not gonna happen," Moray was saying as I approached.

"Don't underestimate us. That's a big mistake." The woman spun around and headed toward the front of the room.

"Ah, Mrs. Farrell." Moray spotted me. "Here to gather more information for your magazine story. I thought we gave you all you needed?"

"I'm primarily interested in hearing what members of the community have to say tonight. Was that Ruby Diamond?"

"Yes. She's arguing now with Commander West and his development officer." He shook his head.

I glanced toward the right side of the room. Ruby's face was flush and her hands gesturing wildly as the two aquarium representatives stood passively, Bradford's hands in his pockets and Commander West's arms folded in front of his chest.

"By the way, is Sam Wong here?" I asked.

"No. He is not."

"You may be the last person who had contact with him before he vanished."

"Vanished? You're a bit melodramatic."

I wasn't melodramatic. If Sam had gone away, he would have contacted Katie. Something happened. I decided to confront Moray head on. "Where did you meet with Sam on Sunday?" When he looked surprised, I added, "I know you phoned and said you had to see him."

Moray frowned. I thought he wasn't going to answer my question. "Sam came to my office. Now, excuse me. I need to touch base with my architect." He turned and maneuvered through the crowd until he reached a woman in a beige suit holding what appeared to be a large set of blueprints.

The police needed to question Moray. I doubted he'd evade their inquiries the way he did mine. It was time for Katie to go back down to the police station and insist on a missing person's case. Tomorrow would be the fourth day since Sam had vanished.

Meanwhile, I had a job to do.

Bradford Monroe and Commander West had wandered off. Ruby Diamond stood by herself. I dashed over before someone else grabbed her attention.

"Ruby Diamond?"

"Yes." She eyed me suspiciously.

"I'm Kristy Farrell with *Animal Advocate Magazine*. I'd like to ask you a few questions." I pulled out my pad and pen.

"*Animal Advocate Magazine*, huh. Let me guess. You're in favor of the aquarium expansion."

"You're not?"

"Leave the land alone. We don't need more development."

"But the expansion will enable the aquarium to work on problems such as pollution of our waters and vanishing marine species.

"It will bring more tourists. Thousands of people will come trampling through."

"It's my understanding that some of the new areas, such as breeding grounds, will be off limits to the public."

"Still, won't work. Listen, I'd like to talk to you but not now. I need to organize my forces before the meeting. Why don't you come to my place tomorrow?" She reached into her bag and handed me a card that read: *Ruby Diamond Pottery.* Underneath was her address followed by the phrase, "*One mile east of the Cove Motel.*"

I noted that the address was down the road from the aquarium. I was pretty sure it was adjacent to the twenty acres that were for sale. I smiled. Who wouldn't want to live next to vacant pristine land?

"I'll be there all day. I live in back of my studio," she said.

"Fine. I'll see you late morning. I'm curious about your organization."

She scooted off and joined two young men—one clean shaven and one with a billy-goat beard. I wandered to the spot in the corner where

Commander West and Bradford Monroe appeared to be wrapping up a conversation with a woman who was holding up a sign that read, NINE OUT OF TEN LIVING THINGS LIVE IN THE OCEAN—SUPPORT THE AQUARIUM.

As the woman departed, Commander West said, "That lady is chair of one of the major environmental groups on Long Island. We have the support of the local university, major science groups, and all local environmental organizations."

"Not all," I said. "What about Friends of the Fish?"

Bradford made a pickle face, then answered. "I question whether that organization exists or if Ruby Diamond has a personal agenda."

Before I could question Bradford about his comment, he and the commander excused themselves to talk with another group of supporters. I turned and spotted Katie Chandler. She appeared to be deep in conversation with two older men. I started navigating in her direction when the sound of a banging gavel stopped me in my tracks.

"Will everyone please find a seat. I'm councilwoman Brady and I'll be running tonight's meeting. Just a reminder. This meeting's purpose is to ask questions, get answers, and dispel rumors."

Katie and I made eye contact, and she maneuvered her way to meet me. "The people I was talking with are Sam's co-workers," Katie said as we both slid into chairs. "They don't know where he is either. Did you find out anything from Moray?"

"No, but I have a strange feeling he's hiding something," I replied in a low voice. "Tomorrow, you should contact the police again. They need to hear Moray's message on Sam's voice mail."

Councilwoman Brady called the meeting to order. The program started with Moray's power point presentation on his condo complex of seventy-five units, ranging in size from one to three bedrooms. The facility included two pools, two Jacuzzis, a tennis court, restaurant, club house, and small marina.

"I hope that pompous twit Bradford Monroe can raise the extra money so the aquarium can buy the land," Katie whispered in my ear. "Moray will destroy the ecosystem."

"Katie, you're contributing six million from your grandmother's will. If the aquarium falls short on its fund raising, can you provide more?"

"Unfortunately, no. Grandma left twelve million for me to distribute in two years to three organizations that she specified. But she also left restrictions. One is that no more than six million can be given to any one group."

"Ssh!" A lady, resembling my third grade teacher, Miss Clump, turned around and frowned.

Chastised, we stopped talking and listened as members of the audience shot off questions to Moray. Commander West came next, his presentation also followed by questions and comments. It was apparent most of the audience had formed opinions and taken sides long before tonight's meeting.

I was reading my notes when a familiar voice on the microphone caught my attention. I jerked my head up and looked toward the podium.

"I'm Ruby Diamond, Chair of Friends of the Fish. Moray Development is just another example of corporate greed. But I want to address the pseudo environmentalists here. I say pseudo environmentalists because that's what they are. Using more bay front for the aquarium is not the solution. This land should NOT be developed and—"

"Ms. Diamond," Councilwoman Brady interrupted. "These twenty acres have been zoned commercial since the 1950s. They are grandfathered in. Whoever buys the property has the legal right to develop it. They'll need to file for permits with the building department. If the plans don't conform to village standards, and a variance is necessary, they'll need to come before the zoning board."

Katie whispered in my ear, "The village council wants the condominiums. As do members of the zoning board. Most are part of Clam Cove's business community. Besides, the tax revenue will far exceed anything that the aquarium could bring in."

"So if Moray succeeds in buying the land, he'll get just about any variance he wants?"

She nodded.

The meeting continued with more speakers. Some were proponents of the aquarium, others in favor of Moray Development. But Ruby Diamond and the two young men sitting next to her appeared to be the only group against either, making me wonder about the size, strength, and legitimacy of Friends of the Fish.

32

During the next hour, those approaching the podium only repeated what had been said before, so my mind wandered back to Sam Wong and Jack Patterson. I leaned over and whispered to Katie. "Could Jack's death have anything to do with the land fight?"

"Jack had nothing to do with the acquisition. He was only a fish keeper."

I still wondered if there was a common thread.

The meeting ended after midnight. I said my good-byes and headed outside, my breath visible in the cool autumn night air. Once in my car, I sped off westward, leaving the village and soon finding myself on a lonesome country road.

Only a slither of a moon and a handful of stars shone in the early October sky. I saw nothing but the dark shapes of trees, haystacks, and pumpkins growing in fields, as well as the outline of an occasional barn or house. At night, this was a desolate area. I turned my lights on bright and slowed down, worried an animal would dart in front of me.

The road curved southerly, now running adjacent to the bay. I passed the aquarium, its dome-like structure transformed by darkness into an eerie sentinel against the sky. Then came the vacant land—the twenty acres of untouched sandy beach and shoreline now bathed in total blackness.

Suddenly, lights flashed from the water.

A boat, I reasoned, probably night fishermen.

But a boat should provide a steady stream of light, not flashes.

The flashing stopped, and once again, I saw only darkness.

Then lights flashed again.

But this time, they came from the beach.

CHAPTER NINE

"You seem in a good mood today," I said to my husband when he stepped into the kitchen the next morning. He appeared happy but preoccupied. He still hadn't asked what my mother was doing here.

"I'm in a great mood." He poured coffee into a mug and gulped some down. "I've figured out a way to generate more business for the veterinary hospital."

"Sounds good. Tell me," I said.

"Not yet. There are a few kinks I need to work out." He winked.

I hated when people winked. Especially people who were members of my family. It always meant trouble.

* * * * *

If I'm anything, I'm a multi-tasker. While driving to Clam Cove for my interview with Ruby Diamond, I confirmed the caterer for the dinner tonight with my mother's fiancé and made an appointment with the aquarium's head fish keeper for my second article for *Animal Advocate* which was entitled "Dangers of the Deep."

As I neared my destination, the road curved, and I found myself driving parallel to the bay with its sandy beaches, occasionally dotted with restaurants, motels, and marinas. I spotted the Cove Motel and slowed down. Ruby's pottery studio was a mile east of here. Soon her pink shingled cottage came into view.

I noted it was only a few yards from the empty stretch of beach where I spotted the flashing lights last night.

A barefooted Ruby, dressed in a green and purple caftan, answered the door, and a strong odor of paints greeted me inside the house. I was thankful the window on the right side of the house was partially open.

I swept my gaze across the room. On the left, was a kiln and potters wheel. Two long tables, with paint jars and a collection of vases, pots, and urns, were placed against the right wall.

"Beautiful work," I said. I wandered toward the last table. "Do you sell these?"

Ruby nodded.

Since the items were for sale, I assumed I could examine her work more closely. I picked up a modern looking, zebra-striped vase. It was heavier than I expected, and it almost slipped out of my hands."

"Please don't touch anything," Ruby said as she grabbed the vase from me and placed it back on the table. "I would hate to see my creation smashed to bits if you accidentally dropped it. Plus, I have a buyer for that item."

"Of course."

"If you want to purchase my pottery, a gift shop in the village sells it."

"Is this how you make your living?"

"Art is more than a job. It's my passion. My parents were both doctors, and they wanted me to follow in their footsteps. I attended medical school for a year. It wasn't for me. I want to create."

"Were your parents disappointed?"

"I guess so. I haven't spoken to them in ten years. Enough about me." She motioned toward an aluminum folding chair, located toward the back of the room. "Have a seat, and I'll tell you about Friends of the Fish. Here's a flyer describing our group."

The paper she handed me was no more than a puff piece providing Ruby Diamond's contact information and stating the organization's goal of keeping the beach pristine. I stuffed it into my bag.

"How many members do you have?" I asked, settling into the chair and pulling out my pen and pad.

"We're not large. But we have hundreds of supporters."

"But how many actual members?"

"We don't pay dues or keep lists so its hard to say. But again, the key is those who side with us. Most are afraid to go public. They're too tied into the establishment."

At last night's meeting, the hall overflowed with residents, some in favor of the aquarium, others were with Moray. But aside from Ruby Diamond and two young men, no one seemed to support Friends of the Fish.

"Would you say you have fewer than twenty members?"

"Probably, but that's not the issue."

"Fewer than ten?"

"I'm not sure."

"How long has your group been in existence?"

"Don't know exactly. I guess we came into being when news of the aquarium's expansion plans became known."

"Okay. Let's talk about something else. I can understand your opposition to Moray, but why are you against the aquarium?"

"It's well intentioned but wrong. Tourists trampling over the dunes." She frowned. "It's not natural."

"But that wouldn't be allowed to happen."

"Not true. There is going to be a camp."

"For scientists. They won't trample or do anything to harm the environment. Besides, you live on the beach."

"I exist as one with nature. Most people aren't aware—"

A sharp rap on the door interrupted our conversation.

"I'm not expecting anyone else." Ruby frowned then eyed me suspiciously. "You didn't bring a photographer, did you?"

I shook my head.

Ruby rose from her chair as the door flung open. The young man with the billy-goat beard who had attended last night's meeting stepped into the room. His plaid shirt hung over a pair of torn jeans, and his feet were encased in flip flops.

"We need to talk now about next Thursday, Ruby. I don't like that it's not on Tuesday anymore and that they're moving the time up two hours—"

"I have a visitor," Ruby said, gesturing in my direction. A look of fear flashed through her eyes.

The man frowned. "What's going on??

"This woman's a reporter for *Animal Advocate Magazine*. She wants information on our organization."

"I'm Kristy Farrell." I extended my arm. "And you are?"

"Kyle." He squeezed my hand, perhaps a little too tightly.

"Are you a member of Friends of the Fish?" I asked.

"Yeah."

"I'd love to get your view for my article." I flipped a page on my notepad. "What's your reason for joining?"

He glanced in Ruby's direction.

"He doesn't want the land developed," Ruby answered. "Right, Kyle?"

He nodded.

"Are you an active member of Friends of the Fish? Are you an officer?"

"Officer?" He stared at me as if he didn't know the meaning of the word.

"We're not organized like a traditional group," Ruby said. "I'm chair of the group, but we don't have a vice chair, secretary, or treasurer. We sort of go with the flow with everyone pitching in when needed."

"What do you do for a living, Kyle?" I asked.

"He runs a kayak rental and sales business," Ruby said as she gently touched my elbow. "I'm sorry, but Kyle and I have work to do. I think I've told you what you need, but if you want more information, call me later. My number is on my card." She ushered me out the front door.

I never liked getting the bum's rush. Something was up.

As I lingered near the doorstep, I noticed Ruby and Kyle watching me through the front window. I headed to my car, but once out of sight, I made my way to the right side of the house where I spotted a garbage can near the open window. I knelt down and hid behind it, straining to hear the conversation inside the cottage.

"I'm worried about the set-up a week from Thursday," Kyle said. "I don't like that it's being moved up to ten o'clock. That's too early—"

"Ssh!" Ruby interrupted.

"Why should I be quiet? There's no one here."

"My window is open because of the paints, you fool. Voices carry. That snoopy reporter may still be hanging around. Let's go in the back to my apartment."

They left, and I was no longer in earshot.

Making my way to my car, I reviewed what had occurred. I'd learned nothing new from Ruby, except Friends of the Fish appeared to have only a few members. Basically the organization existed on paper.

But, more importantly, something was happening a week from this Thursday. Something that Ruby didn't want Kyle to talk about in my presence.

CHAPTER TEN

B ack home, I fed Archie and Brandy, then shooed them into the back yard at my mother's request. God forbid her fiancé should wind up with dog hair on his clothes.

Mom was upstairs getting ready for tonight's dinner party. I plopped myself down by the kitchen table with a glass of white wine, my thoughts wandering to Ruby Diamond, Jack Patterson and Sam Wong when Matt burst through the door. Judging by the spring in his step, his day had gone well.

"Are you ready to hear my idea for attracting new clients?" he asked, grinning from ear to ear. "A fall festival for animal lovers."

A fair? This was his plan to save the veterinary hospital.

He reached into the refrigerator, grabbed a beer, and popped the cap. "I'm not the only one feeling the pinch from the Health and Wellness Center for Companion Animals. Estelle's Dog Grooming, Todd's Canine Training School, and Jackson's Pet Sitting Service are also losing clients."

"When is this going to happen?"

"We're coming together in my parking lot on the third Saturday in October, so residents can find out about our services. People can bring their pets. We'll have an animal photographer for complimentary photos, sample treats, agility competitions with prizes—"

"Who's paying for this?" I was always the practical one.

"We're still looking for sponsors—"

Before he could finish, the front doorbell chimed.

"That must be my brother and Barbara." I rose from my chair and we headed out of the kitchen. "We'll talk about the festival later."

The front doorbell chimed again.

"Yup. Gotta be Tim and Barbara." My sister-in-law's signature was impatience.

I pulled open the door, and Tim and Barbara stepped into the living room. The four of us did the kiss and hug bit.

"I can't believe your mother has a boyfriend," Barbara said, rolling her eyes as Matt poured drinks. "Shouldn't she be busy with Bingo and line dancing?"

"She's always done the unexpected," I said.

Barbara slid down into an armchair, crossing her legs at the ankles, not a blonde hair out of place and not a scuff on her Manolo Blaniks.

"Tim," my mother called out as she made a grand entrance into the room. She hugged my brother, then stepped back. "You're so pale. You need to get out in the sun more. Don't you spend time outdoors with your lizards?"

Tim pushed his glasses up the bridge of his nose. "Most of my work with reptiles is done within the confines of the zoo not out in a desert." My brother was curator of herpetology for the Rocky Cove Zoo.

Once Tim left to help Matt with the drinks, my mother addressed my sister-in-law. "Oh, hello, Barbara. I forgot you were coming. You usually don't attend family functions."

I was about to say something in an attempt to thaw out the frost field between my mother and Barbara when I heard the kitchen door slam shut followed by footsteps. Abby entered the living room and greeted everyone.

"Where's Jason?" I asked.

"His law firm has him working late again. It's a fraud case involving a wealthy client who handed over more than one hundred thousand dollars to a home improvement contractor for services he never performed. Jason is meeting tonight with a detective from the police department's fraud and bunco unit."

"I think Jason is avoiding me." my mother said. "Abby, is there some reason you don't want me to meet him?"

"This is going to be a fun-filled evening," I grumbled under my breath before swallowing more wine.

I was about to steer the conversation in another direction when the doorbell chimed and my mother jumped up. "That must be Paul. I'll get it."

While she bee-lined toward the door, Abby whispered to me, "I spoke with Katie just before I left the house. There's still no word on Sam. It's like he fell off the earth."

"Any word on Jack Patterson's autopsy?"

"Nothing."

"This is Paul," my mother announced as she came back into the room. Trailing her was a tall gentleman with a small mustache matching his silver mane of hair. He wore a navy blazer, gray slacks, and a pale blue turtle neck.

"Ah, our hostess," he said as introductions were made. "I can't tell you how much I'm looking forward to dining with you this evening." He handed me a bottle of champagne.

"Mom says you're in New York on business," I said while Matt fixed Paul a vodka martini.

"Yes. I'm investing in a chain of health spas."

"Isn't that a risky business?" Barbara asked.

"Not in this case. This spa is aimed at overweight teenagers in affluent areas. We've conducted studies, and parents will pay big for this. If it does well in New York, the project will be expanded to other states."

Paul and my mother were sitting on the sofa. As Paul put his arm around my mother, an idea flashed through my mind. I darted into the kitchen, grabbed my phone, and returned to the living room.

"You two look so sweet together." I snapped a photo.

Paul frowned for a split second, then smiled. "I hope that doesn't wind up on social media. People of our generation don't like to share our private feelings with the public."

"I don't mind." My mother winked.

"I'm not going to post this," I replied. "This is just for the two of you. I thought I'd print it out, frame it, and give you both a copy."

"Thank you," he said. "Romance is intimate. It's between two people, not the immediate world."

Especially if you're married to someone else or hiding another secret. While I did feel that many folks gave too much information on the

Internet, I tended to be suspicious of someone who appeared to hide their life from others.

The doorbell chimed. This time it was the caterer. While Matt and Abby arranged the platters on our dining room table, I settled into an armchair across from my mother and Paul.

"Have you lived in Florida for a long time?" I asked Paul.

"A little more than a year."

"Paul has a magnificent condo on the ocean," my mother said.

"Where did you live before Florida?"

"All over. I travel quite a bit because of my business investments. I've lived in more than a half dozen places."

"You have a slight New York accent." I smiled.

"Kristy!" my mother called out. "Don't be rude."

"What? We all have accents."

"I was born in New York," Paul said. "I lived there for many years as well as in California, Colorado, Illinois, Connecticut, and New Jersey. I resided in Europe for a while, too."

My brother had been sitting back, sipping his scotch, and apparently listening to our conversation. He spoke up. "Kristy told me you met our mother at a gallery opening. Are you interested in art?"

"Very much."

"At one time Paul worked as an art appraiser," my mother volunteered. "He's had such an interesting life."

"Dinner is served," Matt announced.

As we sat down for dinner, I noticed Abby, who was sitting on my right, studying her phone. In the next few seconds, her fingers, looking like a spider on Prozac, began flying across the small device. Abby knew that texting during family gatherings was one of my pet peeves. This had to be important.

"What's wrong?" I whispered.

"That was Katie. The autopsy on Jack Patterson. It's done."

"Did he drown?"

Abby shook her head. "No They found a small hole in the base of his skull. Someone drove a needle into his brain."

CHAPTER ELEVEN

"That means Jack's death was premeditated," I said to my daughter in a low voice so the others couldn't hear.

Abby nodded. "Supposedly he was killed by a long thin object, like a knitting needle or an ice pick."

"Any idea of the time of death?"

"Katie didn't say, but since the body was in the water, I'm sure it's hard to pinpoint an exact time."

"Do the police have any idea of—"

"Kristy, Paul wants to tell you something," my mother interrupted.

"I just wanted to say that you set an elegant table," Paul said.

"Thank you." Resigning myself to being a good hostess, I turned my attention back to my guests. But the autopsy had piqued my interest, and questions as to what happened flashed through my mind all through dinner.

* * * * *

Before heading out to the aquarium the next morning, I drove by the new health and wellness center for companion animals. The facility, which had opened two month ago, was more than a half block in length. The other half was a parking lot which, despite the early hour, was almost filled to capacity. A sign posted on the building door read, DOGGIE DAY CARE COMING IN TWO WEEKS.

I drove away, frowning. Today's consumers liked one stop shopping, and this place was meeting all their companion animal needs. Matt's business was declining. I didn't know if his fall festival for animal lovers would be enough to help him compete with this new facility.

* * * * *

When I pulled into the aquarium parking lot, I spotted a Crown Victoria with official plates parked by the front gate. I entered the building, and as I neared my destination, I heard a familiar voice.

"Oh, no," I muttered. "It can't be."

Peeking into an office, I spotted a man sitting wide-eyed behind a desk. He was about sixty, dark hair graying at the temples, and an olive complexion with his face just beginning to show age lines. His desk plate identified him as Oscar Mejas. Standing in front of the desk, waving a sausage sized finger, was the man whose voice I recognized. Receding hairline, pot belly, blond mustache, and a smirk that made me want to slap his face—Detective Steve Wolfe.

Steve was a bully who had gone to school with Tim, constantly picking on my younger brother. After graduation, Tim had no contact with him until this summer when Steve was assigned the murder of the Rocky Cove Zoo director, of which my brother had been the prime suspect. Much to the detective's embarrassment, I proved Tim's innocence by uncovering the real murderer.

Steve spotted me. His face turned the color of a holiday ham, and the blue veins in his neck protruded until I thought they'd pop.

"What are you doing here?" He glared at me.

"I've an appointment to interview Oscar Mejas for *Animal Advocate Magazine*. Why are you here?"

"I wanted to talk to a dolphin. Why the hell do you think I'm here? I'm investigating a homicide."

"Jack Patterson?"

"What do you know about Jack Patterson?" He eyed me suspiciously.

Since I didn't want to say too much, I responded with, "I only knew that he worked here. Do you have any suspects?"

"I'm asking the questions. You want information, get it from the police department press office, not me." Facing Oscar, he said, "I'm finished with you for now. But be sure to get me that list of employees. ASAP."

Wolfe brushed passed me, then stopped in the doorway, and spun around. "I hope you're not planning to interfere with another police investigation."

"I wouldn't dream of interfering. But I'm a reporter. It's my nature to ask questions."

"Don't take this the wrong way, but you're a fool."

"What exactly is the wrong way to take that?"

"You lucked out with the case of the Rocky Cove Zoo director. But murder is dangerous business. Being nosy can cause trouble. Stick to writing about monkeys, seals, and flounders. Leave this investigation to the professionals."

CHAPTER TWELVE

As Detective Wolfe stormed out the door, I turned around and found myself facing a smiling Oscar Mejas.

"That bully needed to be put in his place," He gestured toward a straight back chair in front of his desk.

"Before we start, I want to offer my condolences on the death of your fish keeper, Jack Patterson," I said.

"Thank you. A tremendous loss." He shook his head. "I was planning on retiring at the end of the month, and Jack was in line to take my job as head fish keeper."

"Who will get it now?" I wondered if this was a motive for murder.

"I don't know. Our other two fish keepers are too new and inexperienced. Commander West is doing an outside search, but that will take time. He asked me to postpone my retirement until he finds a replacement."

"Will you?"

"As long as it doesn't take too long. Now, how can I help you?"

"My article is called "Dangers of the Deep." While I will be writing about all types of ocean predators, I'd like to begin with sharks."

He nodded. "Sharks attack about one hundred humans a year. Ten to fifteen of these attacks are fatal. Still, many stories about shark attacks are more fiction than facts. Most species are shy and swim away from any encounter with humans. Sharks are an important part of our ecosystem." Oscar Mejas rose from his chair. "Let's take a walk."

We left his office and made our way down the corridor, stopping at the shark tank. "That's a baby nurse shark," Oscar pointed out. "Born two months ago."

With a full set of teeth.

"A shark's skin is studded with bone knobs called denticles," he went on to say. "A mere touch can make your skin bleed. Sharks often bump objects in the water, and we believe this is deliberate. If the object bleeds, it's a potential meal."

After answering all my questions on sharks, Oscar said, "The ocean is the most dangerous place on earth. It's not only sharp teeth. Groupers, who can weigh up to nine hundred pounds, have grinding plates in their throats and jaws big enough to encompass a human's leg or head. They've been known to stalk divers. Then there's the swordfish who uses its razor-like bill to slash. Now let me show you one of the most lethal creatures in the waters."

We wandered down the corridor and stopped at a tank which housed a myriad of colorful fish and coral.

"What do you see at the bottom?"

I glanced down in the tank. "Nothing but rocks."

"See that over by the right," Oscar asked me.

I spotted what appeared to be a large bump in the far corner. "A brown and gray rock."

"It's not a rock. That's a stone fish," he said. "Its back is filled with venomous spines. Divers who had the misfortune to step on one of these, mistaking it for a rock, suffer muscle weakness followed by paralysis. If not treated, death follows."

We continued walking. "Here's the blue-ringed octopus. Cute little guy, isn't he?" He pointed to the tank on the far left. "Like the stone fish, he's highly toxic. His bite isn't especially painful, but that changes quickly. Your tongue starts tingling and pretty soon you experience paralysis. Within ten minutes, you're dead."

We continued for nearly thirty minutes. At the end of the tour, Oscar's parting words were, "We have more than a dozen species here at this aquarium that could kill you instantly."

* * * * *

The wind gusts off the bay had picked up. Using my hands to shield my eyes from the blowing sand, I made my way to the sea lion amphitheater.

The next show was in two hours, so the arena was empty except for Katie who was on stage with one of her sea lions.

"Come on up," she called. "I'm finishing a training session with Bea."

"Hi, Bea," I called back. The sea lion responded with three loud honks.

"I went to the police station this morning and filed a missing person's report. They finally accepted it." Katie turned her head away, but not before I saw her eyes well up with tears. "I told the officer about Sam's voice mail from Lucien Moray, but he didn't seem interested. I don't think the police will do anything."

"I'll ask Abby to talk to Jason. He has contacts in the county police department—in fact he's working on a fraud case with them now. He should be able to make a phone call that will push matters along."

"Thanks." She rubbed the top of Bea's head like you would with a dog. "But between the officer who took the missing person's report and that nasty detective I just spoke with, I don't have a lot of confidence."

"You spoke to a nasty detective about Sam?"

"Not about Sam. A detective questioned me about Jack Patterson's death. Right here. About thirty minutes ago."

"Detective Steve Wolfe?"

Katie nodded. "I don't think they have any leads in Jack's murder either. I can't imagine any motive. Sure, Jack could fly off the handle, but he never held a grudge. He was the first one to help out if you had a problem. Everyone liked him."

"Did he have a girlfriend?" I asked.

Katie shook her head. "No, girlfriend."

"Was Jack close to anyone? What about friends?"

She paused. "He was close to his older sister Jillian. She runs a horse farm about two miles from here. It's been in the Patterson family for three generations. Jack lived there with Jillian, and he helped her with the horses, too."

"You told me the last time you saw Jack was at dinner with Sam. Did Jack act differently? Was anything bothering him?"

Katie scratched her head, frowning. "Jack was unusually quiet that night. Pensive. And he did ask Sam a strange question."

The hairs on the back up my neck stood up. "What did he ask?"

"It was weird. I guess he questioned Sam because Sam works for Moray who has lots of government and political contacts."

I repeated, "Katie, what did he ask?"

"He asked if Sam knew if the beach was being used for military surveillance."

CHAPTER THIRTEEN

Since my best ideas always come when I'm eating, I decided to stop for an early lunch. Upon leaving the aquarium, the first place I came upon was a white-shingled restaurant on the beach called the Seaside Cafe.

The hostess led me to a screened-in patio with views of the bay. With the autumn breeze coming off the water, I was glad I was wearing a wool blazer. I was seated at a table directly behind two women who were deep in conversation while devouring what looked like Cobb salads. Both women appeared to be in their mid-thirties. One was blonde and preppy, the other dark and exotic looking.

"Jillian must be devastated," the blonde said. "She and Jack were so close. I wonder if she'll postpone the next horse show."

The Patterson Horse Farm. While scanning my menu, I eavesdropped on their conversation.

"I don't see how she can cancel. It's too big of an event," the dark haired woman replied. "From what I heard, she needs the revenue. Taxes are up, prices for grain have skyrocketed, and she's trying to hold the line on boarder fees and riding lessons."

"Jillian can't afford a funeral for Jack," the blonde added. "She's only having a private cremation."

"I also heard she hasn't been able to find anyone to lease Magic or Topper. Magic is great for kids, but Topper needs a more experienced rider which may be difficult to find. How will she be able to keep those horses without leasing them?"

Horse leasing was popular on Long Island with people who didn't want the expense or long-term commitment of horse ownership. For a set fee, you could lease a horse from its owner on a monthly or yearly basis. Matt and I had leased a horse for Abby when she was fourteen and continued until she left for college. She had recently mentioned that she hoped to get back into riding.

Suddenly, a germ of an idea began growing in my mind.

I ordered and quickly devoured a Caesar salad with shrimp. Back in my car, I phoned Abby at the veterinary hospital.

"You're off tomorrow, right?" I said. "What are your plans?"

"Sleeping late, running on the boardwalk, organizing my closet. But why do I think that's not happening."

"How'd you like to see a woman about a horse?"

* * * * *

Back home, I made my way into the kitchen for a well-deserved glass of wine. No sooner had I settled down with my Chardonnay and new crossword puzzle when the two dogs bounded into the room. Archie, all one hundred pounds, sat on my foot while Brandy pawed my lap while whining softly.

"Sorry, guys. Just wine here. No cheese and crackers tonight."

Seconds later, a car pulled into the driveway. The dogs scampered to the door as Matt stepped into the house.

"You appear to be in good mood," I said, noting the smile on his face.

"I've scheduled more activities for the animal lover's festival," he announced, while bending over to greet the canines. When he finished providing belly rubs, he grabbed a beer from the refrigerator and pulled up a chair.

"Who's paying for this?" I asked.

"We're still looking for sponsors, but it won't cost that much. The police canine unit is doing a free demonstration, and a local rescue group is bringing a few of their farm animals."

"But there will be costs involved. You need to advertise. You also should check with your insurance company—"

He held up his hands. "I'll take care of it."

This was a man who could rattle off the name and ailment of every dog, cat, and hamster he'd seen in the last year, but would forget to cash a client's check.

"Why don't we make up a 'to-do' list," I suggested. "I'll help you with an advertising campaign and—"

"You have your own career, Kristy. You don't have time for this."

I bit my tongue. If not properly organized, this fair could be a disaster that could ruin Matt's reputation. But I had to handle this gently.

"It won't take that much time. Besides, it sounds like fun." I felt my nose growing.

Suddenly we both looked up as the door slammed. My mother was home.

Both dogs bounded toward her, waiting for her to acknowledge them. But she brushed past them.

"What are you doing home so early?" I asked, glancing at the clock. "I thought you were dining with Paul."

"Something came up. Business meeting. We had to change plans."

"You can join us for dinner. This will give us a chance to catch up."

"Thanks, but I'll pass. I have a slight headache. I think I'll go up to my room. Goodnight."

As she passed by, I saw she was crying.

CHAPTER FOURTEEN

"She and Paul probably had a lover's quarrel," Abby said as we whizzed along the highway. I had told her about my mother's strange behavior last night.

I nodded. "You're probably right, but I'm worried. She didn't come down for breakfast this morning. Ever since she arrived, she's been so mysterious."

We finally pulled into the gravel parking lot of the Patterson Horse Farm.

"Time to be a Nosy Nellie, Mom," Abby said as we hopped out of my car.

"Learning about the victim often provides insight into the murder."

"I'll ride, you ask questions."

"Where are you meeting Jillian Patterson?" I asked as we hopped out of my car. Abby, at my suggestion, had scheduled an appointment with the horse farm owner to discuss leasing Topper. Dressed in her old striped shirt, riding breeches, and knee high riding boots, Abby lugged her saddle while I carried her helmet and a bag of carrots.

"Jillian said she'd be working in the east aisle."

As we hiked across the parking lot, I gazed at the idyllic country scene. To the back right, nearly a dozen horses grazed in grassy paddocks. To the left, were two outdoor arenas. The stable loomed directly up ahead: a red structure that looked large enough to house more than fifty horses. It was in need of a paint job.

Inside the stable, the horsey scent combined with the odor of manure. Judging by the intensity, it was fresh manure. More than half the stalls were empty and missing names plates, an indication this facility might not be filled to capacity.

Turning into the east wing, I spotted a woman pushing a wheelbarrow stacked high with bales of hay.

"Jillian Patterson?" my daughter asked.

She nodded. Tall, muscular, no make-up, fingernails embedded with dirt, and dark brown hair pulled back in a pony tail, Jillian sported a small horseshoe tattoo above her left wrist and wore a horseshoe pendant on a silver chain hanging around her neck.

"You must be Abby," she said. "I'll be with you as soon as I unload this. Take a look around while you wait. Topper's stall is the last on the left."

Topper, a chestnut quarter horse, sported a white blaze extending down his face. Abby fed him a carrot while I stroked his neck. Minutes later, Jillian returned.

"Topper's a sweetie," Jillian said. "Want to try him out, Abby?" My daughter nodded.

Jillian led Topper out of his stall. While Abby rode, Jillian and I watched from under the shade of a nearby oak tree.

"Sorry to hear about your brother," I said. "I didn't know Jack personally, but Abby's best friend did. Do you know Katie Chandler?"

Jillian nodded. "I've known Katie since kindergarten. But she was especially close to Jack. He saw her all the time since they both worked at the aquarium." She sighed. "I miss my brother something awful. Especially our mornings together."

"Mornings?"

"We both lived over there." Jillian gestured toward a white clapboard house behind the arenas. "I manage the stable. Jack's real love is— was-the sea. But every morning before he left for the aquarium, he'd help me feed the horses and muck the stalls. Then we'd eat breakfast together."

"When was the last time you saw him?"

"Sunday morning. When he didn't show up to help in the barn on Monday, I checked his bedroom. He hadn't slept in his bed.

"Were you worried?"

She shrugged. "More angry than worried." Jillian opened her mouth as if to say more but paused and closed it.

One of the best ways to encourage a reluctant talker is by silence. I didn't say another word.

Jillian continued. "When my brother was in college, he had a drinking problem. But if he had too much alcohol, he was always responsible. He'd never drive. He would stay over somewhere or sleep in his car. He'd been sober now for five years. I thought he had a relapse and was sleeping it off somewhere."

Jillian appeared willing, almost anxious, to talk about her brother. I decided to try a long shot.

"A few nights before he died, Jack had dinner with Katie and her fiancé, Sam Wong. Do you know Sam, too?"

"Sam Wong? Never met him." Jillian rubbed dirt off her chin. "But I think Jack knew him. Sam called here a few nights before Jack's body was discovered."

"Do you know what he wanted?"

"Nope. Apparently, the voice mail on Jack's cell was full, so Sam left a message on our house phone. He asked Jack to return his call."

Jillian went back to work. Since Abby was still riding, I made my way to the barn, passing a paddock, which unlike the one visible from the parking lot, had almost no grass. No horses in it either.

Upon reaching the barn, I spotted a woman, who appeared to be close to my age. She was grooming a light tan horse with white around its muzzle.

"Nice looking horse," I said.

The woman smiled. "Gulliver was a beauty in his heyday. He's almost twenty-five years old now."

"Is he a lease or is he's yours?"

"He's mine. I bought him when he was seven years old."

"Have you always boarded him here?"

She nodded. "Yes, I have."

"My daughter is riding here today. She eventually wants to buy her own horse. In the meantime, she will be leasing Topper. I'm glad because that will give her the opportunity to see what this place is like."

The woman didn't comment.

"If you boarded here for nearly eighteen years, you must be satisfied with the services and accommodations."

She hesitated. "I was. At one time this was a great place. But not so much lately. It's the little things. Jillian is a great gal, but she's cutting corners. The back paddock should be seeded, fences need mending, and there never seems to be enough shavings in the stalls."

"That's terrible," I said.

"Don't get me wrong. Jillian loves the horses. She works twenty-four/seven. But she's facing difficulties staying afloat. It's a vicious cycle. Rising costs mean rising boarding fee. But you can only raise fees so much."

The woman led her horse into a stall, then returned and added," A few years ago, Jillian had to get rid of her barn helper. Couldn't afford the salary. For a while, she had her father. He was on in age but still did light work. When he passed away, her brother returned to assist. I don't know what she'll do now."

CHAPTER FIFTEEN

"I can't believe Katie invited me. Tickets are twenty-five hundred dollars," Abby said the next afternoon as we sped along the highway in her car.

"It's her house. She can invite whomever she wants."

Abby and I were on our way to the aquarium's kick-off fundraiser—a cocktail party at Katie's home. When Katie heard that Commander West had invited me, she asked Abby to attend, too.

"What's Katie doing with Gus today?" I asked Abby as we exited onto a country road. Gus was Katie's thirty-pound Maine coon cat.

"He's at my place. I took him last night. Gus is strictly a house kitty, and Katie is concerned that with all the visitors today Gus might escape and get lost."

Soon our destination loomed in the distance. Katie Chandler's house was located on a half acre of land with views of the bay. The house featured a widow's walk—an enclosed cupola on the top level designed for wives of ship captains to observe vessels returning from sea. A huge tree with leaves turning crimson shaded much of the front lawn.

"I'm glad you're here early. Come in." Katie swung open the door. We entered a room brimming with antiques but comfortable looking. I spotted Commander West and Bradford Monroe under an archway where they appeared to be deep in conversation with a woman holding a clipboard.

"That's the caterer," Katie said. "They're discussing last minute details."

"Who's minding the aquarium?" I asked. The aquarium closed at five-thirty and the cocktail party was from four to six. It was a little past three-thirty now."

"It runs fine without the three of us." Katie laughed. "Commander West and Bradford are often away on business."

"But what about you and the sea lion show? Don't you have one scheduled at four?"

She nodded. "Usually. But Commander West thought it important that I be here to meet and greet the guests, so we substituted a penguin encounter instead. Our seabird keeper is handling that."

Commander West and Bradford Monroe had finished their conversation with the caterer and now greeted us.

"Abby has seen the house many times, but you never did," Katie said to me. "I promised the commander a tour before the guests arrive. Would you like to join us?"

"I'd love it."

"I'll come too," Bradford said. "Katie showed me her house weeks ago when we discussed our set-up for the event. But I can never get enough of antiques. I want to see all these beautiful items again."

"I might as well tag along." Abby shrugged and followed us.

"My great-great-grandfather was a sea captain who traveled the world. That tea cart is from Italy, the rug, Turkey, the vase, China." Katie pointed to different items in the living room. "Oh, the painting above the fireplace is from the southern region of France."

"There are four rooms upstairs," Katie continued as we trekked up the steep stairway. "That's more than I need, so I kept the captain's study just as it was more than 150 years ago, filled with mementos from his travels. It's the most interesting room in the house."

As she swung open the door, we stepped back into the nineteenth century.

On display were Japanese prints, Chinese porcelain, and African sculptures. Katie pointed out more than a dozen objects in the room including an Egyptian cartouche, a Haitian voodoo doll, an invitation to the Governor's Ball in Mauritius off the African coast, and a fourteenth century Samurai sword.

"That sword is worth some bucks," Bradford said. "Sure you won't reconsider, Katie?"

"Reconsider what?" I asked.

"I'm donating a few items to the aquarium's art and antiques auction," Katie answered. Bradford would like me to donate the sword, but I said no. I really want to keep it. That sword was given to my great-great-grandfather by the Emperor of Japan. It has sentimental value."

"You've been more than generous, Katie," Commander West added as he shot a disapproving look at Bradford.

Katie turned toward me. "Jack Patterson helped me select three items to contribute to the auction—a silver box from Mexico, a wooden troll from Norway, and an antique clock from Germany. It's funny. He'd been in this house with me so many times as a child, but he'd never seen this room until a few weeks ago. My grandmother always kept it locked."

"Everything here is truly magnificent," Commander West said. "I'd love to browse further, but I think Bradford and I should go downstairs to greet our guests. You should join us Katie. It's nearly four o'clock, so everyone should be arriving soon."

While descending the stairs, Katie grabbed my shoulder and whispered, "I thought we'd have more free time now, but we don't. It's imperative that we talk after the party. I heard a rumor about Jack that may explain his death."

I nodded. "Of course, we'll stay later. You tend to your guests, and we'll talk once everyone has left."

Katie joined the commander and Bradford while I wandered outside, pausing to take in the magnificent view of the bay. Abby headed to the outdoor bar and returned with two glasses of white wine. She handed me one. I told Abby about Katie's comment.

"Whatever did she hear?" Abby asked.

I shrugged. "Katie used the word 'rumor' so it may or may not be true. But we'll find out soon enough. Meanwhile, I need to locate Bradford Monroe. He's introducing me to some of the guests, so they can tell me why they support the aquarium. Hopefully, I'll get a few good quotes for my land acquisition story."

I went back inside. As I hiked across the room, I noticed a woman stationed by the stairs. She wore a badge identifying her as an aquarium volunteer. Abby had questioned Katie about inviting an army of strangers into her home with so many valuable antiques. Katie had laughed and said she didn't think guests paying twenty-five hundred dollars a ticket would steal.

Nevertheless, Commander West had obtained the services of a volunteer to help. This woman's job was to politely inform guests who started heading upstairs that the area was off limits. She was a retired police officer.

"Excuse me, Kristy," said a voice from behind. "I've someone I'd like you to meet."

I turned and faced Bradford Monroe. Standing next to him was a tall, slender man with a horsey face.

"This is Alan Cummings. He's one of our biggest benefactors," Bradford said. "I thought you might get a quote from him on why the expansion project is so important."

We shook hands. "Any connection to Cummings Electronics?" I asked, referring to a large Long Island chain store.

He grinned. "That's my company."

Although Lucien Moray was one of New York's wealthiest individuals, I realized the aquarium had some heavy hitters on their side.

Bradford left to greet another guest. I whipped out my pen and pad. "Why do you support the aquarium's expansion?"

"I'm especially interested in the portion of land that will be designated as a camp for marine scientist. We need to study our waters. Did you know oceans are the largest ecosystem on earth? They're home to some of our oldest species, such as the shark."

Alan Cummings continued talking, and I jotted down plenty of quotes for my story. This man not only loved the water, but he was knowledgeable on the topic.

"Did you grow up by the shore?" I asked.

"I grew up on Long Island, but I lived further inland. I still do. But I come out here as much as possible. I keep my boat at the Clam Cove Sailing and Yacht Club."

"Wasn't that club in the news recently? Didn't the police find a body?" I asked, innocently.

"Yes." His face darkened and he frowned. "Horrible."

"I read it was the aquarium's fish keeper. How did he get in?"

"We have a big sign at the entrance stating dock access is for members and guests only, but we keep the gates open during the day and only lock them at night, between midnight and five in the morning."

"Why do you think he was there?" I tried to sound as casual as possible.

Cummings shrugged. "Perhaps he was visiting a member."

"But no one came forward to claim they knew him."

His frown deepened. "I really don't know. I'm sure the police will figure it out. For the meantime, we've tightened security. We have a guard at the gate—members must now show IDs and guests must sign in. Do you have any more questions about the aquarium's expansion project?"

It seemed that Alan Cummings didn't want to discuss Jack Patterson's death. After he left, Bradford brought over an aging former television actress who lived a few miles away in the tony Hamptons. She discussed her reasons for supporting the aquarium.

The time went quickly, and I gathered plenty of information for my story. I noticed Abby spending her time with a young man dressed in gray slacks and a maroon polo. Abby was smiling, and their body language indicated they were comfortable in each other's presence.

My mind wandered to thoughts of my daughter's relationship with Jason. Abby and her boyfriend had been living together for less than two months. I wondered how their living arrangements were working. I liked Jason a lot and hoped marriage was in their future.

I sighed and headed to the bar for another wine.

Most of the guests, including Abby's new friend, departed by six o'clock. After saying good-bye to Commander West and Bradford, I was about to pour a cup of coffee before the caterer dismantled the urn. Katie came running up, slightly out of breath.

"The aquarium's security guard just texted me. He was doing his rounds right after closing, and he said something's wrong with Bea."

"What's the matter?"

"He didn't tell me, and he's not responding to my texts. I'm driving over there. Can you wait here until I return? We need to talk."

"It's fine with me," I said, glancing at Abby who had just joined us.

"Jason and I are meeting friends for drinks, but not until much later," she said. "Of course, I'll wait."

"If there's a problem, I'll call," Katie promised. "Meanwhile, just relax and make yourself at home. The caterer needs to finish cleaning up."

Katie dashed out the door. I plopped down on the sofa and kicked off my shoes. Abby sank into a nearby armchair.

"So, I guess you had a good time," I said to my daughter. "It looked like you made a new friend." I was referring to the young man wearing the maroon polo.

Abby shook her head and smiled. "I know where you're headed with this, Mom. I'm not seeking another relationship. Jason and I are fine."

"Oh, I wasn't thinking anything at all."

"Sure you were." Abby crossed her legs. "My new friend, as you refer to him, is the son on the county medical examiner. I questioned him about Jack Patterson's murder. I thought it would help if we knew more about the autopsy findings."

I moved to the edge of my seat. "What did he say?"

"The needle was inserted at a point in the base of the brain that would cause instant death. Whoever murdered Jack was familiar with human anatomy."

Abby and I discussed the murder, followed by a brief and non-revealing conversation about the status of her relationship with Jason. When the caterers finally departed, Abby glanced at her watch. Almost an hour had passed since Katie had left.

"I didn't think she'd be this long. I really need to leave," Abby said. "I think I'll text Katie and see what's happening."

Fifteen minutes later, Katie had not returned Abby's text nor the message my daughter left on voice mail.

"This is not like Katie." Abby frowned. "I hope all is okay with her sea lion."

I heard the front doorknob turn.

"Katie's home," I said.

The door swung open, but it wasn't Katie.

I don't know who looked more surprised—Abby or the young man now facing her.

My daughter rose from her chair. "Sam?"

CHAPTER SIXTEEN

"Sam Wong." Abby said, hands on hips. "Where have you been? Katie's been worried sick."

"I'm sorry. I had no choice. Lucien sent me on an assignment upstate and ordered me not to say a word to anyone, including my fiancée."

"Couldn't you have told Katie you'd be away without providing details or secrets?"

He shook his head. "No. Lucien was adamant. He sent me to initiate talks with the owner of several acres of land upstate he wants to develop into an office complex. He was afraid if I mentioned going away, someone might follow me or somehow discover where I was headed. If Lucien's interest in the property was known, the price would jump. Lucien gave me a special cell phone to use and told me to leave my old one home. He said that while I was away I was only to use the new phone for business. Was Katie really worried about me?"

"Sam Wong," Abby said. "You are clueless."

Ignoring Abby's comment, Sam said, "I just came from a meeting with Lucien, the land owner, and his lawyer. The deal's been sealed, so I can talk now. As soon as I left Lucien's office, I texted Katie, but she hasn't replied. Where is she?"

"At the aquarium," Abby answered. "Her sea lion may be sick."

"Will she be back soon?"

"She hasn't responded to my texts." Abby frowned.

"Sam, I'm Abby's mom, Kristy Farrell. I think we should go to the aquarium."

* * * * *

Sam led the way in his car, a silver convertible, while Abby and I followed. The drive to the aquarium took us less than five minutes. When we arrived, only two vehicles occupied the parking lot—Katie's Vespa and a beat up pick-up truck that looked to be about ten years old. We made our way onto the sand and trekked up the pebbled path to the gate.

The gate to the aquarium grounds was locked, but we could see the outdoor sea lion amphitheater. I spotted several sea lions in the water and a few resting upon rocks. None appeared in distress.

"Katie," the three of us yelled in unison.

There was no response.

"She's here. That's her Vespa," Sam insisted.

As we called out again, I remembered I had Commander West's business card. "Let me call his cell."

"Don't leave," the commander said after I explained the situation. "I only live three miles away. I'll be right down."

Within minutes, Commander West arrived. "Where's the security guard? That's his pick-up truck in the lot."

"No one seems to be here," I said.

The commander unlocked the gate. We dashed to the sea lion amphitheater, but all was peaceful.

"Where could Katie be?" Abby asked.

"We need to check the staff area behind the stage," Commander West replied. He hurried across the bridge spanning the moat. We all followed. The commander unlocked the door at the back of the stage that led to the staff workroom. It was empty.

"Everything in its place, too," he said. "There's no indication of trouble."

"Trouble?" Sam echoed.

"Don't jump to conclusions. Let's try the main building," I suggested. "Maybe Katie went inside to look for the security guard."

"I bet we'll find her having a cup of coffee with the guard." Abby smiled weakly. "She's probably fine. Right, Mom?"

I didn't reply. I had that sinking feeling in the pit of my stomach. Instinct told me she was not fine.

We hurried back to the main building. Commander West unlocked the door and swung it open.

I gasped.

The security guard laid spread on the lobby floor, face down, blood splattered across his head. Aquarium brochures had fallen from a nearby stone table and were scattered across the floor.

The commander knelt down. "He's alive. Call 911."

My hear pounding, I made the call.

"There's a first-aid kit in the top drawer of the ticket taker's desk. Bring it to me," Commander West ordered.

As Sam scooted to the desk to retrieve the kit, Abby and I exchanged glances. I mouthed "Katie." Abby nodded, and we took off down the corridor to search for our friend. Surrounded by nothing but fish tanks, the hallway was eerily silent.

"We should have taken the commander's key, Mom. Without it, we can't get into any of the employee sections."

Suddenly, I stopped. My legs felt like jelly.

"What's wrong?" Abby grabbed me.

I couldn't speak. I pointed to a tank where eel-like creatures glided through the water. But they weren't eels. The sign below the tank read, SEA SNAKES—one of he most venomous snakes inhabiting the planet.

Floating in the tank was a body.

Katie Chandler.

CHAPTER SEVENTEEN

Nausea swept over me.

Abby screamed.

I steadied myself as Sam came running, but there was nothing we could do.

Katie was dead.

"Someone get her out of there," Abby said, sobbing.

Sam's stare was zombie-like. Suddenly, his expression changed. His eyes flashed anger. He clenched his fists. "She didn't just fall in. Someone did this to her."

"You're right," I said, choking on my words. "But before we can find out what happened, the body needs to be removed." Glancing sideways, I shuddered. "With all the sea snakes, this will require special skills beyond that of the police and medical examiner. I'll tell Commander West to contact one of the fish keepers to stand-by."

Before trekking down the hall, I placed my hand on Sam's shoulder, murmuring, "I'm so sorry." Then I hugged my daughter as tears streamed from both our faces. This was the first time Abby experienced the death of a close contemporary. As college roommates, she and Katie shared a special bond. Now that was gone.

As I left to find Commander West, I glanced back at Sam and Abby, clinging to each other in support.

* * * * *

Fifteen minutes later, head fish keeper Oscar Mejas, who had been called in, assisted the police in removing the body of Katie Chandler from the sea snake tank. Paramedics had taken the unconscious security guard to the hospital. The aquarium was swarming with law enforcement— crime scene investigators, medical examiner's staff, and two homicide detectives, including my nemesis, detective Steve Wolfe.

Once Detective Wolfe spotted me, he stopped in his tracks, every blue vein in his neck ready to pop. A nice contrast to his red face.

"You again." He growled.

"I wanted to say "down boy" but I couldn't bring myself to utter anything except "I discovered the body."

He glowered at me for a few seconds, then whipped out a pad and pen. "Start from the beginning. What happened?"

"Katie received a text saying something was wrong with her sea lion, so she hurried over here. It was getting late. When she didn't return texts, we decided to come look."

"Who is this *we*? Who besides you?"

"My daughter Abby and Katie's fiancé, Sam Wong. He just returned."

Detective Wolfe asked a few more questions in an attempt to estimate a time line of Katie's whereabouts this afternoon.

"I don't think anything is wrong with Bea," I said.

"Who the hell is Bea?"

"The sea lion."

"What am I now, the ASPCA? I handle homicides—of humans."

"If Bea is fine, someone lured Katie here under false pretenses. That's probably the same person who murdered her."

Wolfe paused, scratching his chin. "Let me think a minute."

I bit my lip so not to respond to that comment.

"Who sent the text?" he asked.

"Supposedly, the security guard." I shrugged. "But maybe the killer grabbed the guard's phone and sent the message to lure Katie here."

Wolfe jotted down some notes. "As soon as the guard regains consciousness, I'll speak with him." He flipped his pad shut. "That's all for now."

He didn't remind me not to interfere, which was good. I was in no mood to argue.

Once Detective Wolfe departed, Abby came running over. Tears were still running down her cheeks. She had just finished her interview with Wolfe's partner.

"Let's go home," I said. "There's nothing more we can do here."

* * * * *

Abby drove home a little too fast and aggressively for my liking. Any attempts I made at conversation, she cut short with one word responses.

Pulling into the driveway, I spotted smoke arising from the fire pit on our patio. "Your father's in the back yard. Come on."

Entering the yard, the first person I saw was Jason. Abby had called him from the car to tell him what had happened. He ran to my daughter, and they hugged.

Matt rushed toward me. "Are you okay?"

"As well as can be under the circumstances." Quickly, I scanned the scene, relieved my mother wasn't here. I loved her dearly but didn't need her well-meaning interference.

As if reading my mind, Matt said, "You're mom's visiting Marcia Silver tonight." Marcia and my mother had worked together at a local insurance agency for twenty years and were best friends.

"How about you, Abby? Are you okay?" Matt asked, glancing beyond my shoulder, an easy task since he towered over me by more than a foot.

Abby approached with Jason not far behind. "We need to find out who killed Katie. Let's go over everything we know so far."

"I brewed some coffee before you got here," Matt said. "I'll bring us all some."

Minutes later, my hands wrapped around my coffee mug, I huddled with the others near the fire pit, finding warmth against the chilly autumn night air.

"There are so many facts we don't know," I said. "Was the security guard knocked out before or after Katie's murder? How was she lured to the sea snake tank? Or was she knocked unconscious and dragged there? We don't know if she was killed by the sea snakes, or if she was dead before she hit the water."

"We won't know any of this until the autopsy," Abby answered. "Right now, I want to focus on the *why* not the *how*. I intend to ask Sam why he neglected to tell Katie he was going away, and why he never returned her texts or calls."

"But he told you—"

"I know what he said." Abby glared, her eyes as fiery as the flame in the pit. "He should have contacted her despite Moray's admonition. Katie was his fiancé, and Sam supposedly is leaving Moray's employ at the end of the year."

"Still, Moray is not someone you want to cross. I'm sure Sam wants to leave on friendly terms." I fiddled through my bag, finally grabbing my pen and pad from my bag. "Let's list all the people we should question— Katie's friends, co-workers, fam…" I stopped mid-sentence.

"What's the matter?" Matt asked.

"Her grandmother's estate. Katie was executor. What happens now?"

"There's probably a line of succession," Jason answered. "Someone to take over as executor upon her death. That's how it usually works."

"But what about the six million dollar donation?" I felt like a lead balloon had landed in the pit of my stomach. "Has she disbursed it yet?"

Abby groaned. "No. Katie told me she planned to make the donation around Thanksgiving."

"Will it still go to the aquarium?"

"I haven't seen the will, but Abby told me Katie had options involving several charities and the amount she could disperse to each." Jason shrugged. "Depending upon the new executor and how the will was written, the donation could be up in the air."

CHAPTER EIGHTEEN

While sipping my morning coffee, my phone trilled. "This can't be good," I mumbled as my editor's name popped up.

Olivia Johnson didn't phone her writers. That job was reserved for Clara. Plus, it was Sunday, before eight in the morning.

"Olivia Johnson here," she said. "I saw a newscast about the murder of the aquarium's sea lion trainer."

No "hello" or "I'm sorry to bother you on a Sunday." That was Olivia. She went right to the point.

"Yes," I said. "Katie Chandler—"

"A fish keeper was killed a week ago," she interrupted. "What is going on?"

"I'm not sure."

"Well, I need you to find out."

Silence.

"Kristy, did you hear me?"

"Yes. But I'm surprised. When I investigated the murders at the Rocky Cove Zoo, you were reluctant to get the magazine involved."

"I was wrong. The story you uncovered nearly doubled our circulation. We need to show corporate management it wasn't a fluke. We want them to know our readership is increasing. And murder coverage will do that."

Before I could say that this wasn't the type of story we could sustain on a permanent basis, Olivia went on to say, "You and I both know there will not be murders to write about every two months. But this buys us time. I need to keep the circulation high. High circulation means more advertising, which means more revenue. This new corporate management is focused on the bottom line."

"Katie Chandler was my daughter's best friend. Of course, my goal is to find her killer. But I can't guarantee I can do that, especially in time for our October deadline." I knew my voice sounded angry.

"Try harder. I'm sure once people start reading us, they will continue. It's getting them to pick up that first copy." Olivia hung up.

"You look like a cat being forced to swallow a pill," Matt said as he sauntered into the kitchen. "What's wrong?"

"I have a lot of respect for Olivia, but she wants to capitalize on Katie's death." I told Matt about my editor's phone call.

"But you want to find out who killed Katie, too," he said. "Your motives may be different, but your goals are the same."

"You're right," I agreed, reluctantly, after pondering his comment. "I'll never get to the bottom of this if I let my emotions control me." I rose from my chair. "Let's see what the local news media is saying about Katie's murder."

We headed into the living room where I turned on the television. Katie's death was a major story on the Long Island news channel. The police had not ruled anything out, including suicide. I couldn't believe it. *Suicide.* People kill themselves by overdosing on pills or shooting a bullet in their brain. The idea of ending your life by jumping into a tank of venomous sea creatures seemed preposterous.

Dozens of scenarios swirled through my mind. But one thought kept recurring. Jack and Katie, both killed within a week of each other, worked at the aquarium.

Coincidence? I think not.

Did the murders relate to the donation from the Alicia Wilcox Chandler Estate? Or was something else happening at Clam Cove?

Although it appeared that Sam Wong's temporary disappearance had nothing to do with the two deaths, I felt Sam might hold the key to the murders.

I drained my cup, grabbed my phone, and punched in Abby's number.

"Do you know how to contact Sam?" I asked. "Can you set up a meeting with the three of us?"

"Of course. But I have an immediate problem, Mom," she said. "It's Katie's cat, Gus. Owl is terrified of him. She freaked out when she saw him and bee-lined for under my bed. Gus wants to be friends, but Owl will have no part of it. She won't come out if he's around."

Owl was a calico cat my husband had rescued from a dumpster. We brought her to our house, but she turned out to be a real "scaredy cat" when it came to Archie and Brandy, so Abby adopted her. Apparently, Owl felt the same way toward cats as she did dogs.

"Katie once told me that Gus gets along with dogs." Abby hesitated, but I had a good idea of what was coming next. "Katie would want me to be sure I found a good home for him. Do you think you could take him?"

Matt had brought rescued animals home from the veterinary hospital, and our dogs usually were fine. Key word is *usually*. When dealing with animals every situation is different. Odds were Archie, Brandy, and Gus would get along splendidly, but until they met, no one could be sure. "Why don't you bring him here later, Abby, and we'll see how it goes. Meanwhile, don't forget to call Sam."

* * * * *

Matt and I were cleaning up the dinner dishes when Abby and Jason paraded into the house, toting a large cat carrier containing Gus. Archie and Brandy, who were in the backyard, knew something was up. They bounded toward the house.

As Abby released the cat, I slowly pulled open the door and let in the two dogs, one at a time. They both began the butt sniff ritual with Gus. The cat tensed, but none of the animals showed aggression. Finally the dogs trotted off to the living room. Gus remained with us.

"They appear to tolerate each other," Abby said. "Sometimes that's the best you can hope for." She changed the subject. "Sam's agreed to meet with us tomorrow. What's this about, Mom?"

"I know you were Katie's best friend. But Sam was her fiancé. She may have told him something she never mentioned to you. Or vice versa. I think it's important to bring the two of you together to share information."

"Like a puzzle," Jason said. "You put all the pieces together to come up with the picture, right?"

Jason was prone to analogies.

Abby nodded in agreement, then said, "Where's grandma?"

"She's on a winery tour with her friend Marcia Silver. She 's staying at Marcia's place tonight." From the corner of my eye, I spied Gus scampering out of the kitchen.

"Is Paul Andre with grandma and Marcia?"

I shook my head. "I don't think so. I had hoped to ask my mother what was going on, but we haven't crossed paths since she came home crying two days ago."

"Grandma was expecting a ring," Abby said. "Maybe Paul jilted her."

"Possibly. She's got to come home sometime. When she does, I'll find out what happened. Meanwhile, who wants a glass of wine?"

Everyone accepted. Matt poured Chardonnay into four glasses and we headed to the living room. There was Brandy, stretched out on the living room floor, her back touching Archie, whose body was curled up around Gus. The cat's eyes were closed, and I heard a faint purring amid canine snoring.

"I guess they get along well, after all," Abby said with a smile.

* * * * *

Around eight a.m. Monday morning, I pulled into the parking lot of Pirate Pete's Coffee Shop located about five miles west of Clam Shell Cove.

Pirate Pete's was different than most of the restaurants that dominated the area. Overlooking the docks where commercial fishing boats moored, this place was out of the 1950s—right down to its Formica tables.

I spotted Sam Wong in a far corner booth, staring at the ceiling.

"They don't have a big breakfast crowd," I said, upon reaching the table. We appeared to be the restaurant's only customers. "Do they burn the toast?"

"Their breakfast patrons are long gone. They're fisherman, and by this time they're out on the water. That's why when Abby called and said you wanted to meet, I suggested this place. We can talk in private."

"How are you holding up?" I slid into a chair.

His eyes filled up as he shook his head. "I can't believe Katie is dead. We started planning our wedding last—"

"Coffee?" interrupted a buxom blonde waitress, also reminiscent of the nineteen fifties.

Abby had entered the restaurant and was headed toward us. "Make it three," I said to the waitress. She nodded and filled our cups.

Not one for formalities, my daughter slid into a chair and zoomed straight to the point. "Sam, do you know about the funeral plans yet?"

"They'll be a memorial service as soon as the body is released by the medical examiner—at least that's what I'm told," he said, a bitterness in his voice. "I'm not a relative so they don't tell me anything."

"Who do they release the body to?" I knew that Katie's parents had died in a car accident when she was fifteen. Katie was raised by her grandmother, Alicia Wilcox Chandler, who passed away a year ago.

"The body is going to her cousin, Calvin Chandler. He's her only relative. He's the one making the funeral arrangements."

"I can't believe that." Abby slammed down her cup, spilling coffee on the table. "Katie despised Calvin."

"Why?" I asked.

"Calvin is a con artist. Years ago, he was arrested and spent six months in prison for operating a Ponzi scheme."

"That wasn't the first time he'd been involved in illegal activities," Sam added. "He was a wide receiver on his college football team, and he was caught accepting bribes to throw the games. He got kicked out of school."

Abby nodded. "Since he was released from prison, he's worked in a variety of sales jobs. Supposedly, he hasn't been in anymore trouble."

"You look skeptical?" I said.

"Katie told me there were rumors about his use of unethical business practices."

"So what can I getcha?" The waitress had returned, breaking the tension for a few moments while we scanned the menus. Sam ordered oatmeal, Abby, an English muffin, and I selected blueberry pancakes, which according to the signs posted throughout the room, were "world famous." After refilling my coffee cup, the waitress departed, and I asked Sam, "Do you know who will replace Katie as executor of her grandmother's estate?"

"Calvin, unfortunately. Alicia Wilcox Chandler named him as executor in the event of Katie's death. She had a soft spot for the boy. He bamboozled her. She thought he was framed for the Ponzi scheme."

"What about the football bribes? Did she believe that was a frame-up, too?"

"Alicia dismissed that as coming from the rash nature and immaturity of youth." Sam shook his head.

"Did Katie know about this? Didn't she try to convince her grandmother to name someone else as secondary executor?" I asked.

"Katie didn't like it, but she wasn't really concerned. What person under thirty thinks they are going to suddenly die?"

"So, will the six million still go to the aquarium?"

"Probably not." Sam leaned back. "There's twelve million to be distributed. Alicia named three charities—Clam Cove Aquarium, the Seafarer's Museum, and the Clam Cove Lighthouse Preservation Fund. She specified the money was to be divided among them but not necessarily equally. The executor was given the power to determine how much each organization would get. But the will specifies that each group must get at least three million, and no one group can get more than six million."

"Katie thought the aquarium's plan was the most deserving," Abby added.

"There's something that's been bothering me for awhile. Katie worked for the aquarium," I said. "Isn't that a conflict of interest?"

Abby shook her head. "Katie told me that her grandmother specifically stated in her will that she had no issue with her granddaughter's employment at the aquarium. I understand the will was written by an old and respected law firm. Katie said it was ironclad."

I nodded. "But the money has to go to charities. Calvin can't keep it for himself. So why wouldn't he honor Katie's pledge?"

"There's nothing he'd like better than getting in good with Lucien Moray," Sam said. "Calvin has the opportunity to do this now by only giving the minimum to the aquarium. No matter how great their fund raising efforts, it's doubtful they can make up the loss in time to buy the property."

"Leaving Moray free to buy the land?" I completed the thought.

"Moray would probably reward Calvin handsomely." Abby clenched her fists.

For a few moments, we sat in silence. Abby finally spoke, addressing her question to Sam. "Katie told me you were leaving Moray's employ."

"That's right. I've given him my notice. He asked me to stay on till the end of the year, so I could tie up lose ends. I agreed."

"Why did you agree to that?" Abby inherited my bluntness.

"So the parting would be amicable. You don't cross Lucien Moray. I'm not sure what I'll do but, whatever it is, I'll use him as a reference."

I recalled what I'd seen the day I interviewed Lucien Moray. "Sam, your office looked as if you were ready to leave now. Barren walls, no personal mementos or work related items on your desk, not even a computer."

He smiled slightly. "I use a laptop, Mrs. Farrell, and I usually have it with me. I did when I went upstate. As for photos…" He shrugged. "I guess I've always kept my personal life separate from business. A workplace is for work."

Something Jillian Patterson had said came back to me, and I wondered if it was connected to the deaths of Jack and Katie. "I was told you called the Patterson house a few days before Jack's body was found."

"Jack's body?" Sam spit out a mouthful of coffee. "He's dead, too?"

Sam had been out of town when that occurred, and I guessed he hadn't heard the news. "Yes. They found Jack's body in the inlet. The autopsy showed that he died from a needle to the base of his brain."

"Why would any one kill Jack?"

"That's what I'd like to find out. So, what did you want to speak to Jack about?"

Sam fidgeted with his spoon. "Nothing important. I wanted to talk to him about a surprise party for Katie's birthday."

Abby nodded, then explained to me. "Katie's birthday would have been in three weeks. Sam was planning a small party."

It made sense, so I went on to another point. "Do you think Calvin or Lucien could have had anything to do with Katie's death?"

Sam drained what remained in his coffee cup and shrugged. "They both have motive. But as the police say, no means or opportunity. Neither had access to the aquarium."

"That we know of," Abby added.

CHAPTER NINETEEN

As I pulled into the aquarium parking lot, securing a spot in the last row, it dawned on me how quickly law enforcement had cleared the crime scene. The aquarium was a major tourist attraction, and I could only surmise that Commander West had called in lots of favors. There appeared to be lots of visitors today.

With Katie's death weighing heavily on our minds, Sam, Abby, and I had barely eaten any of our breakfast, so I was more than forty-five minutes early for my appointment with fish keeper Oscar Mejas, who was taking me out on the aquarium's tour boat. The purpose was to view from the water the twenty acres of land the aquarium hoped to acquire. As much as my heart ached for Katie, I had to do my job.

With time to kill, I would do what I do best—snoop. I'd start with the staff at the sea lion amphitheater.

A sign swung from the amphitheater gate that read: CLOSED UNTIL FURTHER NOTICE. Peering inside, I spotted five sea lions sprawled out on the rocks, basking in the sun, on the far side of the moat. Directly above, an aquarium employee hosed down the stage. I recognized her from my first visit to Clam Cove. It was Madge, the marine mammal care attendant.

"Hello," I called. "May I come up and talk with you?"

"We're closed," she yelled back.

"I'm not here for the sea lion show. I'm Katie's friend."

She raised her head and stared at me.

"It's important." I said as she continued staring in silence.

"I guess it's okay." She made her way across the moat bridge, unlatched the gate, and moved aside so I could enter.

"Yeah. I think I recognize you," she said. "You were here before, weren't you?"

I hesitated. I wasn't sure I wanted her to know I was a reporter, but I feared she might remember having seen me in Commander West's office the day Jack Patterson's body had been discovered.

"I was with the aquarium director when you came in and told him Katie had run off," I admitted.

"Run off?"

"The day she left here—minutes before the sea lion show."

"Oh, yeah. I forgot. But I knew I saw you before."

Since Madge didn't seem curious as to why I'd been in the director's office that day, I let it drop. At that moment, one of the sea lions climbed off the rock and hopped on the stage.

"Bea is sad," said Madge. "She was Katie's favorite."

I nodded as the sea lion waddled toward me. Maybe it was just her soulful brown eyes. But I knew that animals often mourned, even when the loss was of a different species.

"With Katie gone, what's going to happen with the sea lion show?" I asked, while I rubbed Bea's head.

"We have an assistant trainer. He's been on vacation the past two weeks. But he'll be back on Wednesday." She paused. "Maybe Thursday. That's when we'll start up again. But it won't be the same. Katie was my friend."

"Did Katie say anything to you about Jack Patterson recently?" I asked.

Madge scratched her chin. "Jack Patterson. Yeah, I know him. He was a fish keeper here. Hey, he died, too."

I drew in a long breath. This wouldn't be easy.

"Yes, he died, too. That's why I want to know if Katie spoke about him recently."

"I liked Jack. Sometimes I called him Jacks. He loved the bay and the ocean, just like me. He was always nice to me, too."

"Was he close to Katie?"

"Yeah. I think so. He came up here a lot to talk with her, especially lately."

"When was the last time you saw them together?"

"Madge furrowed her brow. "Maybe two or three days before they found his body. He came here twice that day." Madge held up three fingers. She put one down.

"Do you know what he talked to Katie about?"

Madge nodded.

"Can you tell me?"

Madge ran her hand under her nose. "Yeah. He asked who she had told about the invitation."

"What invitation?"

Madge shrugged. "Maybe the invitation to that fancy cocktail party at her house."

"What did Katie tell him?"

"Dunno. I left to feed the sea lions." She glanced at her watch. "I better go. I gotta feed them now, too."

We said good-bye, and I wandered back to the main facility for my appointment with fish keeper Oscar Mejas. As I stepped into the building, I nearly collided with Commander West who was hurrying toward the door.

"Good morning, commander. Are you leaving?"

"I'm headed to the hospital."

"The hospital?"

He nodded. "The security guard regained consciousness."

CHAPTER TWENTY

Had the police talked to the guard? Did the guard see who hit him? Dozens of questions swirled around my head, but Commander West rushed out before I could ask any.

"If only fish could talk," I muttered, while passing a school of shimmering silver piranhas in the Amazon exhibit. From their location across from where I discovered the guard's body, they had seen everything.

While making my way down the corridor, I shuddered as the sea snake tank came into view. The horrid sight of Katie Chandler's dead body flashed before my eyes, but I willed myself to think of something else.

Bradford Monroe sat behind his desk sorting through mounds of papers, a frown etched on his forehead. I still had a few minutes before my appointment with Oscar, so I rapped on Bradford's open door.

"Come in," he said, his frown fading, replaced by a toothy grin. He leaned back. "What brings you here today?" He motioned toward a chair across from his desk.

"Oscar Mejas is taking me out on the aquarium's tour boat," I answered, sliding into the seat. "He's showing me the twenty acres you hope to acquire, but I wonder if this is a moot point. It looks as if you won't get the six million."

"Don't be so sure." His toothy grin became wolf-like. "I'm setting up a meeting with Calvin Chandler. Hopefully, I'll convince him to honor Katie's commitment."

When pigs fly. "But let's say he refuses. That's a lot of money to make up."

"You're right, which means I have to work extra hard." He winked.

"I need to convince our other wealthy donors to double, maybe triple, their contributions. Many can afford it, but it's a matter of how they allocate their charity funds."

Bradford must have seen the look of skepticism on my face because he leaned forward, elbows on desk, his fingers weaved together forming a steeple. "Under the terms of the will, we still get at least three million. And I've another ace in the hole. I'm told Katie left her estate to the aquarium. It includes one million, originally bequeathed to Katie by her grandmother, and the house, which is worth more than eight hundred thousand."

He leaned back. "There's more. I talked to a couple at the cocktail party about sponsoring one of our exhibits. After leaving Katie's house, we continued our conversation over drinks in town at the Tipsy Toad Tavern. Guess what? They're donating one hundred thousand dollars. In return, their names will be featured above our turtle exhibit. It will be called the Elizabeth and Jerome Mulgrave Turtle Haven."

"That's terrific. But you still need more money."

"This is just the beginning. The Mulgrave donation will start the ball rolling. Once other prospective donors hear about it, they'll want to sponsor exhibits, too. I have several more prospects lined up."

"Commander West must be pleased?"

"He was. After I sealed the deal with the Mulgraves, I called him with the good news. He was ecstatic." Bradford lowered his voice to a whisper. "I'm normally reluctant to call him after hours, but he had told me he was going home to read his new book on military history, so I knew I wouldn't be interrupting a social engagement." Bradford winked. "If you get my drift."

"You certainly are good at your job."

"I was born to fund-raise. It started in high school when I spearheaded a drive to buy new band uniforms. Do you know what my college major was?"

I shook my head.

"Mortuary Science."

"I would never have guessed." When I researched Bradford on the Internet, I hadn't gone back that far.

"My father owns a chain of funeral homes in New England. He

wanted me to go into the business. I worked for him for six months after graduating from college. Worst time in my life. I went back to school and got a professional certificate in development and non-profits. Fundraising has been my career ever since." He slammed his hand on the desk. "It will be difficult, but I will get the money to buy the twenty acres."

It appeared the land acquisition fight was far from over. A long shot, but the aquarium could possibly pull it off.

* * * * *

After saying good-bye to Bradford, I scooted down the hall. As soon as I stepped into Oscar's office he sprung from his chair and greeted me.

"Did you hear about the security guard?" he said, as he sat back down. "I heard he's conscious."

I nodded. "Hopefully, he can identify his attacker."

Oscar shook his head. "I can't understand who would do this. Everyone I know loved Katie."

"But she controlled the charitable donations specified in her grandmother's will. Money is always a motive for murder."

"But we all want the money to go to the aquarium. It means this place will get bigger and better, which means more job security and promotions.

That should be true in most cases. But a thought flashed through my mind. What if someone from the aquarium was on Lucien Moray's payroll?

"Oscar, who has access to the aquarium after hours?"

"Commander West, Bradford Monroe, and myself. Katie had a key, of course, and Jack had one, too. Since I was retiring, he had taken over a lot of my duties, so I had a copy made for him."

Oscar furrowed his brows and continued, "Katie lost her key about a month ago. She was given a new one, but the old key was never found."

"The locks weren't changed?"

"No." Oscar shook his head. "We never had a security problem before."

I sucked in my breath. A misplaced key meant suspects were not limited to aquarium employees.

Oscar rose from his chair. "Are you ready for the boat tour?"

Oscar maneuvered around his desk, and I followed him out the door. We trekked down the sandy beach to the wooden pier where the tour boat docked.

Long and wide with eight rows of benches, the boat, named the *Explorer,* rocked slightly in the high tide. Oscar hopped in, then helped me as I stepped from the pier onto the front bench and to the boat's floor.

"Bill," he called to a young man in an aquarium uniform picking up litter a few yards away. "Untie us, will you?"

Oscar situated himself behind the steering wheel, and I slid down on the far end of the same bench. As I settled in my spot, I spotted a familiar figure further up the beach. It was Ruby Diamond's friend Kyle, the one with the billy-goat beard. He quickly turned away and was no longer facing me.

Oscar started the engine as Bill unhooked the ropes, and the *Explorer* moved slowly away from the dock. Out on the bay, my hair blew, my blouse flapped in the wind, and I felt the spray of salt water on my face. Despite the midday sun, I shivered slightly from the autumn breeze. Looking out on the water, I spotted more than a half dozen boats anchored mid-bay. I assumed the inhabitants were fishing for fluke or flounder. I wasn't sure what fish were in season.

"If you look back on shore, that's the acreage the aquarium wants to buy," Oscar said, lowering the throttle as he began trolling. "That part over there" he said, pointing to the land adjacent to the aquarium, "is the piping plover breeding grounds which are off limits to humans. The marine mammal rehabilitation center will next to that but higher up on the beach."

Oscar continued describing how the land would be utilized. Soon we came to the end of the vacant beach, and I recognized the house next to the property. Ruby Diamond's pink shingled cottage. If the aquarium's plan went through, her home would be adjacent to the research camp for marine scientists.

"I don't know why that lady is so upset," Oscar said. "Scientists are quiet neighbors. It's not like they're partying all night."

Oscar slowly u-turned, about to head back to land. In the distance, I spotted a cigarette boat, its bow bobbing out of the water, aimed in our direction. From the corner of my eye, I suddenly watched all color drain from Oscar's face.

The cigarette boat was picking up speed as it careened directly toward us.

CHAPTER TWENTY-ONE

Oscar, waving his arms, yelled something in Spanish I didn't understand, but I was sure it wasn't good. Moving the engine into high gear, he attempted to get out of the way, but the cigarette boat veered in our direction.

"Can you outrun it?" I shouted over the engine noise.

He shook his head. "Tour boats aren't built for speed."

The cigarette boat appeared to be less than ten yards away from ramming us mid-ship. Suddenly, it swerved to the right and sped off, its wake nearly causing us to capsize. I grabbed the railing to avoid falling overboard.

The *Explorer* continued to rise and dip, then swing from side to side. Little by little, the water became calm again.

I shivered. We were soaked from the boat's wake.

"Crazy kids. Probably drunk," Oscar muttered.

It wasn't kids, drunks, or thrill seekers. I'd caught a glimpse of the person at the helm. The boat's driver was Kyle—Ruby Diamond's friend with the billy-goat beard.

* * * * *

Next was an impromptu stop at the local hospital. I approached a woman with thick glasses sitting behind the visitors counter.

"I'd like to see George Grogin," I said. Before I had left the aquarium, Oscar told me the name of the security guard.

She handed me a pass. "He's in room four thirty-three. Go down the hall, pass the cafeteria, and take the elevator on the left."

I scooted down the corridor. Since I was thinking about what I would ask the injured security guard, I paid no attention to where I was walking. I collided with Detective Steve Wolfe.

"What are you doing here?" he asked through gritted teeth.

"Visiting a patient."

"That wouldn't be the security guard, would it? I told you not to interfere."

"I'm concerned with how he's doing. I discovered his body on the floor. Besides, you told me not to interfere in the Patterson case. You never said anything about Katie Chandler's murder."

As soon as those words came out of my mouth, I knew I'd gone too far. Wolfe's face puffed up like a helium balloon.

"Stay away or I swear I'll arrest you for obstruction of justice. I'm leaving now. I'll walk you out." He went to grab my arm, but I pulled it away.

"I'm headed into the cafeteria for coffee," I said, thinking quickly. "That's not obstruction, is it?"

He sputtered an obscenity and left.

I wandered into the cafeteria and spotted Commander West sitting by a table in the corner, eating a sandwich. I navigated toward him through the crowded room.

"Have you seen the security guard?" I asked upon reaching his table.

He nodded and finished chewing. "I just came from his room. He's in pain but he'll be okay."

"Did he see who hit him?"

"No one hit him. He hit his head when he fell against the stone table next to where he'd been standing."

"I can't believe it was an accident," I said. "That's too much of a coincidence. It's—"

"It wasn't an accident. He fell because someone shot him with a tranquilizer dart. His attacker knew what he was doing. The tranquilizer was enough to put George out for a short time—enough time to do away with Katie. If George hadn't hit his head, he probably would not have needed to stay in the hospital."

Commander West shook his head before continuing. "All he remembers is feeling what he thought was a bee sting. Then he blacked out.

"I wonder where the attacker was hiding?"

"I told the police he probably was waiting inside the admissions room. That's right off the main entrance. It's where we keep our admission tickets, brochures, membership information, and our daily receipts." He frowned. "Detective Wolfe thinks it may be a robbery gone bad."

"That's ridiculous. If it had been an attempted robbery, the thief would have knocked Katie out, too, not killed her. Her murder was a deliberate, calculated action."

As I rose to leave, I said, "I have one more question. Was George Grogin retired from law enforcement?"

"Yes. He had been a police officer. Why do you ask?"

"Because law enforcement personnel are trained to recall details."

* * * * *

Despite Detective Wolfe's orders, when I departed the cafeteria, I went to see the security guard. George Grogin was watching a baseball game on television when I entered his room. I judged him to be in his early sixties.

"I'm Kristy Farrell," I said. "I was with Commander West when we found you at the aquarium."

"What can I do for you?" he asked, eyeing me suspiciously.

"Do you remember what time you were attacked?"

"A few minutes after six. I had finished my closing rounds. I inspect the entire indoor facility after the aquarium closes to the public at five thirty to make sure all visitors have left," he explained. "It takes about thirty to thirty-five minutes."

"What do you do then?"

"I usually station myself in the reception area. About two hours later, I walk through the facility again to make sure there are no problems."

"So as far as you know, all visitors were gone?"

He nodded. "Yup."

"Commander West thinks your attacker had been hiding in the admissions room."

"Most likely. When I check to make sure all visitors are gone, I look in the public areas like the cafeteria and rest rooms. I don't look in staff facilities and offices."

"Could any employees have remained?"

"No. Sometimes employees work late but not that day. It's a small staff. I knew everyone working on Saturday, and I said good-bye to each person." He paused. "I guess someone might have returned through the employee entrance. That's in the back of the administration wing."

I hadn't known there was another door. If Katie entered through the back, she wouldn't have seen the injured guard up front. I still wondered what she was doing in the building. Did she need to get supplies or medicines for her sea lions?

"So, you hadn't seen Katie Chandler?" I asked.

"I just said that I didn't see any employees after closing." He sounded a bit testy.

"Can you recall exactly what happened right before you were struck by the dart?"

He nodded. "Yes. I was standing in the reception area, and the admissions room was directly behind me. I'd only been there a few minutes when I heard the door to the room squeak. Before I could turn, I felt a sharp sting in my shoulder. I blacked out instantly."

I couldn't think of anything else to ask. I gave him my phone number in case he thought of something else.

"Wait," he called as I made my way to the door. "One thing I can tell you. Whoever attacked me, knew I'd end up in the reception area. My attacker knew my routine."

* * * * *

No one was home when I arrived. Matt had texted me earlier that he would be late. My mother had left a note on the kitchen table stating she and Marcia would be having dinner tonight with a former co-worker.

I wondered what was happening between my mother and Paul Andre. Mom didn't appear to be spending time with him. Had they broken up?

Realizing there was nothing I could do now about my mother's situation, I decided to take advantage of the temporary peace and quiet in the house. I slid into the chair in front of my computer, brought up a blank screen, and began listing everyone with a motive to kill Katie.

Lucien Moray. With Katie gone, he became odds on favorite to acquire the twenty acres of land he needed for his condo development.

Calvin Chandler. Control of the trust fund meant he could court favor with Moray. A small time scammer like Chandler might figure he was entitled to bribes and kickbacks. Katie's death was his opportunity.

Sam Wong. I didn't want to believe Sam was involved, but wasn't the lover always a suspect? He and Katie had undergone a rough patch in their relationship. His excuse for disappearing didn't sit well with me. He should have phoned or texted Katie that he was alive and safe.

Ruby Diamond. Something strange was happening with Ruby and her group. I thought of how her friend Kyle had nearly rammed into the aquarium's tour boat. Was he just being a smart aleck or was it a deliberate action to frighten me away?

I sat back and thought about the three aquarium employees that I'd recently met. I jotted down **Commander Conrad West**, **Bradford Monroe**, and **Oscar Mejas**. There was no obvious motive unless one of them was on Moray's payroll.

I wondered about access to the building. Oscar had said that Katie lost her key. Anyone could have found it. Still, it was unlikely that Ruby, Calvin, or Lucien would have access to it. But there was one person who might easily have taken the key from Katie.

Sam Wong.

As I pondered the information I had on each suspect, I was so engrossed that I didn't hear the kitchen door open.

"Why are you frowning? Matt asked as he entered the room and jolted me out of my thoughts.

"I'm thinking about the two murders. Both Jack Patterson and Katie Chandler worked for the aquarium. But that's as far as the connection goes."

Matt pulled out a chair and straddled it. "There must be another common thread. You just haven't discovered it yet. You need to dig deeper into the personal lives of Jack and Katie."

"Our daughter and Katie were best friend. They shared secrets. Abby agrees that the only reason for Katie's murder must revolve around the land acquisition. But Jack had nothing to do with that."

"Are you sure? You and Abby may know a lot about Katie, but you don't know anything about Jack Patterson."

CHAPTER TWENTY-TWO

The next morning, I pulled into the gravel parking lot of the Patterson Horse Farm. I found Jillian Patterson seated behind her desk in her office, an eight by ten room at the end of the barn.

"You're Abby's Mom, right? I'm so glad she's leasing Topper. Is she riding today?"

"No. She's working. I wanted to talk to you about your brother and Katie."

She shook his head, her pony tail flapping from side to side. "I don't understand what's going on. The police won't tell me anything. First Jack, now Katie."

"I think the two murders are related."

"Because they both worked at the aquarium?"

I nodded. "Do you know if there was any trouble at work? Did Jack have problems with any co-workers?"

"He never mentioned any trouble. He loved working with marine life, and he liked the people he worked with." Jillian smiled. "He did say he found the development officer, Bradford something, a bit annoying, but they got along."

I had a feeling most people had the same reaction to Bradford Monroe. "Was Jack involved in the aquarium's expansion project and land acquisition? Did he ever talk to you about it?"

Jillian turned her head slightly, no longer facing me. She fiddled with a paperclip, then spoke, "I don't think so."

As a former teacher, I was fairly skilled at reading body language. Jillian wasn't telling me everything.

"How long has Jack been employed at the Clam Cove Aquarium?"

"Only for the last two years. After college, he taught science at a small private school out of state. His degree is in marine biology."

"What brought him back here?"

"A job opening at the aquarium. His dream had always been to work with marine life. Plus, after our dad died, I needed help with the horses, so he moved back."

"Do you have someone to help you now?"

Jillian shook her head. "No. I can't afford it. I'm doing it all." She rose from her chair. "I better get down to the paddocks. There's a fence that needs mending."

As she moved toward the side shelves and grabbed a toolbox, I glanced at a stack of open mail on her desk. A letter was sticking out. The name on the return address caused me to suck in my breath. It read: *Moray Industries*.

I needed an excuse to stay. Luckily, I'd come prepared.

"Do you mind if I give Topper some carrots?" I asked as we left her office. "I brought a bunch. They're in my car."

"Go right ahead. He's the last stall on the left. As soon as I fix the fence, I'll put him out to graze."

We parted. I retrieved the carrots and headed back to the stable, noting that Jillian was now outside busily engaged repairing a nearby paddock fence.

I opened the door to Jillian's office, and gently pulled the envelope from Moray Industries out of the pile. It had been sliced open, making it easy for me to remove the letter. I read the correspondence.

I gasped. After stashing the paper back in the envelope, I carefully placed it back in the pile of mail just the way I found it and left.

As I made my way to Topper's stall, I thought about the implications of the letter. It was an offer to buy the horse farm. But it was contingent on Moray acquiring the twenty acres of land next to the aquarium.

After feeding the carrots to Topper, I made my way to the parking lot. I was wondering how I could find out what Moray wanted with a horse farm when I spotted Jillian returning from the paddock.

Sometimes the simplest strategy is the right one. "Jillian," I called. "You got a sec?"

She spun around. "Everything okay with Topper?"

"He's fine. Ate all the carrots. I've just one more questions about the aquarium and the land acquisition—"

"I don't know anything about that—"

"Moray wanted to buy your land, too. But only if he acquired the twenty acres adjacent to the aquarium."

"I don't know what you are talking about." She averted my eyes.

"Please, Jillian. I think the land acquisition may be related to the deaths of Katie and your brother."

Jillian's shoulders slumped. "Okay. It's true. He wanted to purchase this place."

"Why? What would he do with a horse farm?"

"Tear it down. He wanted to build a shopping center."

"A shopping center?"

"There are great mom and pop stores in town. But the nearest major shopping area is more than an hour away. Moray thought that with the influx of condo residents, the community could support a shopping mall."

"Would you sell?"

Jillian rubbed her head. "I honestly don't know. This farm belonged to my grandfather, but for the last few years, I've barely made ends meet." She paused, then sighed. "Yes. I probably would sell."

"How did Jack feel about this?"

'It was one of the only things we argued about. Jack was furious that I'd even consider selling to Moray. He also told me it was a moot point since the aquarium was acquiring the land."

"But now, it may not."

Jillian nodded. "Do you think Moray had something to do with Jack's death?"

I couldn't answer. Jack may have opposed selling the horse farm, but Jillian, as owner, would make the final decision. I didn't know how much influence Moray thought Jack had with his sister. Enough to kill Jack to get him out of the way?

CHAPTER TWENTY-THREE

Later at work, I had just settled down in my cubicle when my phone buzzed. While stretching to grab the receiver, I knocked over my coffee.

"I need to talk to you about your mother," my sister-in-law Barbara said.

"And hello to you, too," I wiped up the spill with tissues from my bag. "What about my mother?"

"About the garage sale?"

"What garage sale? I've no idea what you are talking about."

"Your mother asked Tim to help her organize a garage sale for her friend Marcia Silver. She expects me to help, too. Apparently, Marcia Silver, whom I've never met, is selling her house. She's getting rid of most of her belongings, but she's not comfortable selling online, so your mom suggested a garage sale. It's scheduled for two weeks from now. Your mother wants us all to pitch in."

"Mom hasn't asked me for help."

"She will."

With the deadline for my stories looming on the horizon, Matt's upcoming animal lover's festival, and the two murders, the last thing I needed was to serve as a worker bee for my mother's friend. But as I thought about it, I realized my mom and Marcia had always confided in each other. If my mother wasn't telling me what was happening with her fiancé, perhaps by spending time in the Silver home, I could learn more about the mysterious Paul Andre.

* * * * *

A few hours later, my intercom buzzed.

"Detective Wolfe is here to see you," Clara said when I picked up.

"Send him down."

"I'm here." Detective Wolfe had obviously started down the hall before Clara called.

"I need to confirm some facts from you statement." Wolfe wiped his nose, then flipped open his note pad. "The day Katie Chandler died, you claimed you and your daughter were together at the Chandler house from about three-thirty until you both left to go to the aquarium at seven-fifteen. Is that correct?"

"Yes."

"You two were joined at the hip eh?"

"Of course, we weren't together every second."

"So you can't verify your daughter's whereabouts."

"Where else would she be?"

Ignoring my question, Wolfe asked, "How long has your daughter known Sam Wong?"

"Abby met Sam when he and Katie first started dating. Remember, Abby and Katie were best friends."

"How frequently did your daughter see Sam?"

"I have no idea. I think Abby and her boyfriend went out to dinner and movies with Katie and Sam, but I don't know how frequently."

"Abby never saw Sam alone?"

I realized where he was headed but couldn't believe it.

I moved forward in my seat. "What are you saying?"

"I'm saying it's not inconceivable that Abby and Sam were lovers and that they plotted together to kill Katie."

"You are so wrong. You have no basis for such a far-fetched theory."

"But I do. We've recovered a series of text messages from Katie's phone." He handed me a sheet and stood back, smirking.

The print out was an exchange between Katie and Abby. I read the page.

Katie: *I need to know I can trust you.*

Abby: *Of course. All the time.*

Katie: *With Sam?*

Abby: *Why would you even ask?*

Katie: *I have my reasons.*

"Those statements could be interpreted dozens of ways," I said.

"One way is that Katie thought there was something between Abby and Sam."

"Preposterous. Besides, I may not have been with my daughter every moment of the cocktail party, but once Katie left for the aquarium, Abby and I sat in the living room the entire time. The catering staff was cleaning up, so I'm sure they can vouch for us."

"Let's hope so." Wolfe smirked again, turned around, and made his way down the corridor.

No way Abby was the murderer. But had she become Sam's lover? Preposterous. I had seen the interaction between the two, and neither showed a spark of interest in the other. And Abby would never do that to Katie or to Jason. I knew my daughter.

But what did those texts mean? I grabbed my phone and punched in Abby's number.

I explained Wolfe's theory that she and Sam were lovers who murdered Katie. I told her about the text messages.

"They refer to the surprise birthday party for Katie," she said. "The one Sam was planning. Only it wasn't a surprise."

"What do you mean?"

"Katie got wind of the party. She was afraid it might be too over the top. You know how laid back Katie is. I mean was." There was a pause. "She wanted me to talk Sam into doing something simple—like a small dinner with close friends. Her comment 'I need to know I can trust you' meant would I make sure the party was more to her taste and not acquiesce to Sam's extravagant plans."

"What did she mean by 'I have my reasons?'"

"I like big parties. Katie was afraid I'd agree with Sam and wouldn't push to keep the party small and low key." Abby paused before continuing. "The only connection I had with Sam was Katie. You didn't think something was going on between us, did you?"

"Not in a million years. But I wanted an explanation of the text messages, so I can confront Wolfe if he brings up his ridiculous theory again."

"He also doesn't appear to be taking into account Jack's murder. He's treating them as two unrelated cases."

"You're right," I agreed. "I believe the key to the crimes is finding out what tied Jack and Katie together."

After ending my call, I decided to dig deeper into the common thread between Katie and Jack, which was the Clam Cove Aquarium. My research showed the aquarium was solvent. Aside from the struggle to raise funds for the expansion, the daily admission receipts and paid memberships raised enough money for normal operating expenses.

The previous director had left under pleasant circumstances. He had received a job offer at a larger aquarium in northern California where his married daughter and three grandchildren lived. No one employed at the Clam Cove facility had been under consideration as his replacement, so when Commander West was appointed, there was no reason for jealously or resentment.

Did someone on staff hate both Katie and Jack? From what I'd seen the answer was no. But I couldn't be sure, so I called Abby back again.

"Katie and I always talked about our work and the people we came in contact with on a regular basis," my daughter said, "and Katie only had good things to say about her colleagues. Sure, there were little everyday annoyances. She found Bradford to be conceited and Commander West's love of paperwork drove her crazy, but there wasn't enough animosity for someone to kill her."

I realized that the same held true for Jack. According to Oscar Mejas, Jack was well-liked despite his temper. In an institution the size of the Clam Cove Aquarium, everyone would know each other's business.

"Besides the land acquisition, did Katie ever talk about any controversial issues facing the aquarium?"

"Not at all. The aquarium has been part of the community for more than twenty years. It's an integral part of the area." Abby paused. "But remember, Abby and Jack's friendship goes back before either worked at the aquarium. Could the murders relate to something earlier in their lives?"

* * * * *

Back home, I poked my head in the freezer hoping to find something

---

that I could defrost in time for dinner. When I heard the door slam, I spun around.

"Hello, Kristy," my mother said with more enthusiasm than I'd heard from her in days.

"I was just choosing something for dinner," I said. "Will you be able to join us?"

"No, thanks." She winked. "I'm having dinner with Paul."

"Really?"

"You sound surprised. He is my fiancé."

"The way you've been acting recently, I thought you two had a fight."

"We had a minor disagreement, but it's been straightened out."

"Oh." I sat down by the table. "Want to tell me?"

"It was nothing." She grabbed a bottle of Chardonnay from the refrigerator, poured two glasses, handed me one, and slid down into a chair. "Paul wanted me to invest in his health spas."

"Mom, that's a risky venture."

"I know." She held up her hands. "I told him no. He put a lot of pressure on me, but I held firm." Her face darkened. "For a short time, I was afraid he wanted me for my money."

The same thought had flashed through my mind. I sucked in my breath.

"But when he saw I was adamant, he understood and promised not to bring it up again."

"When did this change of heart take place?"

"Today. I was at Marcia's house when he called this morning and pleaded to see me. Marcia suggested he join us for brunch, and I thought that was a good idea. I wanted her reaction.

"Which was?"

"She agreed that if he was a scammer, he wouldn't have given up so easily." My mother raised an eyebrow. "Kristy, you look skeptical."

"Tell me specifically what happened from the moment he arrived at Marcia's home."

"Marcia and I were going through her belongings for a garage sale she's planning. I'll tell you more about that later. Anyway, he helped Marcia carry about a dozen items into her garage. He's so strong. After that, Marcia made coffee, heated up a quiche, and we sat down to eat.

That was when he apologized. He said he wanted to let me in on this opportunity, but if I wasn't comfortable, he totally understood."

My mother frowned briefly. "He said there were lots of people in this world like me who just wanted to keep their money safe and were willing to forfeit a high return. I did feel that was a little condescending, but I'm sure he didn't mean it that way."

"Did he tell you a high return is accompanied by a high risk?"

"Not specifically, but I know that. The main point is he said he wouldn't bring the topic up again."

Even in love, my mother was one smart cookie when it came to finances. I couldn't imagine her handing over money to anyone without first consulting her attorney or financial advisor.

But as far as I was concerned, the jury was still out on Paul Andre.

When my mother went upstairs to her room, I retrieved my phone and searched for the photo I'd taken of Mom and Paul. Then I phoned Abby's boyfriend.

"Jason," I said. "I need a favor."

CHAPTER TWENTY-FOUR

"This doesn't make sense," I mumbled. I was on my computer. Matt had an early appointment at the veterinary hospital, and my mother had left for breakfast with Paul.

I grabbed my phone and called Abby. "Can you stop by?" I asked. "I want to show you something I discovered."

"Sure. I'm in my car, about ten minutes away."

While I waited, I punched in a number from my contact list.

"Louise," I said when a woman answered the phone. "This is Mary's daughter, Kristy."

"Is everything okay with Mary? Is she sick?"

"No. She's healthy as a horse." Louise was my mother's neighbor in Florida, and she was a retired New York City Board of Education truant officer. I'd met her a few times and considered her a good judge of character. Someone who would be difficult to fool. Her husband was a retired New York City detective.

"I was wondering if you knew anything about my mother's friend Paul?" I asked.

Silence. Finally, she said, "I know almost nothing. I only met him once, and that was by accident. I was returning a serving dish I borrowed from your mother when he came to pick her up for a date. Here seemed annoyed I was there."

Louise paused. "Mary never brought him to any of the condo social events which she always did with other boyfriends. She stopped attending, too. When I asked her why, she giggled and said Paul preferred to see her alone. I don't like it when a person tries to isolate someone from their friends."

"I agree. When my mother was alone, did she ever talk about Paul?"

"I didn't see her much anymore. She was always with him. But there was one time, when Paul had a business meeting, that Mary came down to the pool. I asked her about him."

"What did she say?"

"She went on and on about how wonderful he was, but she said nothing informative. I was surprised at how little she knew about his background."

I finished my call as Abby stepped into the house. I told her about my conversation with my mother's neighbor in Florida.

"What are you going to do?" Abby asked as she greeted Archie and Brandy who had bounded into the room in anticipation of tummy rubs.

"I'm going to delve deeper into Paul Andre. I need to find out what he's been up to for most of his life."

Abby poured coffee into a mug and sat down across from me. "Why did you want to see me? Is it about grandma?"

"No. Two other matters. Did Katie ever mention trouble in her youth involving Jack? Car accident? Teenage prank that went out of control?"

Abby furrowed her brows, then shook her head. "No. I've been thinking about that since we talked yesterday. Katie did occasionally talk about her high school days, but she never mentioned any bad incident."

"I don't know how to find out about her past. I did online research and nothing came up."

"Katie had a good high school friend who now lives in Connecticut. She was coming to Katie's surprise party. Sam has her contact number. Why don't I call and ask her about Katie and Jack's younger days? Now, what's the second matter you wanted to see me about?"

"Calvin Chandler. I've been thinking of Sam Wong's statement about the six million dollars from Alicia Wilcox Chandler's estate that Katie planned to donate to the aquarium. Sam said Calvin Chandler would steer that money to the other charities listed in the will. I think that's true, but if I'm to include that in my article on the land acquisition fight, I need to arrange a meeting with Calvin, so I can hear it from him."

"Okay. But how do I fit in?"

"I always research my subjects before an interview, right? I looked up

Calvin, and I'm a little confused with what I discovered." I swung my computer, so Abby could see the screen. "Calvin is a real estate agent. He works for Starfish Real Estate in Clam Cove. But his conviction for running the Ponzi scheme was a felony. You can't get a real estate license in this state if you have a felony conviction. I was hoping Katie had mentioned how this happened."

"She did. He received a Certificate of Relief from Civil Disabilities from the court. That meant he could apply for the license." Suddenly, out of nowhere, Gus, the cat, leaped onto Abby's lap. My daughter rubbed the cat's back. "Calvin got the certificate four years ago. Katie was furious."

"I've heard of these Certificates of Relief," I said, "but I thought they were difficult to obtain."

"They can be, but Alicia Wilcox Chandler was a rich and powerful woman. Katie told me her grandmother called in lots of favors on Calvin's behalf."

"But Alicia Wilcox Chandler had a reputation as an honest and upstanding citizen. She was a community activist, generous donor, a—"

"A grandmother who loved her grandchildren. Calvin had convinced her that he wasn't guilty. He claimed he was a victim as much as the other investors in the scheme and that he had been duped by his partner."

I nodded. According to what I had read, Calvin and his partner, Mark Tanner, bilked sixty investors out of more than five million dollars by promising to triple their money in less than one year through a new and exclusive hedge fund. Of course, there was no such fund. As with all Ponzi schemes, the existing investors were paid with money raised from new investors. When the source of new investors dried up, and large numbers of old investors requested pay outs, the scheme collapsed. Calvin's defense attorney tried portraying Calvin as a victim whose partner kept the numbers from him. He claimed Calvin believed the hedge fund was real.

Alicia Wilcox Chandler believed her grandson. The jury didn't buy it.

"Calvin has held several jobs since the conviction, all in sales." Abby said.

"I know. My research showed that he worked as a used car salesman and was accused by the local consumer affairs agency for using bait and switch tactics. Nothing was ever proven. After that he was employed in a marine yard, selling boats and nautical equipment. His last job before entering real estate was as a pharmaceutical representative."

"You missed one," Abby said. "His first job after being released from jail was at the aquarium. Alicia Wilcox Chandler used her influence to get him a job working on the membership drive."

"I didn't find that information anywhere on the Internet."

"Probably because he didn't have the job for long. I think he was employed there for about three months. Calvin always wanted to work in sales where he could earn commissions. There were no commissions in selling aquarium memberships—he earned a straight salary. He started looking for other work, and when he landed the job at the used car dealer, he took it immediately."

"It must have been awkward for Katie to work along side Calvin."

"She never did. This all happened before she started her career at the aquarium. She was in graduate school."

"I'll still bet she wasn't happy."

"You win that bet. Her plans were to work at the aquarium after graduation. She was afraid Calvin would do something illegal which would put a black mark on the Chandler name and jeopardize her chances. It turned out he didn't do anything legally wrong, but he was not a model employee. Calvin had high absenteeism, was constantly late, and spent most of his time making personal calls."

"At least no one held that against Katie."

"As it should be. But Katie was still plenty upset. You look like you just thought of something, Mom."

"I did. What you just told me means Calvin was familiar with the aquarium layout and procedures."

"You're right." Abby nodded. "He had a key, too. Who knows if he returned it when he left. Now that you know Calvin's history, what's your next step?"

"I'm going to make an appointment for this afternoon to see Calvin and find out his plans for the distribution of the charity money." I grabbed my phone.

"What if he refuses to see you?"

I grinned as I punched in the number for the Starfish Real Estate

Something Fishy

Agency. "Calvin might refuse to see Kristy Farrell, reporter, but Kristy Farrell, prospective real estate client, will easily snag an appointment."

105

CHAPTER TWENTY-FIVE

"Calvin Chandler?" I asked as I swung open the door to Starfish Real Estate. Two men were seated behind desks, one gazing at his computer, the other engaged in a phone conversation."

The man on the phone motioned me toward him. He appeared to be in his late thirties. I slid into the chair in front of his desk as he continued talking.

"Remember, a deal like this comes along once in a lifetime. Think about it but don't take too long, or it will be gone." He ended his call, then swiveled his chair to face me. "I'm Calvin. You must be Kristy? You said yesterday that you wanted to rent a house on the beach. Tell me a little more about what you're seeking."

I started telling him about the type of house I wanted when another phone call interrupted our conversation.

"I have to take this, but I'll be quick." He picked up the phone. "These units will be selling like hotcakes," he said. "If you wait too long there won't be any left. Would I steer you wrong?"

I suppressed a smile at his comment. While he chatted on the phone, I gazed at two framed photos on a nearby wall. One featured Calvin in his college football uniform. Considering the gambling scandal that got him kicked out of school, I was surprised he posted such a picture. But I realized most people wouldn't be aware of what happened back then, yet might be impressed with his hunk-like appearance and athletic prowess. Calvin Chandler was handsome now, but he was even more handsome in his youth.

It was the second photo that grabbed my attention. It was a picture of Calvin flanked by two men, all in tuxedos, with drinks in their hands. I had no idea who was standing to his right. But I recognized the man to his left. It was Lucien Moray.

Hanging near the pictures was a large chart listing five names, one of which was Calvin Chandler. Underneath each name was a series of this month's dates.

"What's that?" I asked when Calvin finished his call. I pointed to the chart.

"The office work schedule."

"I see you worked last Saturday," I said, referring to the day Katie died. "Weather was beautiful. Did you show a lot of properties?"

"I did. I was in and out of here showing homes from early morning until nearly seven o'clock. Now, how about we go look at some houses?" He grabbed his keys from a drawer. "I've three great places to show you. And since you want to rent off-season, I can get you a great deal. Follow me."

We drove a short distance until we arrived at our first destination—a small bungalow on the bay.

"If you want to lease this little beauty, you better be quick. Someone is going to snap up this cottage in a second."

Next to this home was a similar house which had a FOR SALE sign on the front lawn.

I sighed. "I'd love to buy a home instead of renting."

"This area is pricey."

"Oh, I can afford it. But I don't want the hassle that comes with home ownership. You know what I mean, the constant upkeep and repair, especially on waterfront houses."

Calvin smiled. "As I said, this is an expensive area. Very few residents do their own work. There are plenty of contractors for hire."

"You still need to call a different service person for everything that goes wrong. Then you have to wait until they find time in their schedule to fit you in. I wish there were condos here. The condo association takes care of maintenance."

"There may be one in the near future. There are plans to build a large condominium development just minutes from here."

"Oh, I think I remember reading about this. But I thought the developer couldn't get the land. Wasn't it going to an aquarium or something?"

Calvin smiled, a Cheshire cat grin. "That's not happening. The aquarium can't afford the property."

"But I heard they were obtaining money from someone's will."

"Let's just say that fell through." He continued to grin. "A prospectus for the condo will be available soon. If you get in at the beginning, I can get you a fabulous deal."

"You?"

"I'm going to be sales manager for the entire condo development."

* * * * *

Next stop, Lucien Moray's office.

"You don't have an appointment, Ms. Farrell," Mama Grizzly said when I asked to see her boss. She kept pecking at her keyboard while she talked. "Mr. Moray sees people by appointment only."

I was back in reporter mode. "I called four times, but no one returned my call."

"Mr. Moray is a busy man."

"I only need a few minutes. Could I see him now?"

Mama Grizzly stopped typing, looked up, and smiled condescendingly. "He's not in yet. I have your phone number. I'll get back to you with an appointment when he has some free time." She turned back toward her computer.

No way was she going to let me see him. As I exited the building, a thought flashed through my mind. Mama Grizzly had said that Moray wasn't in *yet*. That meant he was expected later. I hopped in my car and drove around the building until I found an empty parking spot in the rear with a sign that read, RESERVED FOR LUCIEN MORAY. Only a few feet from the sign was a door to what I assumed was a private entrance.

I parked nearby and waited as the sky quickly became threatening. I spotted a gray convertible with its top down parked about five spaces away from Moray's empty spot. I hoped the owner would close it up before the rain.

An hour later, the clouds had passed without a raindrop, and the sky was once again azure blue. A good thing for the convertible owner who never came out to put the top up on the car.

I was thinking how detectives need strong bladders, and how I would probably only last a few more minutes, when a Jaguar careened into the parking lot and pulled into the reserved spot.

As Lucien Moray emerged from the car, I hurried over to him.

"Mr. Moray, do you have a minute?"

He frowned, but it quickly faded. "A minute. That's all."

"I'd like an update for my magazine article. What's happening with your attempt to buy the twenty acres?"

"That land will soon be mine. The aquarium is not getting the six million dollars from the Alicia Wilcox Chandler Estate."

"But what if the aquarium raises the money through other means?"

"Highly unlikely. I know Brad Monroe thinks he's the superhero of fundraising, but it's too much to raise in too little time. If the aquarium can't come up with all the money by June thirtieth, the land becomes available to whomever has the funds. And that's me."

Bradford Monroe had less than nine months to raise another six million dollars. Brad might have lots of irons in the fire, but would he meet the deadline?

"Before you paint me as the Big Bad Wolf, I'd really like you to examine what I will be doing for this community. I'm giving a party on my yacht tomorrow night for members of the Clam Cove Business Association. Why don't you join us? You can talk to my guests and find out why they are supporting my project and what the condo development means for the future of this area."

"Thank you. I'll take you up on your offer."

"Good. We board at five forty-five. Slip nine in the marina." He grinned. "I'm sure you could use a night of relaxation. I heard about the little adventure you've scheduled at the aquarium for tomorrow morning."

How did he know about my plans for tomorrow?

CHAPTER TWENTY-SIX

"You look a little green," Oscar said with a wide grin on his face as I stepped into his office. "Don't worry. You'll be perfectly safe." He rose from his chair. "Let's head up to the shark tank."

To provide me with an understanding of one of the sea's most terrifying creatures, I was going down in a shark cage.

This had not been my idea. I had been prepared to get all the information I needed for my "Dangers of the Deep" article from interviews, books, and online sources. But Oscar Mejas had suggested that a close encounter with the sharks would provide me with valuable insight. In a weak moment, I agreed.

"About seventy-five unprovoked shark attacks on humans occur each year," Oscar said, as we made our way down the corridor. "That's not a lot when you consider the millions of people who venture into the ocean. Some shark attacks are believed to be instances of errors in identity where the shark mistakes the human for its usual prey, like a surfer mistaken for a sea lion."

I gulped, hoping that the black wet suit I'd be wearing wouldn't confuse the sharks.

Once we reached the exhibit, Oscar pointed to the largest fish in the tank. "That's a bull shark."

"It's huge. It must be eight feet long." I said.

"It's nine feet."

I shuddered. Known for their hostile behavior, the bull sharks were high on the list of the most feared sharks in the world. They are unpredictable, and that is what made them so dangerous.

"The Great White is what immediately comes to mind when you

think of shark attacks," Oscar said. "But the bull shark is probably responsible for most attacks on humans."

"Wonderful," I mumbled through gritted teeth.

Oscar grinned. "Once we go upstairs, you'll see why you have no reason to worry."

Oscar unlocked a door leading to a staircase, and we began the climb. He escorted me to a room on the second floor overlooking the sharks. I went into a private area where I donned a wet suit. Oscar then helped me put on underwater breathing apparatus.

Another fish keeper, whom Oscar introduced as Sally, came into the room to help. With her freckled face and hair pulled back into one long braid, she looked like she was still in junior high school.

"Here's what will keep you safe," Oscar said, pointing to a large steel cage that hung above the shark tank. "It's impenetrable. These cages are built to withstand being rammed at high velocity."

"Are you going to feed the sharks now?" I asked.

"Absolutely no." Oscar shook his head. "Shark baiting is a controversial issue. Off the coast of South Africa and Australia, a few private diving operations still lure sharks to the site with dead fish and blood. The sharks go into a feeding frenzy and have been known to attack the cage."

"I thought you said the cage was impenetrable."

"It is, but we still don't want to frighten you to death. Plus, it's not good to encourage that behavior. Don't worry. You're going to see plenty of sharks up close, but they won't do more than glide by."

I stepped into the steel enclosure. Oscar and Sally lowered the cable and I descended into the water.

Three sharks were headed toward the tank. I was now staring into the glowing green eyes of the one in front—the nine-foot bull shark.

As it came closer, the bull shark opened its deadly jaws, showing off razor-like teeth. Soon more sharks approached, swimming within inches of the cage. I knew they couldn't get through the metal bars, but still...

Suddenly, the bull shark veered to the left and chomped his jaws down on the side of the cage. I stared in horror.

The bull shark chomped down again.

I remembered what Oscar had said about the strength of the steel bars. I hoped it was true.

The shark chomped down a third time, and I heard cracking. The bar had broken in half.

The opening appeared too small for the shark's head to push through. Still, as I stared at its gaping jaws, I pinned myself to the back of the cage, praying the shark couldn't go further. My legs felt like jelly.

I heard Oscar. "We're bringing you up." I felt the rising motion as I wondered if I would get out of here alive. The bull shark rammed the cage, his eyes focused on me. Once the contraption was lifted half way up, Sally threw a handful of dead fish into the water. The distracted bull shark and his buddies swam toward their meal, and I was pulled to safety.

I couldn't stop shaking. "I thought you said the cage would withstand a shark attack?" I yelled, after Sally had helped me out of the steel contraption and had assisted me in removing my breathing apparatus.

"This never happened before," Oscar said as he knelt by the broken bar. "What the…? This is covered in blood. How could that be? Blood or food is never anywhere near this cage." He gasped.

"What is it?" I asked.

"This piece of steel." Oscar pointed to the broken bar. "It's almost completely sawed through. No wonder the shark was able to break it."

"Who would do this?" Sally asked, her eyes as wide as a poppet's.

"Someone who wants me dead." I sighed. "We need to call the police."

* * * * *

"What's going on?" Detective Wolfe grumbled when he entered the room above the shark tank. He saw me and stopped dead in his tracks. "Please don't tell me this involves you?"

"It does." I told him what happened.

"Going down in a tank in water full of sharks is sheer stupidity. How do you know this wasn't an accident?"

"I told you on the phone," Oscar said, before I had a chance to reply. "Someone had splattered blood on the side of the cage to cause a feeding frenzy and had sawed one of the steel bars, so the shark's jaws could break through."

"Who normally goes down in that cage?"

"No one on a regular basis. Occasionally, we've sponsored shark dives as special events."

"Who knew Mrs. Farrell would be going down in that cage?"

Oscar shrugged. "It wasn't a secret. I had to get approval from Commander West. Bradford Monroe was in the office when the commander gave the okay. Brad was going to look into having monthly shark dives as a way to raise funds. I think he was talking it up among aquarium supporters, so that's a lot of folks who knew."

"All of the other fish keepers knew, too, and I told my friends about this the other day at my yoga class," Sally added. "They thought it was real cool."

News of my shark diving had spread. Then I remembered a comment made yesterday.

"Lucien Moray knew about this," I said. "He commented how I might enjoy an evening of relaxation after my adventure today."

"But Lucien Moray doesn't have a way to get in here." Oscar said. "Only fish keepers and top administrative officials have keys to this exhibit."

"If this was deliberate, it had to be someone who works here." Detective Wolfe snorted, then wiped his nose.

The statements by Oscar and Detective Wolfe's were only partially right. Lucien Moray couldn't saw the bars off a cage because he couldn't enter a staff-only section of the aquarium. But he certainly had the money to pay someone who worked here to do it.

Once again, I wondered if an aquarium employee was on Moray's payroll?

"Are you going to investigate?" Oscar asked Wolfe.

"I was called in here because the brass thought this accident might be related to the deaths of the two aquarium employees. I'm not sure it is."

"Of course it is," I replied. "Do we know anymore about Katie's murder? She didn't just jump into the sea snake exhibit. When will the autopsy be finished?"

Wolfe's face turned from beet red to purple. "I said all I'm going to say about that case. You need to drop this."

My daughter's best friend had been murdered. Now someone had tried to kill me.

I wasn't dropping it.

CHAPTER TWENTY-SEVEN

The incident with the shark tank had unnerved me, but I willed myself not to think about it as I sped off to the marina for the party on Lucien Moray's yacht.

Moray was standing on the deck, greeting his guests as they reached the top of the gangplank.

"Kristy Farrell. Glad you could make it." He grabbed my hand and squeezed it. "Let me introduce you to the President of Clam Cove's Community Business Association, Donna Taylor. She owns the Riptide restaurant."

"I'm Donna," said a well-rounded middle age woman standing to his right. "Lucien told me you're writing a story on the land acquisition. Why don't we get a drink, and I'll tell you why our business community fully supports Lucien's condominium development."

"Our economy is dying," she said after we navigated our way through the crowd to the bar and placed our orders. "Last winter, four stores in town closed permanently. There weren't enough people living here to support them. The condos will increase our population."

"But won't the aquarium help the local economy, too?" I asked. "After a day exploring the sea life, perhaps aquarium visitors would stop for dinner at your restaurant."

"Yes, but they won't use my law firm," said a tall man standing near us. He appeared to be in his early forties, with skin the color of espresso. "I couldn't help hear your conversation. I'm Tyler Sinclair, an attorney with an office on Main Street."

"Tyler is also Vice President of the Community Business Association," Donna said as the bartender handed me a white wine.

"Unlike Donna's restaurant, which might attract aquarium visitors, day trippers would not use our local dry cleaner, bank, insurance agency, florist, or pet supply store. I'm sure you get my point," Tyler said. "The condo owners will support these businesses."

"What if Moray decides to erect his own shopping center? "I asked as thoughts of the Patterson Horse Farm flashed through my mind. "Won't that affect downtown business?"

"Ah, you heard about the offer Moray made Patterson." Tyler smiled. "The type of shopping center Moray is known for consists of high-end retail. That's not what we have downtown. Our residents need to drive to the county center, nearly an hour away, to shop for clothes and home furnishings. So Moray's shopping center wouldn't compete with our village stores."

"What do you think will happen now, Tyler?" Donna asked. "Do you think Jillian will sell her property?"

"Yes. She's in danger of losing the farm to creditors. She might as well make some money. Jillian wasn't happy about it, but she was willing to sell from the moment Moray made the offer. It was Jack who stood in her way. Jack thought Jillian could turn around the stable's finances. Plus, Jack hated Moray."

"I know Jack was opposed to the buyout, but did he have that much influence on his sister?" I asked.

"It's more than influence, dear." Donna sipped her wine. "Jillian may manage the stable, but her parents left it to both children. Jack and Jillian owned the stable jointly. Any contract to sell the horse farm had to have both signatures."

Jillian had neglected to tell me that. "With Jack dead, who inherits his half?"

"I haven't seen the will. But I heard he left everything to Jillian."

"We're leaving the dock now," Tyler said as the yacht started moving. "Shall we get something to eat?"

Donna and Tyler headed for the indoor buffet, but I decided not to join them. I wandered to the railing near the boat's stern. It was cool and a bit windy on the deck, and I was glad I was wearing a jacket.

I was sipping my drink and gazing at the pink/orange sunset over the bay when a young man approached me.

"Are you the writer?" he asked as he pushed a wisp of his blond hair away from his tanned face. He had the sleek build of a swimmer, and he looked to be in his early thirties.

"News travels fast." I smiled. "Kristy Farrell."

"I overheard Moray tell some people he invited a writer. You're the only one here I don't recognize from town, so I figured it must be you. I'm Noah Manning. I own the bait and tackle shop in town."

"May I assume you are a member of the Clam Cove Community Business Association?"

He nodded.

"Let me guess. You're here to tell me why you support Moray's plan to build condos."

"No. I'm one of the few members who doesn't support it."

I fumbled in my bag for my pen and pad. I wanted a quote from this guy.

"Why are you against the condos?"

"My bait and tackle store has been in my family for three generations. I love Clam Cove. I don't want to see its beauty destroyed. The aquarium will protect the marine life. The nature walks will be guided and controlled so no one damages or takes anything away—"

"But your business?"

"There's a tract of land, ten acres further inland, that another developer wants to buy and use to build apartments. It wouldn't be as big as Moray's development and certainly not as high-end, but it would provide a significant increase in the population which would help the commerce in town."

This was the first I'd heard of an alternative project. "Why aren't the other members of the Community Business Association in favor of this?"

Noah shook his head. "Money. The Moray waterfront development is bigger and will house more people who will shop in our community." He paused. "A lot more rich people. The apartment complex has fewer units and would be strictly for middle class residents with not quite as much spending power. But if it will protect our marine environment, I'm okay with that. It's a compromise."

My mind turned to another matter. "What about Ruby Diamond?"

Ever since her friend Kyle tried to ram the aquarium's tour boat, my suspicions about Ruby and Friends of the Fish had increased. "Do you know her?"

"Sure do. One weird duck. She's kept to herself until now. She was never involved in any environmental issues here—even when we had problems."

"What problems?" I raised an eyebrow.

"A few years ago, we had a local company dumping waste. The company ultimately went bankrupt, and the owners went to jail. But during the whole time this issue was being resolved, she never said a word."

"Why do you think she's so concerned now?"

"I think its all about her house." He grinned. "She wants to live next to an empty stretch of beach."

Moray had said the same thing. It made sense but there was something else. I couldn't put my finger on it.

Noah said good-bye, and I decided it was time to get something to eat. I headed to the indoor buffet. When I returned outside, the sun had set, replaced by only a partial moon and sprinkling of stars. I grabbed a coffee from the giant urn and talked to a few more people before wandering to the side deck.

It dawned on me that I hadn't seen Calvin Chandler. If he was the future sales agent for the condo development, wouldn't Lucien Moray include him in tonight's activity? The more I thought about it, the more I realized I did not want to run into Calvin. If I needed to question him further, I'd have a better chance as a prospective real estate client than as a reporter. I needed to find out if he was on the yacht, and if so, stay out of his sight.

I spotted Moray talking to three women. When they left, I headed toward him.

"Mrs. Farrell," he said. "Hope you are enjoying yourself."

"I am. But I was wondering if Calvin Chandler is here tonight?"

"I wouldn't invite that worm. I don't want him near me." Two men approached and Moray turned away from me to address them.

Donna Taylor was standing nearby. She laughed. "Don't look so confused. Lucien despises Calvin Chandler. Calvin may think Lucien is his best buddy, but Lucien is only using Calvin to make sure the six million goes to an organization other than the aquarium. Once Calvin distributes the money, Lucien will drop Calvin like a hot potato."

An announcement over the loudspeaker said dessert was being served inside. Donna headed back in, as did most of the people on the deck, but with all I'd eaten at the buffet, I was full. I remained outside.

Moray's yacht was now headed back to the marina. I saw land in the distance with lights glowing from inside a scattering of houses. Soon we passed the aquarium, then the twenty acres of vacant land. There was nothing now but blackness.

Then it happened.

Flashing lights coming from the water, followed by flashing lights on shore.

CHAPTER TWENTY-EIGHT

My mother was devouring a Danish when I came down to breakfast. The two dogs were on either side, waiting for crumbs. Dogs are such optimists.

"You're up early," I said. Someone, presumably my mother, had made a pot of coffee. I poured some into my mug.

"Early? In Florida, eight in the morning is mid-day. Besides, I've lots to do. Paul and I are spending the day in the city. We're visiting a museum, browsing the shops on Fifth Avenue, and tonight a Broadway show."

"Good." I straddled a chair, facing her.

"Oh, by the way, Marcia is having a garage sale, and we need your help."

"I take it things are still okay between you and Paul," I said, avoiding her comment about the garage sale. "Has he revisited investing in his project?"

"He hasn't said a word about the investment since the brunch at Marcia's house. I really think he thought he was doing me a favor by giving me the opportunity to invest with him."

"Have you met his family?"

"Doesn't have any. He's an only child who never married."

"No distant cousins?"

"Never mentioned any." She frowned. "Kristy, why are you prying?"

"I want to make sure you're not going to get hurt."

"You think knowing his cousins will determine my happiness?" She gave me a hard stare, reminiscent of the stares she gave when I was a teenager.

"But you know nothing about—"

"Paul and I are fine. Now, about the garage sale. Marcia is downsizing. She wants to get rid of several of the items she and her late husband collected through the years. She's holding one big garage sale, and she needs help sorting and arranging her merchandise.

I sighed, realizing I wasn't about to worm any information about Paul from my mom. "How do I fit in with the garage sale?" I asked.

"Can you spare some time to help us?"

"Okay. How's Sunday afternoon? But only two or three hours."

"Wonderful. Barbara and Tim said they would assist, too. But you know your sister-in-law. She'll cancel at the last minute. I haven't had a chance to ask Matt yet."

"Matt will be working. He has office hours one Sunday a month to accommodate clients whose jobs make it difficult to schedule veterinary appointments at other times."

"Sounds like an excuse to me." She eyed me suspiciously. "What about Abby? And her boyfriend?"

"Don't know. You'll have to ask." I wanted no part of this.

"I still haven't met Jason."

"You haven't been around much." I glanced at my watch. "I better get to the office. I've got a staff meeting in less than forty-five minutes." Office gossip said that our editor would be making a major announcement concerning the magazine's future. Every time I thought about this, my stomach knotted up like a pretzel.

I had finished pouring coffee into my travel mug when my cell phone trilled. Abby's number popped up.

"Jason got a call from his friend at the District Attorney's office," Abby said. "Katie's autopsy is finished."

"How did she die?"

"Venom from a sea snake. No surprise there."

"Is there any chance she may have fallen into the tank? An accident?"

"No. The autopsy also showed bruises to her hands and fingers. It looks as if she tried to climb out of the tank, but something came down hard on her knuckles, possibly a baseball bat and—"

"And that caused her to lose her grip," I said, completing the thought. "But how did the killer lure her there? She had returned to the aquarium to check on her sea lions. The amphitheater is outside. It's not anywhere near where she died."

"Katie's degree was in marine biology. She knew about more than sea lions. I'm betting the killer asked Katie to observe unusual behavior with the sea snakes. Katie would have gone willingly and offered her opinion."

"That means the killer was an aquarium employee."

"Probably. But this is only a theory. The point is we don't know, so we can't rule out any suspect. Unfortunately, the autopsy doesn't bring us any closer to solving the crime."

"Not true. Katie and Jack were both killed in different ways, but both methods tell us something about the killer.

"Killer? Just one? You believe it was the same person?" Abby asked.

"I do. And we know the murderer possessed two specific characteristics. First, strength. Katie's killer pushed her into the sea snake tank."

"Good point. Katie only weighed around one hundred pounds, but she was strong and active. She'd put up a fight."

"Several of the suspects would have the capability to overpower her. Calvin Chandler was a former college football star, Brad Monroe competes in a variety of athletic activities, Commander West is a physically fit navy man."

"I bet Katie could have fought off Sam. He doesn't weigh much more than she does. What about Oscar? I never met him."

"Oscar is short and pudgy." I shrugged. "But we don't know enough about Oscar or Sam to draw a conclusion. Don't forget, whoever pushed Katie into the tank probably used the element of surprise which makes it easier to overpower someone."

"You're right," Abby admitted. "And the other characteristic is knowledge of anatomy and medicine, right? The security guard was shot with a tranquilizer dart with just enough drug to render him unconscious. Jack was killed by a sharp object inserted into the base of his brain. Who would know where to insert a needle to cause instant death?"

"Commander West started his career as a medical corpsman and Brad Monroe studied mortuary science."

"Don't forget Lucien Moray. He could afford to hire anyone with the expertise needed," Abby added. "What about Calvin, Sam, and Oscar?"

"As far as I know they have no medical knowledge. But I couldn't swear to that."

"I contacted Katie's friend in Connecticut. She told me Katie and Jack had never been in trouble in their youth. She knew them as far back as elementary school."

"We had to check it out, but in my gut, I felt it had nothing to do with their earlier years."

"I agree," said Abby. "Their murders stem from their work at the aquarium. But what?"

CHAPTER TWENTY-NINE

"Corporate is considering the merger of *Animal Advocate* with their newest acquisition, *Green World*," my editor, Olivia Johnson, stated near the end of the staff meeting, causing me to nearly choke on my donut. I realized our new corporate owners were looking at changes, but I never expected such drastic action so soon. Judging by the "deer in the headlights" stares on most of my colleagues, they didn't expect this either.

"How will this affect our jobs?" asked the production manager, who was sitting across from me.

"If it happens, there will be lay-offs. We could lose as much as fifty percent of our staff. But right now the merger is still in discussion stage. A final decision will be made by the end of December. That's all for now." As Olivia rose from her chair and proceeded to the door, she leaned over me and whispered, "Kristy, see me in my office in fifteen minutes."

* * * * *

As I entered her inner sanctum, Olivia rose from her chair. At almost six feet, dressed in a tailored navy blue suit, and wearing her gray hair in a short no-nonsense style, she was a formidable figure. An African American who grew up in the south Bronx, Olivia had street smarts as well as the reputation of being an excellent editor.

"Anything new on the murder investigation?"

I shook my head. "Too many suspects, and I haven't been able to break alibis. But I'm still hopeful."

I expected Olivia to push more, but instead she said, "How's the land acquisition story?"

"With the death of Katie Chandler, it's up in the air as to who will acquire the property. It's a long shot for the aquarium, but we won't know the outcome until after we go to print."

"That's okay. Cliffhangers can be good for circulation."

Olivia walked around her desk. "The fight over the twenty acres has grabbed media attention. "As my granddaughter would say, 'it's trending.' People will buy this issue of *Animal Advocate* to find out who wins—the aquarium or the developer. If the controversy isn't resolved by then, readers will purchase future issues until an outcome is reached. We need articles like this so we don't go the way of the dinosaur and dodo."

"Of course, I—"

"Dig deep. Find out about special interests. Uncover hidden motives."

* * * * *

Bradford Monroe handed me a cup of coffee, while once again commenting on the cost of his espresso machine.

As we sat down, he leaned forward, spreading his hands across his desk, "Now, how can I help you?"

"I'm updating my land acquisition story. Can you tell me where you are in terms of reaching your goal of ten million dollars?"

"We're on our way to victory."

"I need you to be a bit more specific. How are your sponsorships coming along?"

"We will have the Mulgrave check for the turtle exhibit early next week."

"That's great, but it's just one sponsorship for one hundred thousand dollars. You're still a long way from your goal?"

He smiled. "I'm actively pursuing many leads. Commander West and I have a meeting later this afternoon with another potential sponsor."

"Let's talk about the auction. What types of items will you have for sale?"

"We have merchandise to fit every taste and pocketbook. Last count, there were more than one hundred items, ranging from a collection of art deco jewelry to a painting by a famous Long Island artist. All donated by our generous supporters." He grinned. "We're lucky to be only a few miles from the Hamptons, home to many multi-millionaires who support preservation of our marine environment."

Brad grabbed a paperclip and bent it back and forth until it snapped. "And since the aquarium inherited the contents of the Chandler house, too, we will be auctioning most of the items that Katie's great-great-grandfather brought back from around the world in the 1800s. If you remember, there are fabulous items like the Samurai sword. The auction will be a huge success."

"I'm looking forward to it."

"You're coming?" He looked surprised.

I nodded. "I hope to include it in my article."

"Great," he said. "Be sure to attend the preview? It's an hour before the auction begins. Bring a photographer, too. The more publicity we receive on this event, the better for future fund raising."

With all this talk of Katie's home and its contents, an idea popped into my head. After leaving Brad's office, I phoned Sam Wong.

"Sam," I said. "Do you have the key to Katie's house?"

"Sure. Katie and I both had keys to each others' homes."

"Could you let me in? I'd like to look around."

"Well, uh, I don't know, Mrs. Farrell. The house belongs to the aquarium now. I don't have a legal right to be there."

"It might hold the answer to why Katie was murdered."

"How?"

"The day of the cocktail party, Katie told me she heard a rumor as to why Jack was murdered. What if that is related to her death? I'm wondering if Katie left a clue in her home? A piece of evidence?"

"I guess it's okay," Sam said. "I still have some clothes in Katie's closet. If we get caught, I can always say I was there to pick up my belongings." He hesitated. "But what would you use as an excuse?"

"I'll say I lost a bracelet at the cocktail party." I was getting good at fabricating stories. "When can we go?"

"I'm free in about an hour. Meet you there."

Something Fishy

* * * * *

Sam turned his key and pushed open the door to Katie's house. It
appeared exactly the same as when we left the day of the cocktail party.

"Where do you want to start, Mom?" Abby asked. My daughter, who
had the day off, had been riding Topper at the Patterson Horse Farm
this morning. I had called and asked her to join us, figuring another pair
of eyes couldn't hurt.

"Since the cocktail party took over the entire first floor, I don't think
anything would be down here. Let's start upstairs."

"What are we looking for?" Abby asked.

"I'm not exactly sure. But pull out anything that has to do with the
land acquisition, the aquarium, or Jack Patterson."

We were about to head upstairs when Sam's phoned trilled. "I have
to take this call," he said. "I'll be in the living room. I'll join you when
I finish."

The upstairs consisted of Katie's bedroom, her office, a guest room,
and the captain's study. Abby and I entered Katie's bedroom first.

"Katie was a compulsive list maker," Abby said. "She also loved to
write reminder memos. Look for any scribblings or notes on small
pieces of paper."

We searched the dresser drawers and the nightstand and found
nothing. I got down on my hands and knees and checked underneath
the bed and behind the desk in case a note had fallen.

"I'll bet she cleaned up before the cocktail party," Abby said.

"I wonder if she kept a diary?"

"She did," Abby said, excitedly. "According to Katie, all Chandler
women kept diaries going back to Elizabeth Chandler, mother of the
sea captain. Katie wasn't about to break the tradition although she didn't
write everyday. Sometimes, a week or more would go by before she
penned an entry."

"We need to find that book."

"I know what it looks like. It has a sea lion on a navy blue cover."

"A sea lion?"

Abby grinned. "I found a bunch of diaries in a small gift shop in
Montauk. They all featured a different of marine mammal on the cover.

127

I bought one for Katie's birthday this summer, and she's been using it ever since. At least that's what she told me."

We searched Katie's office as well as the guest room but had no luck. No diary. No other clues.

"I doubt we'll find anything in that captain's study," Abby commented as we emerged into the hall. "The room wasn't used. Katie kept it as a museum to display items her great-great-grandfather brought back from foreign ports."

"You're probably right, but we better look anyway."

We crossed the hall and had stepped into the captain's study when I heard the front door slam.

"What's going on here, Sam? Why are you here?" yelled a familiar voice.

The voice belonged to Detective Steve Wolfe.

I put my finger to my lips, motioning Abby to be quiet. We pressed our bodies against the wall in the study, making sure we were out of sight.

"Some of my clothes are here, sir," Sam answered the detective. "I came to take them back to my place."

"You shouldn't be here."

"Why? I have a key."

Silence. I couldn't see Wolfe, but I envisioned his face beet-red with purple veins protruding from his neck and spittle oozing from his mouth.

"This house is now part of the Chandler estate. You're trespassing. Since you have a key, I'll let you off with a warning this time. But if I see you here again, I'll arrest you."

"Yes sir. Are you checking the house again for clues?"

"No. We're finished with that. I was passing by and saw a car in the driveway, so I decided to investigate. Empty homes are prime targets for robberies. Let's go."

I heard the door slam.

"We better leave before Wolfe returns," Abby said, after a few seconds had passed.

"He won't be back for a while. We have time."

"But Mom—"

"I'll be quick."

At first glance, everything in the captain's study appeared as it did on the day of the cocktail party. Then I examined the desk.

"What's wrong, Mom?" Abby asked, apparently seeing the frown on my face.

"I'm not sure. But something is different."

CHAPTER THIRTY

"This isn't good." I muttered.

"What's wrong?" Abby asked as we slid into the last pew of the Episcopal Church for Katie Chandler's Friday evening memorial service.

"Katie's cousin. Calvin Chandler. He's sitting up front."

"He's a hypocrite." Abby shook her head. "Katie wouldn't have wanted him here."

"It's not that," I said. "He doesn't know I have any connection to Katie. He thinks I'm a potential buyer for the condos. I may need more information from him, and I don't want to blow my cover."

"Don't worry. I doubt he'll turn around, and we'll just be careful when we leave to stay out of his sight."

I was skeptical that I could pull this off. There were fewer than fifty mourners in attendance, making it easy to spot someone.

As I wondered if more people would be coming, Bradford Monroe entered and made his way to the first row where he tried to greet Calvin Chandler. Calvin turned away and began conversing with an elderly lady sitting behind him. Bradford stood silently for a moment, then headed up the aisle and squeezed into a seat next to Commander West.

"Bradford still believes he can convince Calvin to donate six million to the aquarium," I whispered to my daughter.

"Judging by the way Calvin blew him off, I'd say that's not going to happen," Abby said.

I noticed Abby's eyes filling up with tears. She was saying good-bye to her best friend. I grabbed her hand and gave it a squeeze. She let out a small sob.

As we grew closer to the start of the service, more people arrived.

I spotted Oscar Mejas sitting next to Madge, the marine mammal attendant. A few rows behind them, Jillian Patterson fidgeted in her seat and thumbed through a hymnal although she didn't appear to be paying any attention to the pages.

But Sam Wong was not here.

Where's Sam?" I whispered to Abby.

"He just arrived." Abby motioned to the entrance of the sanctuary where Sam stood between the two open doors. He appeared to scan the room.

"Who is he searching for?"

Abby shrugged.

Finally, Sam nodded as if acknowledging someone's presence. As the organist began playing "On Eagle's Wings" he headed down the aisle. When he passed by, I turned my head, blocking Abby from view, too. I didn't know why, but I didn't want him to see us. He slid into an empty pew about six rows from the front.

* * * * *

"This is a good spot to watch everything," I said to my daughter as we sat in my car after the memorial service. "Let's wait a minute before leaving. I want to see if anything interesting happens."

"Interesting?"

I shrugged. "You never know."

Commander West left first with Brad Monroe. Seconds later, Oscar Mejas, Madge, and Sam Wong exited the church and headed toward their cars. Finally, Calvin emerged. They all drove off, except Sam. He leaned against the side of his silver convertible, pulled a cigarette from his pocket, and began smoking. He glanced at his watch.

"Why is he still here?"

"Maybe he didn't want to smoke in his car," Abby said.

I frowned. "I think he's waiting for someone."

"Could be. But who?"

That question was answered when Jillian Patterson emerged from the church, made her way through the parking lot to the silver convertible, and shook hands with Sam Wong.

CHAPTER THIRTY-ONE

I glanced at my watch. Sam Wong was late for our meeting. I had contacted him last night and told him we needed to talk.

Five minutes later, Sam walked through the door of Pirate Pete's Coffee Shop and made his way to my table.

"I can't stay long," he said as he slid into a chair across from me. "I don't know why we couldn't do this by phone."

"I have questions I want to ask face-to-face." I needed to see his reaction. As a former teacher I was good at telling if someone was lying. "I didn't know you had a relationship with Jillian Patterson."

"I'd hardly call it a relationship. I'm working on a business deal for her with Lucien Moray."

"The sale of the horse farm? Is that why the two of you met after Katie's memorial service."

"That's right." Sam rose from his chair and frowned. "But this is business. I really can't discuss it."

I ignored the fact that the waitress was hovering over us while she poured coffee. "What if it is related to Katie's murder?"

All color drained from his face. "What do you mean?" He sat back down.

"How desperate is Jillian for money? Come on, Sam. A real estate developer like Moray doesn't make an offer blindly. He sizes up his opponent's strengths and weaknesses. I'm assuming he had you research the Patterson Horse Farm before making the offer. What did you find out about Jillian's financial situation?"

"It's bad. None of her vendors will grant her credit anymore. The grain company will deliver on a cash only basis. She can't survive without grain. I figure she'll be bankrupt in less than a year."

"Did Jack know about this?"

"Jillian told him. She showed him the books, too. But Jack was a dreamer. He thought the two of them together could overcome the financial adversity."

"That gives her motive to kill both Jack and Katie."

"Ridiculous." He shook his head. "You and I both know whoever killed Katie needed access to the aquarium. Jillian doesn't have a key."

"But Jack did. Think how easy it would be for Jillian to have a copy made." I didn't bother to remind him that Katie's key was missing, which meant anyone, including Sam himself, might have found it.

"But why would Jillian push Katie in with the sea snakes? It's an unusual way to kill someone, and Jillian has no experience with marine life."

"I'm assuming it was done to cast suspicion on an aquarium staff member," I said.

Sam appeared to ponder my point. "That makes sense. Focus the investigation in another direction." He nodded.

"The problem is Jillian would need to be familiar with the facility," I said. "She would have needed to know how to access the sea snake tank. Do you have any idea if she ever visited the aquarium with her brother?"

"She was there for *Friends and Family Day.*"

"What's that?"

"When Commander West first came to the aquarium, he held a small get-together for staff, their families, and close friends. It included a tour of the inner workings of the facilities. I was there with Katie. Jillian attended with Jack."

My mind was racing. Would a one day event provide Jillian with enough familiarity to pull off such a complicated murder? "Let's get back to the purchase of the Patterson horse farm. Sam, are you the go-between for Lucien and Jillian?"

Sam nodded. "Yes. I did all the preliminary work. Lucien never gets involved until the very end."

"I know that originally there was an impasse since Jack refused to sign off on the deal. After Jack's death, who reached out first? Did you contact Jillian? Or did she call you?"

"Jillian contacted me the day I returned to Clam Cove, about an hour before you discovered Katie's body. She said she had been trying to reach me. She had inherited her brother's half of the property and was clear to sell."

"What did you say?"

"We'd keep the offer in mind, but the purchase was contingent on Moray's acquiring the bay front property first. Without the condos, there wouldn't be a large enough population to support the shopping center."

I sucked in my breath. "After Katie was killed, did you contact Jillian?"

Sam paused, then frowned. "No. She contacted me two days after Katie's murder."

"What did she say?"

"She wanted to know when Lucien would be ready to buy her horse farm."

* * * * *

"Let me get this straight. You want another tour of the aquarium?" Oscar asked. I was sitting across from his desk.

"Yes. I'd like to see how the facility operates. How you feed the fish, clean the tanks, and so forth. My article is called 'Dangers of the Deep' and I want to include a section on the risks for aquarium staff in the daily care of marine life."

He glanced at his watch. "Okay. I have some time now, so let me show you around."

We exited his office and headed down the hallway. When we passed the shark tank, the nine foot bull shark was in full view. I shuddered.

"Have you made any progress in finding out who sabotaged the shark tank?" I asked.

Oscar shook his head. "No. The police haven't been back since your incident. I've tried to develop a time line as to what employees were working there, but since we haven't done any shark dives in a while, I've no idea of how far back to look."

At the end of the corridor, we came to a door marked *Staff Only.* "This encloses the staircase to the employee work area," Oscar said as he pulled open the door.

"This isn't locked?"

"Most of the time. But two fish keepers are currently working upstairs, so it's open today."

I trudged up the stairs behind him. Upon reaching the top, we stood at one end of a long aisle. At the opposite end were piles of cartons, shelving, and three large commercial refrigerators. Two fish keepers were tearing open the cartons and placing the contents on the shelves.

"This is where we store our fish food and other supplies," Oscar said.

I realized Katie might have come here to get supplies for her sea lions. Her assailant may have been lying in wait.

On either side of us, for the entire length of the aisle, were the tops of the fish tanks that we had passed when we were below. As we headed down this aisle, I looked down into the exhibits featuring fish from around the world including the coral reef of the Caribbean, the Amazon River, and the North Atlantic Ocean. When I came to the sea snakes, I shivered. The image of Katie was etched across my mind.

"We feed the fish from here." Oscar smiled. "Lots of tasks that we perform involve risks. But feeding the fish is pretty safe."

I made my way to the edge. The glass sides came up to my hips, making it almost impossible for someone to accidentally fall into the water.

But pushing a body into a tank was a definite possibility.

CHAPTER THIRTY-TWO

"**A**re you here to watch Abby ride?" Jillian asked. I was at Patterson Stables, where I'd run into Jillian who was pushing a wheelbarrow loaded with horse manure.

"Yes. I was at the aquarium, so I thought I'd stop by," I said. I trailed behind her as she shoveled manure off the ground. "Speaking of Abby, what's going to happen to her horse lease if and when you sell this place?"

"She won't have a problem. She only signed a lease for three months. I'll be here a lot longer than that."

"Did the deal to sell fall through?"

"Not at all. It's just that Moray won't buy my land until the twenty acres of bay front property is officially his. Without the condominiums, he feels there is no need for a shopping center."

"So, it's up in the air." I knew this but wanted to see her reaction.

Jillian shook her head. "The owner of the twenty acres has given the aquarium until the end of June to come up with the money. No way they can do that. Once the deadline arrives, Moray will step in. As soon as he seals the deal, he'll buy my property."

"June is less than nine months away. Can you afford to operate the stable for that long?"

She shoveled another pile of manure into the wheelbarrow. "I don't think it's any of your business."

"It's my daughter's business. It's the business of anyone who leases or boards a horse here. Do your clients have any idea that you're thinking of selling?"

Jillian narrowed her eyes and clenched her fists. I flinched. The woman was physically intimidating. But then she sighed, releasing all physical signs of tenseness. "Jack had a small life insurance policy, and I was the beneficiary."

I must have looked surprised, because she quickly added, " It's not a lot of money, but its enough to support this place for roughly a year."

"What are you going to do once you sell?"

"I'll probably move. With Jack gone, there's nothing holding me here anymore." She smiled wistfully. "I've been cleaning out his room. I think Jack kept everything he owned since kindergarten. He had a collection of shells, comic books, bottle caps, stamps, and postcards." She shook her head. "Postcards. That's a thing of the past."

Her sad looking brown eyes reminded me of a Basset Hound, making me wonder if my suspicions about her were right. She appeared genuinely distraught over the loss of Jack. Could a woman like this murder her brother?

But some people possess remarkable acting skills.

She continued, "If I do move, it will be to an area with horses. I'll look for a job at a stable. I have training as a veterinary technician. I'm great with horses but not with managing money, so I'll probably be better off working for someone." She paused as she appeared to scan her surroundings. "But I do so love this place."

"Jillian, do you have a business manager or an accountant helping you?"

She shook her head. "Jack and I always did everything by ourselves."

I pulled out my phone. "I'm giving you the name of my husband's accountant. Before you make a final decision, why don't you talk to him? I'll let him know to expect your call." I don't know why I did this. Jillian could be the murderer. But if she wasn't, I didn't want to see her lose this horse farm which she loved.

Jillian put the information in her phone, and we said good-bye. I headed to the outdoor arena to watch Abby ride Topper over two-foot wooden jumps. Since Abby had to get back to work, she cut her session short, and we made our way back to the barn, Topper in tow.

At the far end of our aisle, a horse on cross ties was being groomed by a young teenager. A woman, whom I assumed was her mother, stood nearby, handing her daughter grooming tools from a nearby tack box. I made my way toward them.

"Beautiful horse," I said, as I gazed at the chestnut with a black mane.

"Lucky's a love," the girl replied. "And he's a really good horse. I won a blue ribbon with him at the horse show here a week ago."

"A week ago?"

"It will be exactly a week tomorrow."

That was the day following Katie Chandler's death.

I remembered when Abby competed in horse shows. The day preceding the big event was a busy day at the host stable, and barn help was usually there in case complications arose. Jillian had no staff, so it's likely she would have been here to provide assistance. That would have given her an alibi, depending upon how late she stayed here.

"So, I guess you were busy grooming Lucky that Saturday. Was Jillian here?" I asked.

"Yeah. She came around a few times to make sure all her riders were prepared for the next day."

"Except for the hour we couldn't find her," her mother added. "I was so annoyed at the time we wasted."

My ears perked. "What happened?"

"My daughter couldn't find her curry comb. There are extra grooming supplies in the tack room, but when we went there, it was locked. We tried to find Jillian but she was gone." She shook her head. "That was irresponsible. She knows a million things come up before a horse show."

"It all worked out, Mom," the girl said, rolling her eyes. "No reason for panic. Another rider was still here, and she lent me her comb."

"Several riders were running late," the mother said, shaking her head. "She shouldn't have left until we were all gone."

"What time did this happen?"

"As I said, we were running late. I don't know exactly what time she left, but we were looking for her a little after six."

The same time Katie left her home to go to the aquarium.

CHAPTER THIRTY-THREE

"But she had to have had a good reason to run off from the stable the day before a horse show," I said. "Could murder be that reason?"

I was sipping my favorite alcoholic beverage, a pomegranate martini, on the patio of the Nautical Inn overlooking the Great South Bay. Matt and I were waiting for Tim and Barbara to join us for dinner.

"Did you ask Jillian why she left?" Matt asked as he swished the scotch in his glass.

"Didn't have a chance. I also don't know if I would believe anything she told me."

A puzzled expression spread across Matt's face. "But, Kristy," he said. "Would a woman have the strength to push Katie in the sea snake tank?"

"This woman would. She's nearly six foot tall and has more muscles than most men I know. You should see her toss hay bales in the stable."

"Have you told the police about this?"

I shook my head while gazing at the orange sun setting on the water. "It won't do any good. Detective Wolfe is handling the case, and he would disregard any leads that come from me. The police haven't the foggiest notion who committed the crime." I sighed. "Neither do I, but I intend to find out."

"Kristy, be careful." Matt ran his hand through his thinning sandy hair. "Two people have been murdered, and you could have been killed in the shark tank, and—"

"This conversation seems way too serious," a voice interrupted. It was my sister-in-law, Barbara. Bringing up the rear was my brother, who looked more disheveled than usual. His thick eye glasses had a crack in the right lens.

"Sorry, we're late," Barbara said. "Tim was delayed at the zoo."

"Dental problems with one of my crocodiles," my brother added as he slid into a chair.

"We were just talking about the murder at the aquarium," I said.

"What is it with you and murder? Let's talk about something else," Barbara sat down and rubbed her hands together. "How about your mother and Paul Andre? What's going on there?"

"I think your mother really loves him, Kristy," said Matt.

"Or she loves the idea of being in love." Although my mother had lots of friends in Florida, I think she missed male companionship.

"Is Mom out with Paul tonight?" Tim asked.

"No. She and Marcia went to the movies. Paul couldn't make it because he was meeting with a prospective financial backer."

"On a Saturday night?" Matt swallowed what remained of his scotch.

"We no longer live in a Monday to Friday work world. Business is conducted seven days and nights."

The waitress approached, took drink orders from Tim and Barbara, and asked us if we wanted to be seated inside for dinner or stay on the patio. Although the restaurant with its dark paneling, subdued lighting, and fresh flowers on every table, was gorgeous, nothing could beat the Harvest moon, which soon would be visible in the sky above the Great South Bay. Since space heaters had been placed on the patio to ward off the chilly autumn night air, we opted to dine outside.

After the waitress handed us menus, I excused myself to use the rest room. As I entered the restaurant and wandered down the hall, my eyes adjusting to the diminished light, I heard a familiar voice coming from a nearby alcove.

I stopped and listened.

"Just one more week. I promise you this is the last time," the voice said. And you're going to love Paris. We'll have a wonderful time. A wonderful life."

It felt like tiny spiders crawling in my intestines.

I peeked around the corner, so I could peer into the alcove without being seen.

The familiar voice belonged to Paul Andre.

Paul was sitting with an attractive blond, probably thirty years younger than he was. The way his hand was placed on hers, this didn't look like a business meeting.

I hurried back outside and told my family what I'd seen.

"Are you sure?" Barbara's eyes widened. She rose from her chair. "A love triangle. I'm going to take a look."

I grabbed her arm. "Wait. You need to be sure he doesn't see you."

"Why?" Barbara furrowed her brows. "Don't you plan to confront him?"

I shook my head. "We need to get to the bottom of this first. If we don't, and if we cause a break-up, Mom will never forgive us."

Barbara sat back down. "What are you going to do?"

"I don't know yet. But tomorrow Mom and I are going to Marcia's house to help sort out items for the garage sale. That's when I'll pry a bit and come up with a plan."

CHAPTER THIRTY-FOUR

"Do your really think someone will buy a statue of an owl with a clock in its stomach?"

"Who knows?" My mother shrugged. We were in Marcia's basement sorting through items for the garage sale. Marcia had gone upstairs to fetch us coffee.

"This is really a pile of junk," I mumbled under my breath.

"I heard that." My mother smiled. "You know what they say about one man's trash being another man's treasure. Besides, Marcia has already sold a few items online."

I looked at my mother. "I thought you had said she wasn't comfortable with online selling."

"She's not. My Paul is helping her. So far, he brought in more than six hundred dollars. He's taking care of everything including mailing the merchandise to the buyers."

"What's he sold?"

"Some small kitchen appliances, a few books, and, oh, her doll collection."

"Marcia has a doll collection?"

My mother nodded. "She has about a dozen dolls. Marcia's father started the collection for her. He traveled on business when she was a child, and he always would bring back a doll from the state or country he had visited. She has a beautiful porcelain doll from Japan, an Indian warrior doll from Arizona, an Eskimo—"

"Here's your coffee," Marcia interrupted as she descended the stairs. She handed us cups, then got down on the floor to help with the sorting, a difficult task since she suffered from arthritis.

"Are you seeing Paul today?" I asked my mother.

"I'm meeting him at his hotel in about an hour and a half for an early dinner. After that he has a business meeting, so I'll be back at your house. Will you and Matt be home?"

I nodded absentmindedly as I wondered what sort of business. Would it involve the blonde from last night?

An idea popped into my mind. "Where's Paul staying?"

"The Weeping Whale Hotel."

The Weeping Whale was a boutique hotel located about ten miles from here.

I devised a plan. I'd go to the Weeping Whale and wait outside the hotel. After Paul finished dinner with my mother, I'd follow him to his meeting.

"Oh, look at these pictures. You'll get a kick out of these, Kristy," Marcia said, interrupting my thoughts. She was sorting through an old photo album.

Marcia handed me the album, and I began thumbing through the pages, examining the black and white pictures, so different than today's digital photography.

One photo caught my eye. I stared at it for a few seconds. "What are you doing with these albums?" I asked Marcia who, along with my mother, had moved to the other end of the basement where they were attaching price tags on old barbecue utensils.

"I'm keeping them, of course," she said. "For the time being, I'm placing them in the big carton by the stairs. I'll take that to a storage unit I recently rented. Once I move to my new place, I'll bring everything home."

While Marcia and my mother continued pricing items, I slipped a photo out of the album and stashed it carefully in my bag.

* * * * *

Later that day, I sloughed behind my steering wheel in the Weeping Whale Hotel parking lot waiting for Paul Andre to emerge. I had positioned my car in a prime spot in the guest parking area with a good view of the main entrance. Before leaving Marcia's house, I had asked my mother what type of auto Paul was driving. She said a black Chrysler LeBaron.

I hoped to stay out of Paul's sight, but I wanted to be prepared just in case. I had put my hair in a French twist and donned a pair of oversized sunglasses. He'd only met me once, so hopefully he wouldn't recognize me.

"They've been here for way more than an hour. They should be finished with dinner by now," I mumbled as I glanced at my watch impatiently, then drummed my fingers on the steering wheel.

Fifteen minutes later, I was beginning to wonder if Paul had left through another door when he and my mother emerged from the front of the hotel. He escorted her to her rental car, then walked through the lot until he reached the black LeBaron located about ten cars down from where I was parked.

As he drove off, I followed. I didn't have a real plan. I simply wanted to see where he went next. I hoped he wasn't going too far. To my luck, he drove for less than a mile and pulled into the parking lot of a popular watering hole called the Blackbird Inn.

I hopped out of my car and followed him at a safe distance as he entered through the front door and strolled through the lobby to the taproom. He appeared to scan the dimly lit room, then headed to a table in the far corner. As he slid into a chair next to the blonde he had been with last night, he reached over the table and greeted a man sitting across from the woman.

"What the hell is going on?" I mumbled.

Paul was shaking hands with Bradford Monroe.

CHAPTER THIRTY-FIVE

" I'd like to see Lucien Moray's proposal for development of the land adjacent to the aquarium," I said to the clerk in Clam Cove's Office of Planning and Zoning. Tall, skinny, with a beak-like nose and large hands, he reminded me of Ichabod Crane.

"It will take a moment. While I retrieve them, please fill this out." He handed me a form and disappeared into a back room.

Although Lucien Moray's presentation at the Village Hall meeting two weeks ago provided a rendition of his new development, I wanted to examine the plans more closely. I knew I was grasping at straws, but maybe I had overlooked something that served as a motive in Jack and Katie's deaths.

The clerk returned with the plans, which showed pretty much what Lucien had talked about at the meeting—seventy-five condo units, restaurant, club house, tennis court, two pools, two Jacuzzis, tennis court, and small marina. Lucien had promised to donate an acre to the aquarium and his plans did show that area. But at the opposite end of Moray's project, another acre of land also appeared to be set aside. I had missed this during Moray's power point presentation. Or maybe he hadn't mentioned it.

"Do you know what this acre is for?" I asked the clerk.

"Moray is using that as a nature preserve. Sort of a buffer between his development and the residential and commercial establishments down the beach."

The preserve was next to Ruby Diamond's home. This would leave her with an acre of untouched land between her cottage and the condominium development. Next to this vacant land was the tennis court, then the pools. The condo units were located at the end closest to the aquarium.

No wonder Ruby seemed to hit harder at the aquarium than the condominiums. With the aquarium, she would be next to a camp ground, even if its use was severely restricted to marine scientists. Although she wanted the twenty acres to remain vacant, an acre of natural land was better than a camp.

But was it enough to kill for?

* * * * *

I wandered out of the zoning office intending to get a quick bite to eat. While strolling down the street I noticed pottery in the window of Gracie's Gift Shoppe.

I remembered Ruby Diamond's comment about a store in town that sold her products. As I stepped inside, and glanced at my surroundings, I had a feeling this was the shop.

In addition to the pottery, the store featured an eclectic array of merchandise. The smell of incense permeated the shop and was a bit too strong for my liking.

"Are you looking for anything in particular?" asked a young woman. With her raven hair, alabaster skin, and vermilion lips, she looked like a character from a Gothic novel. "I'm Grace. This is my shop."

"This is beautiful." I pointed to a ceramic jug painted in several shades of blue. "Is this Ruby Diamond's work?"

Grace nodded.

"Is all this pottery from Ruby?" I asked. There were more than a dozen pieces displayed on a shelf situated against the front window.

"Yes. She is the only potter whose work I sell."

"I'll bet it sells quickly."

"Not as quickly as I'd like. I sell about two or three pieces a month."

Three pieces a month would only bring in a few hundred dollars. That was before the shop owner took her commission. The property taxes on Ruby's beach house would be considerably more than what she made from the sale of her pottery. Then there was her electric and phone bill, car insurance, gas, and food. The point: where was Ruby getting the money to support herself?

While strolling down the aisle examining merchandise, I spotted an a large storage closet. The door was ajar, so I looked in. Sitting atop a shelf were seven pieces of Ruby's pottery. A vase, painted in blues, tans, and white with a sea shell motif, caught my eye. It would fit perfectly in Abby's home.

"Are those items for sale?" I asked, pointing to the pottery in the closet. "If so, how much is the vase with the sea shells?"

Grace's eyes widened. "Oh, no. Nothing back here is for sale." She shut the closet door. "Those pieces have been sold. We keep them in storage until we ship them out."

"Could I at least get a closer look at the sea shell vase? Maybe I could get Ruby to create a similar one for me."

"I can't take a chance," Grace said. "What if you dropped it, and it broke?"

"I only want to—"

"If you describe this vase to Ruby, I'm sure she can duplicate it for you," Grace said as she guided me toward the front of the shop.

As I left the store, various scenarios ran through my mind. I hadn't asked to pick up the vase, I only asked if I could get a better look at it. Was I becoming paranoid, or did Grace really want to get me away from those vases? But those thoughts quickly disappeared as I passed the Starfish Real Estate Agency. I glanced in the window and spotted Calvin Chandler. He appeared to be deep in conversation with a man who was sitting across from his desk.

"I don't believe it," I mumbled, while positioning to get a better view. It was the aquarium's head fish keeper. Oscar Mejas.

Talk about strange bedfellows. Yesterday, I discovered Paul Andre and Brad Monroe together. Today it's Calvin Chandler and Oscar Mejas. What was going on?"

* * * * *

After grabbing a chocolate ice cream cone in town for my lunch, I sped off to the aquarium. Upon arrival, I knocked on the open door of Oscar's office.

"Come in," he said, barely looking up from his computer keyboard.

I slid into a chair across from Oscar while noticing a half-eaten sandwich and a can of cola on his desk.

"Didn't have time for lunch in town?" I asked.

Oscar stopped pecking at his keyboard and looked up. "I beg your pardon."

"The sandwich on the desk. I'm guessing you didn't have time to grab a bite in town. I saw you there less than an hour ago."

"I decided on a working lunch." He stared at me quizzically.

"I didn't know you were friends with Calvin Chandler," I said.

"Friends? I would hardly classify us as friends. Why would you suggest that?"

"Because I just saw you in his real estate office. I was surprised, considering he's the one who is diverting Alicia Wilcox-Chandler's money away from the aquarium."

Oscar sighed. "I'm planning on downsizing once I retire. I'm selling my current home, but I plan to stay in Clam Cove—"

"Are you using Calvin Chandler as your real estate agent?"

"Absolutely not. I would never use a sleaze like him."

"But you were in his office."

Oscar sat back. "Chandler is only a sales agent. The owner of the agency, Thad Tucker, is a friend of mine, and he's my broker. I needed to drop off some documents today. Since Thad knew he wouldn't be in the office, he asked me to leave them with Calvin."

It made sense, but I wasn't totally convinced.

"Oscar, where were you the night Katie died?"

He frowned. "Yes. I remember Katie talking about you. She told me that you solved a murder at the Rocky Cove Zoo this summer. I guess you consider yourself to be an amateur detective."

"I consider myself a friend of Katie. I'd like to find out who killed her."

He nodded. "I liked Katie, and I had no reason to kill her. On the day of the murder, I had left the aquarium a few minutes early at about five-twenty—I usually leave that time on Saturdays. I waved good-bye to the security guard. He saw me leave. You can check with him. I grabbed pizza in town and then attended my grandson's weekly basketball game at the community center. Game started at six-thirty, and I arrived there about a half hour before, so I could grab a good seat."

"Did you go by yourself?"

"Yes. My daughter and son-in-law came later. They missed the first quarter because they had to work. I missed the end of the game because I received the phone call from Commander West to return to the aquarium and help the police remove Katie's body from the sea snake tank."

The pizzeria and community center were less than ten minutes from the aquarium. Katie was alive at six. We found her body at close to seven-thirty. Would Oscar's alibi for that time check out?

As I left Oscar's office and headed down the corridor, I spotted Bradford Monroe coming toward me. I wanted to ask him about his meeting yesterday with Paul Andre and the blonde, but he was accompanied by a middle age couple, so I knew I wouldn't be able to question him now.

"Kristy Farrell. I'm glad you're here," he said with bounding enthusiasm. "I want you to meet our first sponsors, Elizabeth and Jerome Mulgrave. Their names will be above our new turtle exhibit."

Before I had a chance to say hello, Bradford turned to the couple. "Kristy Farrell is a reporter for *Animal Advocate Magazine,* and she is doing a feature on our proposed expansion plans." He turned back to face me. The man moved around like a wind-up doll. "You should mention the Mulgraves in your article. They should get recognition for their generosity. And who knows. That could lead to future sponsors."

As much as I wanted to aquarium to succeed, my job was not to act as a cheerleader for their cause. But certainly, some quotes from the Mulgraves on what led to their decision to become sponsors belonged in my story.

"That's not a bad idea," I said. "Why don't—"

"Let's go to my office now." Bradford whisked us down the hall.

The Mulgraves, who both were short, squat, and ruddy faced, sat on a couch while I slid into an armchair. I smiled at them, while wondering if married couples really do begin to look like each other as they age.

Once situated behind his desk, Bradford started talking. I had had enough of his rhetoric and knew it was time to take control.

"I'd like the Mulgraves to tell me in their own words why they decided to become sponsors," I said.

"We both grew up in Clam Shell Cove," Mrs. Mulgrave replied. "We now live about an hour away, but much of my family is still here, and we visit frequently. We believe strongly in the work the aquarium is doing in helping endangered species and in educating the public."

"We also gave Bradford a list of our friends and business associates who believe strongly in similar causes," Mr. Mulgrave added. "We're going to help Bradford convince these friends to become sponsors, too."

"You should get a photo of the Mulgraves for your story," Bradford said.

"Well, I guess—"

"We'll do it by the turtle exhibit. Let's go." He hopped out of his seat. As we exited the room, Bradford whispered to me, "Since I'm responsible for the donation, I'd like to be in the picture, too. I should get credit."

"Do either of you work in the field of marine science?" I asked the Mulgraves as we made our way down the corridor.

"No. We own a car dealership near the county seat," Mrs. Mulgrave said. "We also have investments in other businesses. We recently became part owners in a chain of health spas. It's aimed at overweight teenagers. It should do quite well."

CHAPTER THIRTY-SIX

"I've news." Matt greeted me when I arrived home later that night. "It's about your mother. She told me this morning, she and Paul have been shopping for an engagement ring."

I frowned.

"There's more," Matt said. They talked about eloping. She said you might have a stepfather soon."

"I'm racing the clock. I need to expose him before my mother does something she'll regret for the rest of her life."

"Expose what? His relationship with the blonde?"

"It's more than that. He's up to something."

"Like what? Isn't it possible he and the blonde were meeting for a legitimate business reason?"

"You don't hold hands with a business associate." I frowned. "Paul Andre has no intention of marrying my mother. He's using her for something else, and I need to find out quickly. I keep going back to an investment scam, but my mother swears he hasn't approached that topic since she told him no."

"So what are you going to do next?"

"I need to meet with Bradford Monroe and ask him why he met with Paul and the blonde."

"Do you think he'll tell you?"

"Doesn't matter. If Bradford and Paul are involved in a scam, by confronting Bradford, I might scare them off. Maybe Paul will leave town without my mother. I'd like to find out what type of scheme he's hatching, but my first goal is to protect Mom."

"Could Bradford be a victim, too?"

I shrugged. "I doubt it."

"Why?"

"Because the Mulgraves—they're big contributors to the aquarium—recently invested in a chain of health spas catering to overweight teens. Coincidence? I think not. I'm guessing Bradford is supplying Paul with lists of wealthy donors."

"You can't be sure Paul's health spa project isn't legit."

"I'm pretty sure. Call it gut instinct. Do you want something to eat?"

"Thanks but I'll heat up Sunday's leftovers. Right now, I've a ton of work to do on the festival. I need to crunch the numbers to find out how much I can spend on advertising."

I gulped. "Shouldn't your accountant be crunching the numbers?" I knew advertising was imperative to get crowds to the event, but I didn't want him to go overboard.

"Arnold doesn't have a flair for marketing or advertising," Matt said, referring to his accountant.

And you do. "When you have everything figured out, I think you should run the numbers by him."

"Yeah, maybe." Matt rose and headed toward his study.

I poured a glass of white wine, sat back, and thought about my husband and his uphill battle to keep his veterinary hospital afloat. Finally deciding it was time to get back to work, I trudged upstairs and propped myself up in bed with my laptop. I opened it to the screen where I'd previously listed potential suspects in Katie's murder. I had learned a lot since then. For the next hour, I deleted and added information. When Matt came into the room, I showed him what I had.

Lucien Moray. He had motive. He believed Alicia Wilcox Chandler's donation was all that prevented him from acquiring the twenty acres. With Katie out of the way, this was no longer an obstacle. Jack Patterson, too, was a major stumbling block to another Moray project. With Jack dead, Moray could easily convince Jillian Patterson to sell the horse farm for a shopping center.

"As for means and opportunity, Lucien Moray certainly wouldn't do the dirty deed himself," I said. "But he had plenty of money to hire a killer. On the other hand, would a man like Moray risk everything for a building project? Wouldn't he just seek out another location?"

Next I showed Matt what I had written about the three aquarium employees who had keys to the facility. There appeared to be no motive—unless one of them was on Moray's payroll.

Commander Conrad West. The man was a decorated hero with an impeccable reputation. Yet, the commander was the suspect I knew least about. All the information I'd gathered on him came from naval press releases and professional websites. Perhaps there was a more personal motive.

He didn't have an alibi for Katie's murder either. From the time he left the fund raiser until I called him, Commander West was supposedly home alone.

Oscar Mejas. Fish keepers, even those in supervisory positions, didn't earn huge salaries. Ready to retire, extra money from Lucien Moray would come in handy. Yet, he seemed to love his work, and I found it difficult to believe he'd do anything to jeopardize the aquarium's goals. As for an alibi, Oscar claimed he stopped for pizza and then attended his grandson's basketball game.

Bradford Monroe. He had expensive tastes. Money could be this man's motive. But his family owned a chain of funeral homes, so he could be independently wealthy. And what about his alibi? At the time of Katie's murder, he was drinking with the Mulgraves at the Tipsy Toad Tavern. The tavern was only a few minutes away from the aquarium.

"Was there opportunity for Brad to leave and commit murder?" Matt asked.

I shrugged. "Unlikely but possible."

"The next four names on the list normally would not have access to the facility. But since Katie's key was lost, and no one bothered to change the locks, all bets were off."

Calvin Chandler. For an opportunist such as Calvin, administering the trust and denying the money to the aquarium would greatly enhance his relationship with Lucien Moray. He supposedly was showing homes at the time of the murder, but I hadn't verified his alibi. Since he once worked for the aquarium, it was possible he had a key.

Sam Wong. He remained the biggest enigma. Although Sam and Katie seemed to love each other, their opposing roles regarding the land acquisition had created increased tensions. Sam's employment with

Moray didn't sit well with me. He could have easily taken Katie's key, too. But what would be his motive for Jack's murder? And what about opportunity? Was he really upstate for the time he claimed? Or had he returned early and committed the crimes?

Ruby Diamond. She was adamant in her opposition to the aquarium's effort to acquire the twenty acres next to her property. She and her friend Kyle appeared to be involved in a secret activity, too. It could be perfectly innocent, but my gut told me it wasn't.

Ruby had attended medical school before embarking on an art career. She would have knowledge of human anatomy and medicine.

"How she would obtain access to the aquarium?" Matt asked.

"That's the puzzle. For Ruby to find Katie's lost key would be like finding a needle in a haystack."

Jillian Patterson. She hadn't been on my original list, but I had enough circumstantial evidence to add her now. Jillian was in extreme debt, and the sale of her horse farm might be the only way she might avoid bankruptcy. Two people stood in her way—her brother, who refused to sign off on the deal, and Katie, whose donation to the aquarium would thwart Moray's goal of obtaining land for his condominium development and therefore eliminate his need to buy her horse farm for a shopping center. Her brother had a key to the aquarium. After he died, she might have taken it.

Jillian had mentioned she was a veterinary technician. That meant she had some medical knowledge. But the anatomy of a horse was different than that of a human. Would she know where to stick a needle in the brain to cause instant death?

Matt held up his fingers and ticked off the three items a detective looks for in solving a crime. "Most of your suspects have motive. Some have means. But as for opportunity..." He shrugged.

"I need to delve deeper into alibis."

"Kristy, be careful. You're dealing with—"

"I know. I'm dealing with a murderer. I'll watch out." As I powered off my computer, Matt made his way toward our bathroom shower. Looking for something to read before going to sleep, I rolled over to his side of the bed and began sorting through a pile of magazines on his nightstand. In addition to sports and news publications, I came across several copies of the last issue of *Animal Advocate.*

"Are you taking *Animal Advocate* into work?" I called out to ensure he could hear me above the running water.

"I want them for the reception area," he called back. "A few clients have said that they enjoy reading the publication. One person asked if he could take the magazine home so he could finish the article on wildlife smuggling."

The running water stopped and Matt emerged, wrapped in a large towel. "You did a terrific job on that one," he said as he donned the sweats that he wore to bed. "My clients are amazed when they read about the strange ways wildlife is smuggled into the country."

He stretched across Archie who was snuggled next to me. He kissed me good-night and said, "That was one dangerous assignment. I was worried about you."

I smiled. Matt would worry over a hangnail. Yawning, I decided I was too tired to read. As I turned off the light and pulled up the comforter, my husband's comments whirled around my head. Something he'd said bothered me, but I didn't know what. I finally fell asleep.

Three hours later, I woke with a start. I knew what Ruby Diamond was doing.

CHAPTER THIRTY-SEVEN

"I need to be back at the veterinary hospital in two hours," Abby said as we made our way down Clam Cove's main street.

"This won't take long, "I said.

"A lot could go wrong with this scheme," Abby warned me.

"We won't know till we try." I pulled open the door, and we stepped inside Gracie's Gift Shoppe.

"This is Ruby Diamond's pottery," I whispered to my daughter as I picked up a vase from the front display and examined it.

"May I help you?" asked the same Gothic looking woman that was here the other day. I remembered she was Grace, the store owner.

"We're just browsing."

"Please be careful." She pointed to a sign that read, "*If you break it, you've bought it.*"

I placed the vase back on the shelf and nudged Abby.

"Perhaps you can help me?" my daughter said to Grace. "I'm looking for a house warming gift for a friend. I have no idea what to get, but I want something with a beach motif."

"Our shell art might be perfect. It's on the left. Follow me."

Once Abby and Grace were out of sight, I scooted to the back of the store. After checking that no one was looking, I quietly opened the door to the storage closet and peeked inside. Ruby Diamond's pottery still sat on the back shelf. But instead of the seven pieces I'd spotted the other day, this time, there were only five.

I glanced back, noting that Abby and Grace were examining the shell art. Grace's back was facing me.

I stepped into the storage room and grabbed one of Ruby's vases. It was the same size and shape as the one displayed in front of the store—the one I'd picked up and examined a few minutes earlier. Only this vase was heavier.

I placed the vase back on the shelf and made my way toward the front, casually approaching my daughter and Grace.

"Did you find anything you like, Abby?" I asked.

"Not sure." She turned to Grace and said, "Thanks, but I think I'll look around a little more. I may be back."

Once we were outside the store, Abby asked, "Okay Mom, did you get the information you needed?"

"I certainly did. I'm pretty sure I know what Ruby is up to, and it has nothing to do with keeping the land pristine." I told my daughter what I had discovered.

"You still need more evidence."

I grinned. "We'll get that Thursday night."

* * * * *

Abby hopped into her car and scooted off to work. I was hungry, so I stopped at the Tipsy Toad Tavern. Since it was a little early for lunch, only two tables were occupied. A senior citizen couple were eating in a booth in the far right corner. In the left corner booth was a man who was drinking what appeared to be a martini.

"Commander West," I said. "May I join you?"

He motioned toward a chair. "If you want, but I'm not good company today."

"What's wrong?" I asked.

"What's wrong?" He slammed down his martini, spilling much of the liquid. I was surprised the glass didn't break.

"I'll tell you what's wrong," he continued. "Two of my employees are dead. The aquarium is being screwed out of several million dollars from the Alicia Wilcox-Chandler estate, my head fish keeper is retiring, and I can't get a replacement. No one wants to be associated with an institution with such high odds of producing murder victims."

"At least Oscar agreed to stay on until you find a replacement."

"There's a slight problem." He gulped what remained of his drink and motioned the waitress for another. "I may need someone right away."

"Why?"

"I guess you haven't heard. I only found out this morning." He burped. "Excuse me. I might as well tell you as you'll hear about it soon enough. Oscar Mejas is a person of interest in Katie Chandler's murder. Rumor says his arrest is imminent."

"What?" I could hardly sputter out the word.

"They found a crowbar in Oscar's office. There's blood on it. Testing showed the blood belongs to Katie. The theory is Oscar used it to bang on Katie's hands as she tried to climb out of the sea snake tank. This case is unraveling like a soap opera."

"How did the police find the crowbar?"

"Detective Wolfe was questioning Oscar when one of the fish keepers came into the office. She needed to look up information in Oscar's fish care manual. She grabbed the book off his shelf, and there was the blood covered crowbar. It had been hidden behind the manual. Now it was in plain sight."

"What did Oscar say?"

"He claimed the crowbar wasn't his, and he didn't know how it got behind the book."

"It's pretty damaging evidence."

"Oscar almost never locks his door, and the fish keepers constantly refer to that manual, so it's possible that someone other than Oscar put it there."

"Did the police find fingerprints?"

"No. Whoever handled it probably used gloves."

"What about his alibi?" I asked. "Oscar claims he was eating at the local pizzeria and attending his grandson's basketball game at the community center. If Oscar's alibi can be verified for the time of Katie's death, that should prove the weapon was planted."

"The pizzeria and community center are less than a ten-minute drive from the aquarium. It would have been easy for him to sneak out during the basketball game. At a busy sporting event, who would notice?"

"But why would Oscar murder Katie?"

"Money, my dear, money. The police believe he was paid to do this.

Oscar needs money. Money, money, money."

"Needs or wants?"

"Needs. Several years back, Oscar's grandson developed cancer. He's cured now. I don't know the whole story since this happened before my time here, but, supposedly, his son and daughter-in-law didn't have health insurance. Oscar helped with the medical expenses. It put him in big debt."

I sat back and let the facts of the case seep through my mind. "What about Jack Patterson? I believe whoever killed Katie also murdered Jack. Oscar has no motive for killing Jack."

"Oh, but he does. Detective Wolfe is looking into Oscar for that murder, too. Supposedly, Oscar and Jack had a huge argument a few days before Jack's body was discovered. That's why Detective Wolfe was in Oscar's office. He was questioning Oscar about the fight."

"But Jack was stabbed in a specific spot in the base of the brain. A spot that would cause instant death. Would Oscar know how to do this?"

The commander shrugged.

The waitress delivered another martini to Commander West. She asked me if I wanted a menu, and I shook my head no. My appetite was gone. I said good-bye to the commander and made my way out of the building.

Although Oscar had been on my suspect list, something didn't sit right with me. Why would he be careful enough to wear gloves, but then leave the blood splatter on the murder weapon? Why would he leave it in his office?

* * * * *

My final stop of the day was the aquarium. I spotted Madge, the marine mammal attendant, coming up the path.

"I miss Katie," she said. "The other sea lion trainer is okay, but it's not the same. Everything is different now. Oscar will be retiring. I don't know when. I hope he stays awhile."

She obviously didn't know about Oscar's impending arrest.

"I hope he does well in his new career," Madge said.

"What new career?"

She frowned. "Not sure. Oscar enrolled in college for the next semester. He told us about it a few days ago."

"Us? Who did he tell besides you?"

"Bradford Monroe," Madge said. "You know him, right?"

I nodded.

"Bradford set up a photo shoot with the sea lions and some old guy who's giving money to the aquarium. Bea and Barney didn't like the guy. He didn't want to feed them the fish from his hand—"

"Oscar was at the photo shoot?"

She shook her head. "We ran into Oscar as we were leaving. We were coming down the path, just like I ran into you now. Hey, isn't that funny."

"So, what exactly did Oscar say?" I was trying to keep her on track.

"He was real excited. Said he was going to ask Commander West if he could leave by spring, so he could start day classes. Oh, nursing."

"What about nursing?" I felt a headache coming on.

"That's what Oscar was studying. Said he always wanted to be a nurse. I better go. Bea and Barney are waiting to be fed."

* * * * *

Oscar Mejas was making his way up the path toward me. He looked as if he had aged ten years.

"I guess you heard the news," he said, after we exchanged greetings.

"You mean about the crowbar on your bookshelf?"

"I swear it's not mine. Someone planted it there."

"Can I ask a question?" Before Oscar could reply, I said, "I heard you and Jack had been fighting the Saturday before Jack died. What was that about?"

"The police asked the same thing. I told them we weren't fighting." He shook his head. "Jack wasn't angry at me. He was venting."

"Venting?"

"Jack had barged into my office. I could tell he was upset. He said Katie wasn't with her sea lions, and he asked if I knew where she was. I told him she had gone into town to pick up supplies."

"Why did he want to see Katie?"

"He didn't say. But he became agitated. His face turned red and he muttered something under his breath. He said he was going to see Commander West. When I told him I'd spotted the commander leaving the aquarium only minutes ago, Jack pounded his fists on my desk and started cursing. I asked him what was wrong, and he said he'd tell me later. He needed to find Commander West and talk to him. But he needed to warn Katie first."

"Warn Katie? That was the phrase he used?"

"Yes. I told him to calm down, but he stormed out of my office. He said he couldn't wait for Katie now, but he'd talk to her during the weekend."

"But he was killed before he had the chance," I said, thinking out loud. "Do you have any idea what he wanted to tell Katie?"

"Not really." Oscar hesitated. "I wonder if it was related to his phone call earlier that morning? I heard Jack on his cell. He was furious."

"Did you overhear his conversation?"

"Only some of it. I heard Jack say, 'Remember, I knew him years ago' and 'he's up to his old tricks.'"

"Who did he know? Who was up to his old tricks?"

Oscar shrugged. "I haven't a clue."

CHAPTER THIRTY-EIGHT

Since Matt was working late and my mother was dining with Paul, I drove to the Village of Clam Cove and entered the local pizzeria, where I hoped to accomplish two goals.

One goal was dinner. The other could determine Oscar's fate.

It was still early, so only a few tables were occupied. I placed my order with a young woman behind the counter.

"Dad, will you heat up one slice of mushroom pizza," she called to an older man who had picked up a remote and was changing channels on the small flat screen television facing the dining area.

"Is this a family business?" I asked, smiling.

"Been in the family for more than twenty years."

"You must know lots of people in town."

She nodded. "We get some tourists, especially in the summer, but our business is mostly locals."

"Do you know Oscar Mejas?" I asked as she handed me a diet cola.

"Oscar is a regular. He comes here every Saturday before his grandson's basketball game."

"I know," I said as I nodded and smiled. "He told me he gets here at five-thirty, and he leaves at six. I don't know how he can be so precise."

She pointed to the television. "That's because he and my Dad are big fans of the quiz show *Stumper*. They bet on who gets the most answers right. *Stumper* airs on Saturday from five-thirty to six. Oscar usually comes in right after the emcee introduces the contestants. He leaves as soon as the show ends. He always eats the same thing, too. One regular slice and a calzone."

The security guard claimed he was attacked and rendered unconscious after he completed his rounds at about five minutes after six. If I could verify that Oscar went straight from the pizzeria to the community center, Oscar would be in the clear.

After gobbling up my pizza, I bee-lined to the Clam Cove Community Center which was directly across the street. I made my way straight to the gym where a young Asian man was setting up a volleyball net. He stopped what he was doing and headed in my direction.

"May I help you?" he asked.

"I'd like to talk to someone about the basketball game two Saturdays ago."

He grinned. "The Jumping Jellyfish beat the Lucky Lobsters. Our middle school division. It was a close game."

"I take it you were here?"

"I certainly was. I'm director of the center." He held out his hand and I shook it. "Jimmy Chang."

"Kristy Farrell," I said. "Do you know Oscar Mejas? He's a friend of mine."

"Of course, I know him. Oscar's a great guy. I'm so happy that he's planning on staying in Clam Cove."

"You mean when he retires?"

Jimmy nodded. "Selling his house and moving in with his son's family is the perfect solution."

"Perfect solution?"

"You have no idea what I'm talking about, do you?" Jimmy frowned. "I thought you said you were Oscar's friend."

"Oh, you mean his financial problems," I said, guessing that was what Jimmy meant.

"Right. The money he'll make selling his home will pay off all his debt and will leave him with enough to build an extension on his son's home. He'll have enough to pay for nursing school, too, which is something he's wanted to do since his grandson had his bout with cancer."

"I'm happy for Oscar, too," I said. "I was wondering if you saw him at the basketball game two Saturdays ago?"

"That's a strange question." Once again, Jimmy frowned and eyed me suspiciously. "Why do you want to know?"

I sighed, but decided to open up, at least partially. "I'm a writer for *Animal Advocate Magazine.* I've been doing some research at the aquarium. A lot is going on there. Something happened that night, and I want to verify if Oscar has an alibi."

"The murder of Katie Chandler. Everyone in town knows about that." He narrowed his eyes. "So, you're not Oscar's friend. You're just a snoopy reporter."

"I am a reporter, but I like Oscar and want to help him."

"How?" The look on his face said he didn't believe me.

"I want to find out—"

"Something that is not your business," bellowed a familiar voice coming from behind me. I spun around and found myself facing Detective Steve Wolfe.

"What are you doing here?" He wagged a finger in front of my face as spittle came out of his mouth. "Didn't I tell you to stay away from this investigation?"

Ignoring his comment, I said, "I heard you were looking at Oscar as a person of interest. Oscar says he has an alibi."

"That's exactly why I'm here," Wolfe replied. "I'm wrapping up the case. I'm looking for holes in his alibi so some smart aleck lawyer doesn't get him off. I doubt if anyone can verify he was here the entire time."

"Excuse me," Jimmy interrupted. "I can verify that Oscar was here."

Wolfe narrowed his eyes. "Not just verify that he came here but also when he arrived and when he left."

"Oscar was here at six o'clock. Maybe a minute or two later, but no more than that."

"Oh, yeah. Did he punch a time clock?"

"Admission to our basketball games is free, but we sell snacks to offset costs. One of our volunteers didn't show up. She needed to be here by five forty-five. By six, when we start selling, I had to find a replacement. I was about to search the stands for someone to help when Oscar arrived. I put him to work immediately."

"Sorry, Detective Wolfe." I grinned. "I guess you need to look somewhere else for your suspect."

Detective Wolfe took several steps toward Jimmy and leaned in. "You're sure you didn't look for a replacement closer to six-thirty?"

"Absolutely not," Jimmy said. "We don't sell refreshments once the game starts. We sell exactly one half hour before. Oscar was here at six. He sat next to me during the game, so I know he was here until he got a phone call a little after seven-thirty."

"That was when Commander West contacted him to help assist the police in removing Katie's body from the sea snake tank," I reminded Wolfe.

It appeared Oscar was in the clear.

CHAPTER THIRTY-NINE

"Dad told me grandma will be leaving in a week," Abby said as Archie pulled on the leash in an attempt to chase a squirrel who was scampering toward a nearby tree.

I nodded as we stopped walking, so Archie and Brandy could sniff a nearby pile of leaves. "She told us that a few nights ago. But there's more. She'll be engaged to Paul Andre unless I can prove he's up to no good."

"Why not tell grandma about the blonde you saw—"

"Because Paul will tell her it was a business meeting. He'll say the blonde was investing in his health spas."

"You're sure it's not that?"

"He told the blonde they'd have a wonderful life together." I shrugged before we continued walking the dogs. "Maybe he's scamming her, too."

"Either way, isn't that proof enough to make grandma suspicious that his intentions are less than honorable?"

"No. Paul will twist it and claim he told the blonde she'd have a wonderful life because of all the money she'd rake in with her health spa investment." I shook my head. "I saw them holding hands. But Paul will deny any romance with the woman, and I'm afraid my mother will believe him."

"I don't get it, Mom. What's Paul's angle with grandma? Once she said she didn't want to invest with him, he stopped pressuring her. So how is he scamming her? Do you think he wants to marry her for her money?"

"Possibly, but I don't think so. She has the condo and a pretty decent nest egg, but that's not enough for a man like Paul Andre. She's financially comfortable, but he wants to be rich. Trust me, if he were marrying for money, there are far wealthier women in Florida. Whatever he has in mind for my mother is happening quickly, and I don't know what it is."

I had an idea. But before I said anything to Abby or anyone else, I needed to check it out. When we arrived back at the house, Abby left to go to work. After I made sure the dogs had water, I grabbed the picture I had snatched from Marcia Silver's photo album earlier in the week. Then I went on the Internet and clicked onto my favorite search engine. When finished, I grabbed my phone and punched in a series of numbers.

"Jason," I said when I reached my daughter's boyfriend. "I need your help again."

* * * * *

The next night, Abby picked me up at home, and we drove to Clam Cove.

"You sure this will work?" she asked as we traveled parallel to the bay, passing the Clam Cove motel.

"No, but it's the best chance we have."

We pulled off the road and trekked down to Ruby Diamond's cottage. Night had fallen, but the light from the waning moon and a twinkling of stars provided the illumination we needed.

Once we reached the edge of Ruby's property, we crept partially down the embankment, and hid behind tall sea grass. From this spot, we had a close view of Ruby's house as well as the water.

"What do we do now?" Abby asked.

"Wait."

I pulled binoculars out of my bag and scanned my surroundings. The bay appeared like a sheet of glass, the stillness broken only by an occasional ripple.

Thirty minutes later, I spotted a small boat maneuvering around the curve. As I adjusted my lenses, I made out the silhouette of a figure in the boat. I thought it was a man, but I wasn't positive.

Seconds later, lights flashed from the boat, followed by lights flickering from inside Ruby's cottage. After a short period of darkness, lights appeared again, first from the water, then the house.

"You're right, "Abby whispered in a voice so hushed I could hardly understand her. "This is a code."

A figure emerged from the back door of the house. I was sure it was Ruby. She wandered to the water's edge, using a flashlight to illuminate her path. She flashed it on and off twice.

As the boat came closer, I recognized it as a kayak. I watched as its sole occupant paddled into shallow water, hopped out, and pulled the boat to shore. I could now see everything clearly without binoculars.

I sucked in my breath as I realized the boat's occupant was Kyle, Ruby's friend with the billy-goat beard. They were talking, and I was able to make out snatches of the conversation.

"Thursday... earns... farmer."

Kyle turned his face, and I couldn't hear anymore. Ruby handed him what looked like an envelope and he gave her a package. He pushed his kayak back in the water, hopped in, and padded away. Ruby returned to her cottage.

"What do you think farmer means?" Abby asked while we trekked back to where we had parked.

"I've no idea. There's a farm adjacent to Moray industries."

"There's also a few on the outskirts of Clam Cove. But what could she be bringing in from a farm? I never heard of illegal pumpkins or apples."

"I feel in my bones that Ruby is involved in a smuggling operation. Or something else involving illegal merchandise. But what?" I frowned as I hopped into the car. Whatever was going down was happening next Thursday. I had a week to figure it out.

"Uh, oh, I'm almost out of gas," Abby said as she turned on the engine. There's a twenty-four hour station about a mile east of the aquarium. I think we better go there, then double back. I don't know what else is open this late."

"Okay," I said. Abby had a reputation for never filling up her tank until it was near empty. Right now, we were probably coasting on fumes.

As we drove down the road, I gazed up at the sky, noting streaks of orange and yellow in the distance.

"What's that?" I asked.

"It looks like fire."

"Oh, no." I gasped. "It's the aquarium."

CHAPTER FORTY

We sped down the road, halting at the spot where fire trucks, police cars, and emergency vehicles blocked traffic from moving further. I hopped out of the car and raced toward the barricade with Abby behind me. I coughed from the smoke in the air.

"Are you going to ask a fire fighter what happened?" Abby asked.

I shook my head. "I'm not bothering them while they're working. But maybe someone else can answer my questions."

I scanned my surroundings, finally spotting Commander West. He stood alone, staring straight ahead. The flames had begun to subside, replaced by heavy waves of black smoke.

"Commander West," I called. "How did this happen?"

He turned around and made his way in my direction. "Don't know. The administration wing went up in flames. Luckily, I think it's contained to that section. It's not hitting any of our marine life."

"Will the damage be minimal?"

"Hopefully, but it will still cost a pretty penny to repair." He shook his head. "We have insurance but there is always extra costs and we need every dollar to put toward our campaign to purchase the twenty acres. We can't afford any additional expenses."

"Do you think it was deliberately set? Or an accident?"

"Tomorrow, the arson squad will begin an investigation." He frowned. "This building is up to code so I don't think its an electrical fire. It's a non-smoking facility, too." As he spoke, I saw the anger in his eyes. "I don't believe this was an accident."

* * * * *

The next day, I drove to the office that housed the arson division. Three years ago, Matt had performed life-saving surgery on a Golden Retriever and had earned the gratitude of the dog's human family. That grateful dog parent, Ben Barone, was chief investigator of the arson squad. Matt had called this morning and made an appointment for me to interview him.

"I told Matt I'm glad to help, but this is an ongoing investigation," Ben said as we shook hands. "That means—"

"That means it's arson."

He rubbed his well trimmed mustache. "You're right. This wasn't an accident. It's arson, but there is a lot we don't know yet. Which means I'm limited in what I can tell you."

"I'm not asking for any information that would impede the investigation. Can you tell me how the fire started?"

He nodded. "We believe it began in the trash can."

"But couldn't that be accidental?" I thought back to a fire in my community where a teenager, hanging out with his friend in a mall parking lot, threw a lit cigarette into a garbage receptacle full of paper. The fire spread quickly and destroyed several stores.

Barone shook his head. "An accelerant was used. We found traces of it in the parking lot. It's a fuel that is common in camping stoves and lanterns. The arsonist must have spilled some before starting the fire. And the trash can had been moved up against the—"

"Whatcha got?" a booming voice behind me called. "I heard you have a preliminary—"

He stopped mid-sentence. I found myself facing Detective Steve Wolfe, who looked like he was about to have a stroke.

"You!" He wagged a finger at me. "You're interfering with an investigation. I warned you." He pulled out his handcuffs. "You are under arrest."

"Hold on," Ben said. "I invited her. This investigation in currently under the jurisdiction of the arson squad and that is me."

Judging by Detective Wolfe's beet-red face, he knew he couldn't stop Ben from talking with me. He put his handcuffs away.

"Why are you here?" Ben asked Detective Wolfe. "You're a homicide detective. This fire didn't involve murder, only property damage, and not that much since it was extinguished so quickly."

"The brass thinks this case is possibly related to a homicide at the aquarium. I'm not so sure."

Something had been bothering me, but up until this moment, I couldn't put my finger on it. Now I knew what was wrong.

"I always thought fire spreads quickly," I said. "But this fire was contained to one section. How come it didn't spread through the entire aquarium?"

"Because we probably arrived within seconds of the fire igniting," Ben said. "A contingent of Clam Cove fire fighters had just put out a small oven fire in a house up the road. They were returning to town, and as they drove past the aquarium, a few of the fire fighters noticed flames by the building. If they hadn't been there at that moment, I think the whole facility would have been destroyed."

"Did the fire fighters see anyone driving away from the scene?"

"Yes. But we've been unable to identify the car or driver. The fire fighters saw a convertible, possibly silver or gray, speed out of the parking lot just before the fire trucks turned into the entrance.

"A silver convertible?" I repeated.

Sam Wong drove a silver convertible.

CHAPTER FORTY-ONE

"What's so urgent that you needed to see me today, Mrs. Farrell?" Early the next morning, Sam Wong slid into a chair across from me at Pirate Pete's Coffee Shop. Abby had called him and set up this meeting.

"Where were you Wednesday?" I asked. "A little before midnight?"

"Why do you want to know?"

"There was a fire at the aquarium."

"What? You think I did it?" His eyes blazed with anger.

I'd been too blunt. I wasn't the police, and he didn't have to respond to my questions. But tact had never been my long suit.

"The fire fighters noticed a convertible, possibly a silver one, whizzing out of the parking lot around midnight," I said. "You have a silver convertible."

"The aquarium borders on the Hamptons, Mrs. Farrell. Lots of people here have convertibles."

"So, you're not going to tell me where you were?"

"Of course, I'll tell you. He sighed. "I was home redoing my resume. I've officially resigned from Moray Industries. I walked out the door Tuesday at five for the last time."

"Can anyone verify that you were home Wednesday night?"

Sam shook his head. "No. I was alone. Mama Grizzly delivered a bonus check from Lucien Moray but that was early evening. A little after six."

"Mama Grizzly delivered your check? That's service."

He grinned. "She lives down the road from my house. But to tell the truth, I was surprised. Mama Grizzly never goes out of her way for anyone, except Lucien Moray. He probably told her to bring it to me. Lucien can be considerate when he wants." Sam paused. "I didn't expect the check. It was a generous gesture."

"I thought you were staying with Moray through December?"

"I was. But I finished what I was working on. Moray is in-between projects, so this is a good time to leave."

Sam glanced at his watch, then rose from his chair. "If there's nothing else, I need to get going."

"Just one more quick question," I said. Sam frowned but didn't leave, so I quickly spoke. "Wouldn't it have served you better to leave after you landed another job?"

Sam shook his head. "No. I just would have been assigned another project, and Lucien doesn't take kindly to staff leaving in the midst of an assignment. Since I plan to use him as a reference, I need him to think highly of me. Besides, if I were still there, I'd procrastinate about leaving. I need a change in my life now."

"What do you plan to do?"

He paused. "I'm not sure. I may not stay in law. I'm going to take my time. I'll probably move to Connecticut and work part-time as a judo instructor in my cousin's jujitsu and karate school until I make my decision. Combined with my bonus check, that should keep me going for a while."

A thought flashed through my mind. I had assumed that since Sam was small and slight, he wouldn't have the strength to push Katie into a tank of sea snakes. But if he had expertise in martial arts, that made it a different story.

Sam left, and the waitress refilled my cup. I sat back, gazing through the window at the whitecaps on the bay and sipping my coffee. I recalled all that had transpired the last few weeks.

I vaguely remembered seeing another convertible recently. I had spotted the car in the Moray Industries parking lot. But it wasn't Sam's car. His convertible was silver while this one was ash gray.

What Sam had said was true. Convertibles were popular on eastern Long Island—there were certainly more than two.

Moray had a vested interest in seeing that the aquarium didn't reach its financial goal. Monday, I would search the Moray Industries parking lot for the convertible and the employee who owned it.

* * * * *

"Why are you concentrating so intently?" I asked Abby as I stepped inside my house. My daughter was sitting in the kitchen, pencil in hand, newspaper spread open on the table. "And why are you here?"

"I'm here because I had to drop off papers for Dad and talk to him about the animal lover's festival. But he's in the shower, and you know how long that takes. Anyway, I'm working on the crossword puzzle while I wait."

"You appear stumped."

"I am. What's a fifteen letter word for prescription drugs? The sixth and seventh letters are *c* and *e*."

I thought for a moment. "Pharmaceuticals," I said. I loved puzzles.

As I headed toward the refrigerator, I stopped in my tracks.

"That's it." I snapped my fingers. "That's what Kyle was saying."

"What are you talking about?"

"Don't you remember, Abby? The night we hid in the tall grasses by Ruby's cottage when Kyle kayaked to the beach. We overheard snatches of conversation."

"I remember. We made out three words: *Thursday, earns,* and *farmer.*"

"Right. Only it wasn't farmer with an *f*. It was a *ph*. We couldn't hear the rest of what Kyle said but I bet it was 'ceutical'. Pharmaceutical."

Abby's eyes widened. "Of course. Ruby and Kyle are smuggling prescription drugs. No wonder she doesn't want a research camp adjacent to her property."

I nodded. "Scientists staying at the camp might be out exploring at night and notice the flashing lights. With Moray's condominium development, there's the vacant land that acts as a buffer. Adjacent to the vacant land is the tennis court, which according to Moray's proposal has no lighting—"

"So it wouldn't be used at night." Abby completed the thought. "What are you going to do now?"

"First thing, I need to clear my schedule for next Thursday night. I need—"

"Mom, are you crazy? You can't take down a drug smuggling operation."

I held up my hand. "On Monday, I'm calling the Drug Enforcement Agency. I'll let them handle it. But I'll be hiding in the tall grasses watching them make an arrest."

"Why must you be there?"

"I need to see what happens. Whoever would have thought the controversy surrounding the land acquisition involved drug smuggling? You have to admit, this is a terrific addition to my story."

CHAPTER FORTY-TWO

I arrived late at the Fall Festival for Animal Lovers. Once I saw my husband's face, I immediately knew something was wrong.

"What's the matter, Matt?" I asked.

"The costume contest is about to begin and we've a problem with the entry forms. The goat ate nearly half a dozen."

"The goat?"

"From the animal rescue group. He got loose and chewed the papers before we could step in. Now I have no idea who is entered, and who is in what category. We're giving prizes for the most original, scariest, funniest..." Matt ran his hand through his thinning hair. "We were able to salvage three forms, but they're still a little wet and—"

"Don't worry. I'll straighten it out. Where's the entry table?"

I bee-lined for the table where I quickly made an announcement over the loudspeaker. More than two dozen humans and their costumed canines and felines lined up as I reissued applications. I chuckled at the sight of a dachshund dressed as a hot dog and a Bernese Mountain Dog wrapped in orange and covered with green leaves while sporting the sign: WORLD'S FRIENDLIEST PUMPKIN.

After collecting the new entry forms (and making sure they were no where near the goat) I decided to take a short break and visit the different booths.

"Kristy, wait up," a voice called. It was my mother.

"I thought you were spending the day with Paul." I said.

"Later. I wanted to support Matt's project. Unfortunately, Paul has allergies. He claimed he really suffered a bad reaction to your dogs when we had dinner at your house. Anyway, he decided this wouldn't be the best place for him. But we have lunch plans."

I didn't remember any signs of an allergic reaction when Paul visited us. Was he trying to avoid my mother's family? Did he think we suspected that he was up to no good?

"What is it, Kristy? You look like you want to say something?"

"Only that I'm sorry he couldn't make it," I lied. My Internet research had provided me with a plausible theory as to Paul's scam, but I was waiting for more evidence before I said anything to my mother.

"I've been here for an hour. I think I've been a supportive mother-in-law. I'm going back to your place now to freshen up for my lunch date with Paul."

We said good-bye and I headed toward the booths.

"These are beautiful," I said as I stopped by a table which featured animal sculptures. I examined a carving of a wolf with two cubs. The price tag said one hundred, twenty-nine dollars.

"This is just a sample of what I have to offer," said the woman behind the table who was wearing a name tag identifying her as Sandy. "I don't bring the more expensive ones to shows because of possible breakage. Be sure to take catalog with you."

I picked up one of her catalogs and began to thumb through it. I was amazed at the price range. "Wow. You have an item that costs ten thousand dollars."

Sandy nodded. "Yes. That horse is an antique. It's a magnificent piece."

"Ten thousand is still a lot."

"I once sold a bronze tiger figurine for more than forty thousand dollars. That was my biggest sale ever. I purchased it for twenty dollars from a garage sale upstate New York. The woman selling it had no idea of its value. I wasn't sure at the time if it was a real antique, but for twenty dollars I decided to take the gamble and it paid off. I researched the piece and discovered it was from seventeenth century Japan."

I frowned as I thought of the unsuspecting woman who sold her the piece for twenty dollars.

Sandy must have read my expression. She added, "I didn't take advantage of the woman. When I found out how much it was worth, I returned and told her. She took the tiger back and reimbursed me the twenty dollars. Then I offered to sell the figurine for her for a ten percent commission, which is my standard fee."

"Did she accept your offer?"

"The woman wasn't familiar with art at this level and realized I'd get a better deal than she would on her own, so she agreed. I only made four thousand dollars, but I think we both did well."

"You certainly did."

Before Sandy turned her attention to a prospective customer, she handed me a business card. "If you have merchandise you think may be valuable, call me."

The world of antiques was fascinating but complicated. To make money, you had to know your stuff. Not everyone was as honest as Sandy, and I was sure there were people who had sold valuable items to antiques collectors for white elephant prices.

My mind wandered to next weekend's art and antique auction to benefit the aquarium. I assumed Bradford Monroe would research all items before putting them up for sale.

"Mom."

I was jolted out of my thoughts as Abby and Jason sprinted toward me. Abby had a worried look on her face.

"You need to hear what Jason has to say, Mom. He's been talking about the aquarium to his friend in the District Attorney's Office."

"About the murders or the fire?"

"Right now, the fire."

"We have to find out if Sam Wong has an alibi for the time the blaze started," Abby said.

"He doesn't. He was home alone."

"That's not good." Jason shook his head.

"An alibi would be better, but there's no proof he started the fire."

The expression on the faces of Jason and Abby said otherwise.

"What aren't you telling me?" I asked.

The District Attorney may seek an indictment against Sam for the fire."

"I know he has a silver convertible, but none of the fire fighters were able to read the license plate. How can they identify him?"

"My contact wouldn't go into specifics, but I understand new evidence has popped up."

Abby nodded in agreement. "Really damaging evidence."

CHAPTER FORTY-THREE

My first stop on Monday was the aquarium. It had been closed for the last three days because of the fire, and I wondered how that would impact this month's admission revenue. Lots of events were scheduled in autumn, especially on weekends, and it was my understanding that Saturday night's *Sleeping with the Fishes*—an indoor sleepover for a local scout troop—had been canceled.

When I arrived, I spotted Commander West immediately. He was greeting visitors outside the main entrance.

"We're back in business," he said. "All exhibits, inside and outside, are open." He pointed to a trailer at the front of the parking lot. "That's the temporary office for staff. We'll be there until the administration wing is rebuilt."

I spotted what appeared to be two men in work clothes, one carrying a toolbox, scurrying into the building."

"I take it reconstruction has started."

He shook his head. "No. That won't begin for awhile. The architect is coming today with plans for rebuilding."

"But the two men I saw entering—"

Those two men are installing security cameras."

"Security cameras?"

"Talk about closing the barn door after the horses have gone, right?" Commander West shook his head. "But something tells me attacks on the aquarium are going to continue, so maybe this will help in the future."

"How will the fire affect you financially?"

"We've received an outpouring of support from the community, including commitments for some very substantial donations. Since most damage is covered by insurance, we should be okay."

"What about your fundraising events? Isn't the art and antique auction scheduled for this Sunday?"

"That will go on as planned. It's at Katie Chandler's house, so it doesn't affect anything we do at this facility." He looked up and nodded in the direction of a woman in a tailored suit carrying a set of large papers. "Excuse me, Mrs. Farrell. The architect has arrived with the blueprints and I need to talk to her."

I had a little time to kill, so I made my way to the sea lion exhibit. I don't know why, but perhaps I felt closer to Katie when I was there.

As I neared the outdoor exhibit, I spotted Madge exiting the facility, her head down, barely picking up her feet as she trudged up the path.

"Are you okay, Madge?" I asked.

"What? Oh, hi. Yeah, I guess I'm okay, but I'm still sad. I miss Katie."

"We're all sad."

"I guess so. But not Bradford. He's happy."

"He's happy?" I repeated.

"Yeah, I think so. He's always walking around here smiling."

"He's a professional fundraiser. They tend to put on a cheerful demeanor."

"Meaner. He's not meaner."

"Demeanor. He smiles and acts like he's in a good mood even if he's not."

Madge furrowed her brows. "That doesn't make sense. I heard Oscar talking to one of the fish keepers. Oscar said Bradford is in a good mood because he's going to raise enough money to buy the land. Is that true?"

I shrugged. "Bradford believes he can do it, and maybe he can."

I wanted to talk to Madge longer, but I didn't have time. "Do you have your phone with you?" I asked.

She nodded and pulled a pink case out of her pocket.

"I want you to take my number. This way, if you ever need me, you can reach me."

"Why would I need you?"

"If you see something strange happening here. Or if you just want to talk to a friend."

I realized that Madge might know more about what was happening behind the scenes than she realized.

* * * * *

My next destination was the Moray Industries parking lot. Upon arriving, I searched for the ash gray convertible and located it in the same row as last time, about five spots down from Lucien Moray's reserved space. I jotted down the license number and then called Abby.

"Don't you have client who works for the Department of Motor Vehicles?" I asked.

"Jane Zimmer. I take care of her two Siamese cats, Lin and Lu."

"If I give you a license plate number, can she look up the car owner?"

"She can, but I don't know if she will."

"Please, will you ask? It may lead to whoever started the fire and that could open the door to finding Katie's killer."

Abby paused. "I'll ask."

I left the parking lot and began the drive home. As I walked into my kitchen I heard a beep and glanced at my phone. It was a text from Abby. I gasped.

It read: Sam Wong arrested.

CHAPTER FORTY-FOUR

"Sam called and told me everything," Abby said as she barged through my kitchen door two hours later. "He's out on bail now. It was just like Jason said. Sam was arrested for arson. The police found evidence."

"I can't believe—"

"He was framed."

"Are you sure?" I grabbed a bottle of wine, poured some into two glasses, and we sat across from each other at the kitchen table. "We don't know Sam that well. Maybe he did set the fire."

"I'm pretty sure he's innocent," Abby said. "You're right. I don't know Sam well, but I do know he's not stupid."

"I agree. But even smart people do stupid things."

"Not like this. You don't leave evidence in plain sight, and if you do, you don't give the police the right to search without a warrant."

"Is that what happened?"

"This is what he told me. Supposedly, there's a witness. We don't know who the witness is yet, but someone claims to have seen Sam drive into the aquarium parking lot a few minutes before the fire. This witness also claimed Sam kept cans of fuel in his garage, the same type used to set the fire. Based on that information, the police questioned Sam and asked permission to search his premises."

"And he agreed? He's a lawyer. He should know better."

Abby nodded. "He wanted to get this over with. He was innocent and thought if the police searched and found nothing, they'd be finished with him. He's also a corporate lawyer not criminal—"

"Any lawyer would know you insist on a search warrant." I shook my head. "Did they find the accelerant?"

Abby nodded. "Same type as used in the fire. Its most common use is in lanterns and camping stoves. Sam has neither."

I groaned. "You're right. He wouldn't have granted permission if he knew the accelerant was there."

"It gets worse. The police found his shoes covered in Canadian goose poop—"

"That's not evidence. Canadian geese are all around Long Island.

"But they're especially common around the aquarium grounds. While you would avoid stepping in it in daylight, it's something you might not notice while sneaking around in the dark and—"

"That's still not evidence. They—"

"There's more. There were spots of accelerant on these shoes."

I sighed. "Does Sam have any idea who planted this evidence?" I asked after processing what she had just told me.

Abby shook her head.

"We need to meet with him," I said. "Can you contact Sam and make arrangements while I feed the dogs?"

Ten minutes later, Abby said, "Sam doesn't want to meet at Pirate Pete's Coffee Shop. He's afraid the press might confront him there. He says to come to his place tomorrow morning around ten. But he told me he doesn't know a thing."

"Sometimes, the best information comes from clueless people put in stressful situations."

* * * * *

Seconds after I had pulled into Sam's driveway, Abby arrived at his house. We had driven here in separate cars since my daughter was due at the veterinary hospital this afternoon, and I was spending the day in Clam Cove.

"Let's go in the living room," Sam said. "I'll get us some coffee. Unless you want something stronger."

"Not at ten in the morning. Coffee is fine."

While Abby and Sam wandered off to the kitchen, I plopped down on the sofa and gazed out the sliding glass doors at a sailboat gliding on the bay while wondering who would want to frame Sam. And why? Was it personal? Someone seeking revenge? Or was the real arsonist simply trying to cast suspicion on someone else?

Of course, in the back of my mind, was the thought he could be guilty.

My thinking was interrupted when Sam and Abby returned.

"Do you have any idea who might have stashed the accelerant in your garage?" I asked, as he handed me a steaming mug.

He shook his head. "To tell the truth, when I'm home, I don't always lock the garage door." He paused. "I usually keep it open about a foot. There's a stray cat that hangs around, and I leave a dish of cat food inside."

"But wouldn't you have heard someone pulling the door up?"

"Depends. Since Katie died, I've been having trouble sleeping, so I've been taking sleeping pills. They really work. And my bedroom is far away from the garage. If I were zonked out, I wouldn't have heard anything."

"What about the goose poop and accelerant on your shoes?"

"It wasn't shoes, it was boots. When I was working on the deal upstate, I traipsed through the mud. I changed into my office clothes when I returned for my meeting with Moray. The boots were so filthy that when I brought them home, I left them in the garage. Whoever left the accelerant could have tampered with them."

"Point taken. Do you have any idea who started the fire?"

He shrugged.

"Didn't you say Lucien Moray paid your bail?" Abby said to Sam. "Don't you find that suspicious?"

"Not really. Lucien and I left on good terms. When I resigned he told me if I wanted to come back after I sorted things out, I should give him a call. The bail was a drop in the bucket for him. I think he put it up as a way of cementing the relationship between us."

"But isn't Lucien worried that the aquarium still might be able to raise the funds to buy the twenty acres? That gives him motive to set the fire."

I agreed with my daughter. "You're right. He might have hired someone to do it."

Sam shrugged again. "Possible, but I don't think it's him."

While Abby and Sam tried to brainstorm a list of people who might want to frame Sam, I excused myself to use the bathroom.

"Down the hall, on your left, past the first bedroom," Sam said.

On my way back, I noticed Sam's bedroom door was ajar. I pushed it slightly, so I could peek inside.

There on the nightstand was a book. Its cover was navy blue, and it featured a sea lion on the front.

Katie's diary. Sam has Katie's diary.

I could hear the voices of Abby and Sam echoing from the living room. Since they were deep in conversation, I darted into the room, grabbed the phone from my bag, and began snapping photos of each page of the diary, starting at the last page and working forward. Since Abby gave Katie the book this summer, it went back less than four months.

I'd taken pictures of eighteen pages when I heard Sam say to Abby, "I have an appointment with my attorney in twenty minutes."

Realizing it was time to leave, I stashed my phone in my bag and made my way to the living room.

Abby rose when I returned. "We should get going, Mom."

"Sure, but did you come up with any ideas as to who might want to frame Sam?"

"No really," Abby said. Sam nodded in agreement.

As Abby and I headed out the door, my phone trilled. I didn't recognize the number that popped up, but I answered the call. It was Madge from the aquarium.

"Mrs. Farrell," she said, gasping for breath. "You said I could call you if I ever wanted to talk."

"Of course. Did you think of something about Katie's murder? Is something wrong?"

"Yes. Something is wrong."

"What?"

"The turtles are dead."

CHAPTER FORTY-FIVE

M adge was standing by the parking lot, waiting for me.
"Oh, Mrs. Farrell," she said. "It's awful. They think the turtles ate something bad."

Poison. "Let me see what I can find out. I'll—" I stopped talking and scowled at Madge.

"What's the matter?" she asked.

"Where did you get that necklace?"

"I didn't steal it. Honestly, I found it."

"Where?"

Madge didn't answer. She looked down at her shoes.

"You're not in trouble," I said. "This is important."

"I found it on the ground near where the fire took place. I know no one is allowed there, but I just wanted a peek. I started looking around after work the other day, and I dropped my gum wrapper. I didn't want to litter, so I picked it up. That's when I saw the necklace. Are you sure I'm not in trouble?"

"Positive. But the necklace belongs to someone else. Why don't you give it to me, and I'll return it to its real owner."

Madge unclasped the necklace and placed it in my hand. "Tell the person I'm sorry, but it's so pretty, and I didn't know who owned it."

"Don't worry. I'll talk to you later," I said. "Meanwhile, let me see what I can find out about the turtle poisoning."

"Okay. I better get back to my sea lions."

The turtle exhibit was inside the aquarium, near the front entrance. The area had been roped off. Two security guards were keeping the public away.

"I heard what happened," I called to Bradford Monroe who was inside the petitioned off area along with two uniformed aquarium workers. "Can I come in and talk to you?"

He nodded. I ducked under the rope.

"Three of our turtles are dead," he said. "Why couldn't this have happened one day later? The Mulgraves were coming in late this afternoon with their check for the sponsorship of this exhibit. Now they may back down."

"Three dead? Last time I was here, I saw five turtles. What happened to the others?"

"They appear to be okay. We removed them temporarily, and our veterinarian will keep a careful eye on them for a few days."

"What caused the deaths?"

"It looks like poison. To find out definitely, we're going to perform a necropsy."

I knew from my brother, curator of reptiles at the Rocky Cove Zoo, that a necropsy is the animal equivalent of an autopsy.

"How could these turtles have been poisoned?" I asked.

Bradford shrugged. "Don't know. But at least now we have security tapes. We only installed the system the other day. Maybe we can see what happened."

"Have you looked at the tapes yet?"

"No. Commander West wants to see them, too, but he had to make some calls first. We're planning on looking at the tapes in about ten minutes."

"Can I watch with you?"

I could see his mouth about to form the word "no" but he paused, then said, "That's up to Commander West. You need to ask him."

"You've called the police, right?" I asked.

He sighed. "Yes. Turtles aren't their top priority, but since we had a murder at the aquarium, plus arson, the police are taking this fairly seriously. They're sending a detective out later today."

Bradford looked up. "Commander West is here now."

* * * * *

Commander West did not look happy. No one likes to be in charge of a crumbling empire.

I asked if I could view the tapes.

"That's highly irregular." He frowned.

"But I may be able to help. I've talked to tons of people about the land acquisition. Maybe I'll recognize someone."

He hesitated, then nodded. "I guess that makes sense. Follow me."

Since the administration wing was still uninhabited because of the fire, he led us to a small room behind the sting ray exhibit. The room appeared to be about ten by ten. A security guard stood behind a table.

"The turtles were alive when the aquarium opened today," the guard said as he turned on a monitor. "The poisoning happened sometime this morning. Since large crowds don't normally arrive until after eleven, this is a break for us. It means we should be able to get a decent look at everyone in the area, and see if there is any suspicious behavior."

We reviewed the tapes. Most visitors to the exhibit today, which was a school day, were families with preschoolers. But twenty minutes into the tape, a lone figure appeared on the screen. The figure appeared nervous, constantly looking right, left, and behind. When the only other people viewing the turtles, a woman with two young children, moved on, the figure quickly threw something over the three-foot Plexiglas fence surrounding the exhibit.

"That's it," Commander West yelled, pounding his fist on the table. "Can we get another look at her face?"

The security guard rewound the tape, freezing it at a spot where a side view of the figure's face appeared.

"I have no idea who this is?" Commander West said, shaking his head.

I did.

Before I could speak up, my phone binged. I glanced down and saw that Abby had texted me the name of the owner of the ash gray convertible.

"Excuse me, commander," I said. "But I may have the answer as to who poisoned the turtles and started the fire. I believe it's the same person. I'll get back to you." The commander stood with his mouth open as I scooted away.

* * * * *

"Mr. Moray is not here today. Even if he was, I told you that you can't see him without an appointment," said Mama Grizzly as I stood in front of her desk. She eyed me as if I were a cockroach she wanted to squash.

"I'm here to see you," I said.

"I have nothing to say to reporters. Contact our corporate press office if you need more information about the land acquisition and condominium development."

"It's not about the land acquisition. It's about the crimes committed at the aquarium. I know you're responsible for the turtle poisoning and arson."

"How dare you." She rose from her seat. "Get out, or I'll call security."

"You do that. Why don't you call the police, too? I have proof. A few days ago, the aquarium installed security cameras at their exhibits. I viewed the tape of the turtle exhibit and saw what you did."

Mama Grizzly's face turned ghostly white. She obviously didn't know about the cameras. She twisted her hands together.

"You're also responsible for starting the fire?" I said.

"You can't prove that."

Abby's client, who worked for the Department of Motor Vehicles, had gotten back to her. The text I had received from my daughter listed the owner of the gray convertible in Moray's lot as Helen Eubanks—Mama Grizzly's real name. I knew it wasn't enough, but I had more evidence.

"Recognize this?" I pulled out the necklace from Madge. It was a cameo on a gold chain. "This was found on the ground in the area near where the fire occurred. I saw you wearing it the first time I met you. I remember because my grandmother had a necklace just like this."

Mama Grizzly quickly gained her composure. "Then maybe it's your grandmother's. You can't prove it's mine."

I decided to lie and see if she would call my bluff. "The police found your fingerprints on the accelerant in Sam's garage."

Mama Grizzly sank into her chair, defeat evident on her normally haughty-looking face.

"I did it for him. The turtles. The fire. For Lucien," she said with a sigh. "No one was hurt."

"Tell that to the turtles," I mumbled under my breath.

I don't think she heard me, or didn't care, because she continued. "It looked as if the aquarium might actually raise the money to buy the twenty acres." She shook her head. "Bradford Monroe was on a roll with his sponsorships and had to be stopped."

She paused. "My sister, who lives upstate, goes camping and used this particular accelerant for her camp fires. I decided a fire would be a good way to stop the aquarium's momentum, so I took a can. I just wasn't sure when I'd commit the act. When I dropped off Sam's bonus check, his garage door was partially open. He told me he fed a stray cat. Can you believe that?"

I ignored her remark. "I take it this was when you decided to frame Sam?"

She nodded. "I set the fire that night, then returned to his place and stashed the open can in his garage. When I spotted the boots, I sprinkled them with accelerant." She shook her head. "I thought I wiped off my fingerprints off the container."

I wasn't about to tell her I made up the part about the fingerprints. Meanwhile, one thing didn't make sense. "Damage caused by the fire could hurt the aquarium financially. But why the turtles?" I asked.

"I heard about the Mulgraves, and I hoped this would head-off their sponsorship." She hesitated. "Mr. Moray needs this project. He had some financial setbacks, and the condos would be a real money maker. I know how worried he's been. He's developed an ulcer, and he's preoccupied all the time."

I sucked in my breath. "Did he ask you to commit these crimes?"

She shook her head. "He has no idea what I did. As gruff and hard nosed as he is, he wouldn't break the law. He said there are too many government agencies looking at a man of his stature, and he didn't want to spend his final years in jail. But I knew nobody would be looking at me. I figured I would tell him what I did after everything was settled, and he'd be so pleased. Maybe he'd realize how much he needed me."

Mama Grizzly was in love with Lucien Moray.

Helen Eubanks, AKA Mama Grizzly, had committed the arson and turtle poisoning, but there was more.

"If Katie hadn't been murdered, there was no way Moray could acquire the land," I said. "You had motive to kill her."

Mama Grizzly's eyes dilated to the size of marbles. "Oh, no. I didn't do that. I'd never murder someone.

I don't know why, but I believed her.

CHAPTER FORTY-SIX

I phoned Ben Barone, the arson squad supervisor, and told him about the evidence and Mama Grizzly's confession. It turned out it was Mama Grizzly who had made the call to the police. She claimed to have seen Sam drive into the aquarium parking lot a few minutes before the fire. Of course, that was a lie. By the day's end, Mama Grizzly had been arrested for arson. She was also charged with the turtle poisoning. All charges against Sam Wong were dropped.

As for the murder of Katie Chandler and Jack Patterson, there was no direct evidence linking Mama Grizzly to the crimes, but Ben stated he would contact homicide detective Steve Wolfe. Ben didn't believe she committed those murders. But based on her actions against the aquarium, he felt Wolfe needed to initiate a thorough investigation.

As far as I knew, Detective Wolfe never investigated anything thoroughly. Wolfe had a reputation for laziness and sloppy work, always looking for the easiest solution, which in this case would be arresting Mama Grizzly. But if Mama Grizzly didn't kill Katie or Jack, someone else did, and that person would get away with the murders.

When I arrived at my office, Clara was away from her desk. I made my way to my cubicle, pulled my phone from my bag, and turned to the photos I'd taken of Katie's diary.

The last time Katie had written in the book was three days after the body of Jack Patterson had been discovered.

She wrote, *My first reaction to the discovery of Jack's dead body was relief that it wasn't my Sam. Although I am still worried sick about Sam's disappearance, I find myself thinking more and more about Jack. I know he wanted us to be more than friends. If it wasn't for Sam, that might have happened. Now, I'm wondering if deep down, I really loved Jack. Is it possible to have two great loves? Was my relationship with Sam more about passion? Was Jack my soul mate? The pain of his loss in my life has become unbearable.*

I sat back and tried to digest this new information. The major motives for murder were greed, jealously, blackmail, and revenge. I had been focused on greed and the land acquisition fight. Was that the wrong track? Perhaps the reason Jack and Katie were killed was jealously.

Long before he got hold of the diary, Sam may have suspected Jack and Katie of having feelings for each other. Was Sam afraid of losing Katie to her childhood friend? Did he feel betrayed?

Did he murder Jack? And Katie?

Next, I came across an earlier section where Katie had expressed doubts about her relationship with Sam Wong. She wrote: *I met him at a party about one month before Lucien Moray made public his interest in buying the twenty acres of land for condominiums. At first, Sam and I never discussed business. Then he started talking about how wonderful the condos would be fore the growth of Clam Cove.*

Sam also tried to convince me that the Clam Cove Lighthouse Preservation Fund needed money more than the other organizations specified in my grandmother's will. At one point, I wondered if my chance meeting with Sam at the party and our subsequent relationship had been a set-up. Did Sam really love me? Or was he using me to get information and steer me away from donating six million dollars to the aquarium?

This must have been the rough patch Abby had talked about. But according to my daughter, Katie and Sam had settled their differences and were very much in love. From what I had seen, that seemed true. Katie didn't appear to realize her feelings toward Jack until he was dead. Still, I wondered.

I sat back and stretched while dozens of scenarios squirreled through my head. To get to the bottom of this, I needed a caffeine fix. I made my way to the coffee machine located on a table near the entrance to the editor's office.

Clara was back at her desk, pecking at her keyboard. I said hello, but she barely acknowledged me as she continued focusing on her computer.

"Is Olivia in?" I asked.

"Nope."

"Will she be in later?"

"Don't know."

"Okay, Clara. What's the problem?"

"Nothing." Clara didn't look up.

"Not true. Tell me what's wrong." I poured coffee into a mug.

"I'm busy. That's all. Why do you think something is wrong?"

"You haven't bombarded me with questions, and you haven't filled me in on the latest gossip. This is unlike you. Your office nickname is Chatty Clara. Stop staring at your computer and start talking."

She spun her chair to face me. "I need to type our financial data into a report for Olivia. She has another meeting at corporate headquarters tomorrow." Clara sighed. "The more I type, the more depressed I become."

"I'm guessing our financial situation is bleak?"

She nodded. "Our big problem is that our advertising revenue has plummeted."

"Any idea why?"

"For the last year, John hasn't been aggressive in seeking business. Thank God, he's retiring."

John Williams was our advertising manager. When he first started here he was a dynamo salesman, but he lost his wife two years ago, and ever since, his work went downhill. I had heard he was moving to Delaware to be closer to family, and I hoped he would find happiness.

I was about to question Clara when my phone binged. Clara went back to her keyboard while I read the text. It was from Olivia and it read: "The Baumgarten Museum is featuring a special exhibit this weekend on the history of sharks. Visit it before completing your article 'Dangers of the Deep.' Might add an interesting twist to your story."

Although my article was almost complete, I knew when Olivia made a suggestion, she expected it to be followed like an order.

My thoughts were interrupted by Clara, who said, "Olivia has hired a new advertising manager. I hear he's a real go-getter."

"That's great."

Clara shrugged. "Revenue will play a key role in whether we merge with *Green World*. That will be decided in December, which is only two months away. Olivia is asking for more time to turn our finances around before corporate management comes down with its final edict. I don't know if the big brass will grant her the extension. My gut tells me our new advertising manager is coming too late."

* * * * *

"So, where's grandma tonight?" Abby asked. She and Jason were eating dinner at my house. We were sitting around the kitchen table. Archie and Brandy were playing in the backyard. When I last saw Gus, he was curled up on my bed.

"She's with Paul and Marcia," I said.

"That's become quite a threesome." Matt pulled the white cartons out of the Chinese take-out bag and placed them on the table. I was not known for home cooked meals.

Abby frowned. "For an engaged couple, they almost never spend time alone."

"Marcia Silver is your grandmother's best friend," I said. "They only see each other when grandma visits, so I understand why they want to spend time together. Grandma and Paul will have lots of time alone when they return to Florida." The thought of the two together unnerved me. I changed the subject. "Have some garlic shrimp, Abby." I passed the carton to my daughter.

After dinner, I suggested we have our coffee in the den.

"This is a perfect night to use the fireplace. Abby, why don't you and your father bring in some logs and start the fire. Jason, you can help me with the dessert."

Jason looked surprised to be assigned cake duty, but he followed me into the kitchen.

"Did you get the information yet?" I asked as I sliced a cheesecake and placed each piece on a plate.

"Not yet."

"My mother and Paul are leaving for Florida on Monday. For this plan to work, we need the information by this weekend."

Jason nodded. "I'll call again."

After we settled in the den, I gave my family a filtered version of what Katie had written in her diary. I did not mention any of Katie's comments about Jack, but I focused on Katie's thoughts concerning her relationship with Sam. I was interested in Abby's take on that situation.

"There was a period where Katie did question if Sam loved her of if he had deliberately been put into her life by Lucien Moray." Abby hesitated. "At one point, she considered breaking up."

"But she didn't?"

"No. When Sam said he planned to leave Moray's employ, Katie decided he was on the up and up. From that moment on, the relationship seemed to be going smoothly. They were about to plan their wedding."

Jason, who returned from the kitchen with his second piece of cheesecake, said, "Do you think Sam was legit? Was he in love with Katie or was it an act?"

Abby appeared to ponder the questions before answering. "I think in the end, he really loved her. But I don't know how it started. There appears to be lots of inconsistencies in Sam and Katie's relationship."

* * * * *

The next morning, I put my investigation into the murders on hold as I headed into Manhattan, to check out the shark history exhibit at the Baumgarten Museum.

Sharks had been on this planet two hundred million years before dinosaurs, making them one of the oldest creatures on earth. I marveled at the exhibit featuring the fossilized teeth of the Megalodon. The Megalodon had been the largest prehistoric sea creature in the history of the world. Its tooth was the size of a human hand. According to the information packet, this ancient shark may have been more than forty feet in length, making the Great White look like a guppy. Shark history would be a great addition to my story.

As with most museums, my visit ended at the gift shop. A special section was dedicated to merchandise with a shark theme. What caught my eye was a collection of shark postage. Each stamp sold for between twenty and twenty-five dollars. Collector items. I silently chuckled at the sight of a "shark and jellyfish love" wedding stamp. The wedding stamp made me think of Abby and Jason. I wondered if there would be nuptials in their future. If there was, I was pretty sure there wouldn't be images of sea creatures anywhere near their wedding invitations.

I moved on and while I was gazing at some shark themed jewelry, a thought flashed through my mind. I grabbed my phone and checked my favorite search engine.

"Got it," I mumbled under my breath as I stashed the phone back in my bag. I flew out of the museum and took the subway downtown.

Twenty minutes later, I entered a small, dimly lit shop in Greenwich Village. I was glancing at the display case when a man behind the counter approached.

"May I help you?" he asked as he maneuvered his wheelchair to face me.

I told him what I was seeking. He pulled out a book, placed it on the counter, and began thumbing through the pages.

"Aha! Here it is." He spun the book around so I could see where his finger pointed.

"Can you get me one of these?"

"Can I get you one?" he repeated as if he hadn't heard correctly." This isn't a doughnut. Have you any idea how rare this is? And expensive?"

"I can get the money," I lied.

He shook his head. "I wouldn't know where to start the search."

"One is on the market."

"That may be." He closed the book. "But I know nothing about it. As they say, it's above my pay grade. I can't help you."

CHAPTER FORTY-SEVEN

"What about jealously as a motive? Did Katie have any significant relationships before Sam?" I asked Abby early the next morning. We were sitting in my kitchen drinking coffee and eating cinnamon rolls, the aroma wafting through the air. The two dogs were under the table, hoping for crumbs.

Abby shook her head. "During college, Katie dated, but nothing was ever serious. She met Sam after graduation."

"What about her relationship with Jack Patterson?"

"Jack?" Abby paused. "They were nothing more than good friends."

"You seem unsure," I said, noticing the way Abby had furrowed her eyebrows. I proceeded to tell my daughter about what Katie had written in her diary concerning her feelings toward Jack.

Abby smiled slightly. "I always suspected Katie and Jack had a thing for each other."

"Why?"

Abby leaned back and explained. "Jack visited Katie in college one weekend when we were freshman. That was the first time I met him. Katie introduced him as the brother she never had. But sometimes I caught her glancing at him with a look that was more than brotherly."

"Didn't you believe that the relationship was platonic?"

Abby paused, as she appeared to be gathering her thoughts. "There was a strong bond between them. It may have started off as a friendship, but I think it grew into love. But I honestly don't think Katie realized how strong her feelings were until Jack died."

"Could Sam have suspected anything?"

"I doubt it. Sam is brilliant, but he's not the type to notice romantic nuances. And Katie was one hundred percent loyal to Sam while they were together."

"Okay. No motive. Let's move on. What about professional jealously at work. Rivalries? Did Katie face competition for promotions?"

"No." Abby shook her head. "Katie was the most laid back person I'd ever met. She didn't care about money or power at all. She simply wanted to train her sea lions. By nature, she wasn't ruthless or backbiting."

I nodded. "I remember you telling me that when her grandmother brought up the idea of leaving most of her money to charity, Katie encouraged her to do so."

"Right. Katie told me her salary at the aquarium was more than enough to cover her needs. Plus her grandmother was willing the house to her along with one million dollars." Abby grinned. "The point is she was satisfied. She didn't want more."

"Did Katie have any personal enemies?"

"Absolutely not."

There appeared to be no reason other than Alicia Wilcox Chandler's money for someone to murder Katie.

"Jack Patterson appears to be the unknown in this equation. I'll check on him when I get to the office which I should do now," Changing the subject, I said, "Your father seems happy lately. Last night, he told me the animal lover's festival was a success."

"It was." Abby beamed. "We've several new clients. Apparently, a lot of folks are not happy with the new animal health and wellness center."

"Why?" I put down my cup.

"A few people thought the veterinarians working there pushed for expensive diagnostic tests before ruling out other causes. Some complained about the failure to keep scheduled appointments on time. For most, however, it was about impersonal service. You rarely get to see the same veterinarian, so no one gets to know your dog or cat."

"Well, whatever the reason, I'm glad your father's business is picking up." I paused. "Do you know what the festival cost?"

Abby smiled. "That's more good news. With all the sponsors it cost less than two hundred dollars."

"I was surprised by the types of sponsors," I said.

"Types? What do you mean?"

"I understand the pet food company and the store that sells dog beds, but there was a bank, an auto repair shop, and even a shoe store. Those businesses have nothing to do with animals."

"But people with companion animals deal with those vendors. They have bank accounts, mortgages, and loans like everyone else. They buy cars and clothing. They're just another segment of the marketplace."

Another segment of the marketplace. That thought stayed with me as I grabbed a light sweater and threw it over my shoulders. Abby and I left the house, and went our separate ways. While stopped at a traffic light, an idea popped into my mind.

I slammed my hand on the steering wheel. "That's it."

* * * * *

"I've got it."

"Got what?" Clara looked up from the papers on her desk.

"The solution to our problem."

Clara scratched her head, messing up her short, gray hair. "Problem? Which one?"

"Advertising revenue. Is Olivia in? When does the new advertising manager start? Did she get an extension from corporate? Did she—"

"Slow down." Clara held up her hands. "You're acting like a caffeinated squirrel. Yes, Olivia is in. The new manager started today. Olivia only got a one month extension from corporate headquarters, but that's better than nothing. Now, what is your idea?"

"I'll tell you later. I promise." I bee-lined to Olivia's office and knocked on the door.

"This must be urgent," Olivia said, as I stepped into her inner sanctum.

I caught the sarcasm. Staff didn't drop in on Olivia without an appointment. "I heard you hired a new advertising manager?" I said.

Olivia nodded. "Evan Hale. He started here today. You'll meet him at next week's staff meeting. What did you want to see me about?"

"What about approaching non-animal related businesses for ads?" I told her about the sponsorships at Matt's festival, then added, "More than half the readership of *Animal Advocate* comes from Long Island. I'll bet lots of our local business leaders would love to attract that segment of the market. Why can't the new advertising manager go after them?"

Olivia frowned. I sucked in my breath. I was a writer not an ad salesperson. Would Olivia tell me this was none of my business?

"You may have a point," she said. "When *Animal Advocate* first was published, we did have a few ads from local banks, car dealers, department stores and so on. Gradually we moved toward animal related businesses in a national market, but most of our magazine sales are on Long Island."

Olivia picked up her phone. "Let's give it a try. I'll call Evan now and make sure he incorporates community businesses into his strategy. Is that all?"

This was my cue to leave. "Yes," I said as I headed out the door.

I scooted off to my cubicle, booted up my computer, and searched for Jack Patterson. The stable posted a website that listed both Jillian and Jack as owners. Jillian had not yet taken down Jack's biography.

According to the information, Jack had been involved with horses since he was a child, and he had worked at the stable his entire life, except for a four-year period when he attended college in Pennsylvania, followed by a three year stint as a biology teacher in a small prep school in Philadelphia. He had returned to Clam Cove about two years ago, and although he worked full-time at the aquarium, he still taught riding classes, assisted with the care of the horses, and helped with the general maintenance of the stable.

"Nothing here I didn't know," I grumbled under my breath as I sat back in my chair and stretched. Still, something bothered me. I stared at the screen. Suddenly I saw it—a connection between one of the murder suspects and Jack.

I continued my research going from screen to screen until the intercom trilled. I picked up and heard Clara's voice.

"Detective Wolfe is here. He wants to see—"

"He just arrived in my cubicle," I said as I looked up and saw his frowning beet-red face looming over my desk.

"We need to talk." He narrowed his eyes. "While Sam Wong was in custody, he and I had an interesting conversation."

"What was so interesting?"

"He told me that on the day I came across him in Katie Chandler's house, which was less than a week after her death, you were hiding in one of the rooms upstairs."

"I wasn't hiding. I lost a bracelet the day of the aquarium fund raiser, and I went back to the house to search," I lied. I didn't think it was a good idea to tell him that I was looking for clues to Katie's murder.

"Really? The fund raiser was in the bedroom?" He smirked.

"Before the cocktail party had started, Katie showed me some of her great-great-grandfather's possessions, which she kept in a room upstairs. I thought I lost the bracelet there."

"Did you touch anything?"

"I'm sure I did, but since the police had finished with the investigation of the premises, I didn't think that was a problem."

"But the property now belongs to the Clam Cove Aquarium. I didn't know that then, but now I do. You were trespassing." He pointed a fat finger at me.

I didn't like where this was headed. I needed to change the conversation's focus.

"What have the police found out about Helen Eubanks?" I asked, referring to Mama Grizzly by her real name.

"Her alibi for Katie Chandler's murder checks out. She was attending a wedding for her niece upstate."

"Did you check if she was there for the entire time?"

Detective Wolfe's face blew up like a puffer fish. "Of course, I checked it out. Don't tell me how to do my job."

He turned to leave but paused. "By the way, did you find it?"

"Find what?"

"Your bracelet. The one you were searching for in Katie's house."

"Oh, yes," I added quickly. "I found it at my home." I smiled.

He smiled, too. I was surprised until he opened his mouth to speak. "I'm headed to the aquarium now," he said. "I will be telling Commander West that you were trespassing in Katie Chandler's house. Since that property now belongs to the aquarium, Commander West may want to press charges. I intend to encourage him to do so."

His grin became wider as he added, "If so, I'll be back. With handcuffs."

CHAPTER FORTY-EIGHT

During the drive to the Patterson Horse Farm, I watched the light drain from the sky as dusk approached. Upon arrival, I located Jillian in the stable filling buckets with grain.

"Can I talk with you?" I asked. "It's important."

She nodded. "As long as you can do it while I work. I gotta feed the horses."

"I need information about the school where Jack worked. I know this is a long shot but do you know anyone there who might talk to me?"

"I do. Her name is Sara Goldstein. She's administrative assistant to the headmaster. She was one of Jack's closest friends at the school, and they still kept in touch."

"Do you have her phone number?"

Jillian filled the bucket in the last stall before answering. "It's on Jack's phone. Give me a moment and I'll get it."

* * * * *

Sara picked up the phone on the first ring.

"I'm so distraught about Jack's death," she said after I introduced myself and told her why I was calling. "I hadn't spoken to him in about six months, then a few days before he died, he called."

"Any particular reason?"

"His call was odd. Jack asked if I had a phone number or address for Rupert Cunningham."

"Who?"

"Rupert Cunningham is the estranged brother of Marshall

Cunningham, the man who bequeathed his five million dollar estate to our school."

"Why did Jack want this information?"

"All he said was that Rupert may have been right." Sara paused. "When Marshall died, Rupert went ballistic upon discovering the estate was going to the Throckbrush Academy and not to him. Rupert had planned to contest the will, but his attorney told him he would lose. Then Rupert began defaming the school. At one point, he accused staff members of stealing from the estate, but that was never proven."

"Wait a second. Couldn't forensic accounting prove or disprove that?"

"No. We're not talking about financial embezzlement. We're talking about out and out stealing. Stocks and bonds accounted for only half of Rupert's estate. The other half consisted of his home, worth nearly two million, and his prized coin collection. That was valued at half a million, but Rupert claimed it was worth more. He said a 1943 copper wheat penny appraised at close to nearly one hundred thousand dollars was missing."

"Did Rupert accuse any staff member in particular?"

"No. He only said that it was taken by someone from the school's administration."

"How did he know the coin was missing?"

"The headmaster held a press conference when the coins were sold. Rupert contacted the person who purchased the collection. He pretended to want to buy it back and discovered the penny was missing."

"But if Rupert was estranged from Marshall, how did he know it hadn't been sold years ago?

"He claimed it was his brother's prized possession and that Marshall would never have sold it. Of course, the problem was that the police couldn't take Rupert's word. They investigated but couldn't prove the item wasn't sold prior to Marshall's death.

"Were you able to provide Jack with information on Rupert?"

"I gave him what I have on file in the office, but I don't know if he made contact."

"Can you give me his address and phone number? I guess I'll call. I'd love to talk to him in person, but I don't have time to drive to Pennsylvania."

"You don't need to. He doesn't live down there. Marshall's home was outside of Philadelphia, but Rupert lives on Long Island."

* * * * * .

I pulled up in front of Rupert Cunningham's home. A colonial in a middle class neighborhood, I had a feeling it was nothing like the two million dollar mansion belonging to his late brother Marshall. This house was in need of a paint job and the landscaping was overgrown.

"May I help you?" asked a stout, middle age woman in a nurse's uniform who answered the door.

"I'm a reporter doing a piece on coins, and I'd like to ask Mr. Cunningham a few questions about his late brother's collection."

She didn't step aside. "I don't know if—"

"Who's at the door, Bertha?" a male voice bellowed.

"A reporter."

"What does she want?"

The nurse hesitated.

"I asked, what does she want?"

"She has questions about your late brother's coins."

"Send her in."

The nurse stood her ground for a few seconds, sighed, and stepped aside. I followed her to the living room where I faced an elderly man sitting in a wheelchair. Judging by his bulbous nose covered in purple veins, I had the feeling he was a heavy drinker. That thought was confirmed by his next comment to me.

"Did you bring any scotch? All she gives me is water or tea." He pointed a thumb at the nurse.

"Sorry." I smiled.

"No harm asking. What do you want to know about the coin collection? It should have been mine."

"I understand it included a 1943 copper wheat penny."

"At one time it did. The coin was stolen."

"How do you know that? Maybe your brother sold it before he died."

Rupert's face turned red as he shook his head. "Absolutely not. That copper penny is the reason we were estranged."

Rupert hadn't told me to sit, but I slid into a nearby chair as he began his story.

"I never had nearly as much money as Marshall, but I was comfortable. Then I faced financial adversity. I received a stock tip. I put all of my money into one stock and purchased more of it on margin." He narrowed his eyes. "Do you know what that means?"

"Yes. Basically, you borrowed to buy the stock, hoping it would go up in value."

"Instead it tanked. Embezzlement scandal with the CFO, but no need to get into that now. Point is, I received a margin call. That meant I needed money immediately to pay for what I owed—I needed three hundred thousand. I scraped together a half, and I asked my brother to loan me the rest. He refused. Said he didn't have cash available. The market was on a downward trend, and he'd take a beating if he sold any of his investments."

I leaned forward in my seat as he continued.

"I knew his copper wheat penny was worth nearly $100,000. I asked him if he would sell it and one other coin worth $50,000. After all, he didn't have a spouse or children. I would be getting his money when he died. Or so I thought."

Rupert coughed, then took a sip of water from a glass on an adjacent table. He continued. "Marshall refused. Said the penny was his most prized possession. As long as he had a breath in him, he would keep the coin and every other one in the collection. I stormed out of his house and never spoke to him again. I had to empty most of my retirement account. I lost everything. All I have is this house. There's a reverse mortgage on it. I use that money to pay the nurse and medical expenses not covered by Medicare. I'm living on social security and a small pension."

"He didn't leave you anything when he died?

"The day I walked out of his house, he changed his will and left everything to that prep school. Did you bring scotch?"

CHAPTER FORTY-NINE

Ten o'clock at night, and I was hiding among the tall beach grass on a dune next to Ruby Diamond's cottage. I shivered as I buttoned up my jacket. Only a week since I'd last been here, but autumn temperatures drop quickly as late October approaches.

I watched through my binoculars as it came into view—a boat occupied by a sole individual. Seconds later, lights flashed from the boat's bow. Then came lights from Ruby's cottage followed by darkness. The pattern continued.

Exactly as it happened last Thursday, Ruby Diamond emerged from her house with a flashlight and made her way to the shore line.

The boat now was at the water's edge. I recognized the occupant as Kyle. He hopped out and pulled the craft to shore. He handed a large box to Ruby, and she handed something to him.

Suddenly, lights flooded the beach. Above me, the sound of a whirling helicopter filled the sky.

"This is the Drug Enforcement Agency," a voice called over a loudspeaker. The helicopter hovered directly over the spot where Ruby and her companion stood. "Stay where you are with your hands up."

Four cars with sirens blasting drove up to the beach and nearly a dozen men and women in uniform, guns out of holster, emerged from their vehicles.

Glued to my spot, I watched as an agent grabbed the package, tore it open, and nodded to an associate who promptly handcuffed Ruby and Kyle. The two were escorted to a car while three Drug Enforcement Agents headed into her cottage where I presumed they would be conducting a search.

I was still watching the action when a voice behind me said, "Turn around slowly with your hands up."

I did as told and found myself facing a Drug Enforcement Agent. She appeared to be more than six feet tall and was pointing a gun at me. She did not look happy.

It's okay," I said. "I'm the one who called Agent Colby and gave him the tip about the drugs. I'm a reporter. My name is Kristy Farrell. My identification is in my bag."

"Keep your hands up." Her gun was still pointed at me. "Agent Colby is down below. We'll see him now and sort this out. But even if you gave him a tip, I'm sure he didn't give you permission to be here. Let's go."

She marched me along the beach to the cottage.

"Agent Colby, I found this one hiding in the tall grass near the embankment," she said to an agent standing near the back door of Ruby's cottage. "Her name is Kristy Farrell. She claims she's the reporter—"

"You can put down your gun," he said. "She's telling the truth." He frowned at me. "But you shouldn't be here. This is dangerous."

"I wanted to see what happened, so I could include it in the article I'm writing."

"If Ruby had seen you she might have aborted the entire operation, and we would have had nothing." He shook his head. "Get out of here. Agent Zipser, escort her to her car and make sure she leaves."

I spotted a slight smile on his lips as he added, "But thanks for the tip."

"So, you're a reporter, eh," said Agent Zipser as we hiked back to my car. "How did you get the tip about the drugs? An informer?"

"No. I had a strong hunch based on several factors. I had spotted flashing lights coming from the bay and from Ruby's cottage. I figured it was a code. I also overheard Kyle talking about changing Tuesday's operation to Thursday. Ruby made it clear she didn't want to have that conversation in front of me. And Ruby's argument about keeping this land pristine didn't ring true. While Ruby protested the aquarium move to acquire the property, she only gave token opposition to Lucien Moray's development. A true environmentalist would be against Moray."

"What does her environmental stance have to do with this?"

"The aquarium was planning a research camp on the land directly next to Ruby's cottage. That meant there would be people present at night who might get curious. Meanwhile, Moray's plan included a buffer of vacant beach adjacent to Ruby's land."

"All this is still a hunch. Agent Colby wouldn't approve tonight's operation without proof."

"Oh, there's more. I had written an article two months ago on wildlife smuggling. One of the most common means of bringing contraband into the United States is in hidden compartments. Ruby's vase in the storage room in Gracie's Gift Shoppe was much heavier than the vase for sale out front, but they were the same size and shape, so I suspected a false bottom."

"How did you know it would be drugs? Why not something else, like diamonds? Or counterfeit money?"

"I came out here last Thursday and overheard a conversation between Ruby and Kyle. The word pharmaceuticals was used."

"You came out here yourself to confront a drug dealer," Agent Zipser said. "That was a stupid thing to do. "

"I had no intention of confronting anyone. I just wanted verification before reporting it to the Drug Enforcement Agency. You said yourself what proof did I have."

Agent Zipser shook her head. "Go home."

We had reached my car. I was happy to oblige.

CHAPTER FIFTY

"You're a charmer," I said, glancing into my rearview mirror. "We'll work as a tag team. You start them talking, and I'll steer the conversation. And stop whining. We're almost there."

I was talking to my collie, Brandy, as we sped along the main highway to the Village of Clam Shell Cove. Many people are reluctant to start a conversation with a stranger. One exception is if the stranger has a dog in tow. Dogs are great ice breakers.

My goal today was to collect information. I firmly believed most rumors held at least a smidgen of truth. I wasn't sure how I would segue "Does your dog shed a lot?" into "Who benefits from Katie Chandler's death?" but I would come up with something.

I had chosen Brandy as my conversation starter instead of Archie. Although my bear-like mixed breed was a gentle giant, he was young, exuberant, and jumped when excited. I figured having a one hundred pound dog staring directly into your eyes while his paws rested on your shoulders might scare people off. Eight year old Brandy was beyond that stage.

When we arrived in the village, I parked myself at a dog-friendly outdoor café, making sure to secure a table near the sidewalk. While I sipped my cappuccino, Brandy rested on the floor next to me.

So far, nothing was happening. I debated getting another cup when I heard a youthful sounding voice say, "Mommy, look at the Lassie dog."

Thankful that *Lassie* was now in reruns, I smiled at a boy, who appeared to be about six, and a woman, I presumed was his mother. I said, "You're right. This is the same type of dog as Lassie. This is a collie. His name is Brandy."

"Does he shed a lot?" the mother asked.

"He does, but he is such a love. I take him with me when I can."

This was the opportunity for my segue. "Only problem is that my friend called five minutes ago and invited me to join her at the aquarium. Of course, the aquarium doesn't allow dogs, so I can't go."

"Too bad. The Clam Cove Aquarium is terrific."

"The sea lions are my favorite," said the young boy, who was now petting Brandy.

"My favorite, too." I looked at the mother. "I'm glad none of the animals or marine life were injured in the fire."

"That was lucky," the woman said. "But the damaged portion of the building is such an eyesore. I wish the village would stop playing games and issue permits so they can rebuild."

"Playing games?"

She nodded. "The mayor claims budget cuts have resulted in a backlog in the building department and that it takes time to finish the paperwork. He said permits should be issued soon, but I think he's stalling."

"Why would the mayor stall?"

"Everyone knows the mayor supports the condos and will do whatever is necessary to ensure the development gets the green light. If that means causing problems for the aquarium, so be it. Construction delays cost money." She shrugged. "We better go. Brian has gymnastics in five minutes. Nice talking to you. Brian, say good-bye to the dog."

"Bye Bran." Brian gave my collie one last pet and scampered down the street with his mother.

"Good work," I said, patting Brandy. "Keep on looking adorable."

I ordered a second cappuccino and had almost finished it when I spotted two familiar figures strolling down the street.

"Hello. Aren't you the reporter from *Animal Advocate*?" Mr. Mulgrave said.

"Beautiful dog," Mrs. Mulgrave added.

"Thanks. And yes. I'm Kristy Farrell. Are you on your way to the aquarium?"

"Maybe later. We had lunch in town, and now we are going to visit Elizabeth's mother at the nursing home. It's about ten minutes from here."

"My mother has Alzheimer's disease," Mrs. Mulgrave said.

"I'm sorry."

"It's rough. That's why we want to visit early in the day. She has sundowner's syndrome and is a lot worse at night. The day of the cocktail party at the Chandler house, we didn't get to visit her until after six, and she was not doing well."

"Six o'clock? I thought you met Brad Monroe at the Tipsy Toad Tavern."

"Oh, that was later. The staff at the nursing home starts preparing everyone for bed around seven-thirty, so we had go to see her first. We met Bradford at the tavern around seven-fifteen, right, honey?"

Mr. Mulgrave nodded. "We were a few minutes later than that because we ran into Commander West coming out of the liquor store across the street, and we stopped to talk. He was chatty, but he received a phone call and had to leave."

At the time of the murders, Commander West was supposedly home alone. Bradford Monroe claimed he had been at a meeting in the Tipsy Toad Tavern. The Mulgraves had just knocked out the alibis for two suspects.

CHAPTER FIFTY-ONE

When I arrived at the garage sale, Marcia Silver was standing by the front steps of her house talking with a woman who was wearing a colorful poncho. I located my mother sitting behind the jewelry table, sipping coffee. She had stayed overnight at Marcia's home, so the two could set up early. She and Marcia had sorted the merchandise into categories and had arranged everything on six-foot tables placed in long rows on the front lawn.

"Good morning," my mother greeted me cheerily as I strolled up the walkway. "Why don't you go into the kitchen and get coffee before the crowds arrive." She handed me her mug. "You can get me a refill, too."

I smiled. "Isn't that a customer with Marcia? I thought you didn't open for another thirty minutes."

"That's probably an antique dealer," my mother whispered as if she were trading in government secrets. "We posted ten as the time we would open, but antique dealers come early to find bargains."

After I filled coffee mugs, including mom's refill, I decided to browse. Marcia had finished her conversation with the lady in the poncho and came over to greet me.

"Did you make a sale?" I asked.

Marcia shook her head. "No. But I'm sure business will pick up."

"I noticed lots of items here the other day that are now missing, "I said, not adding that much of what remained appeared to be junk.

"Paul Andre sold most of the better items for me. He's such a dear. Your mom is so lucky."

"Did he sell online?"

"Some items but not all. He made a few private deals for me. He's got great contacts in the antique field. He sold my doll collection privately for four hundred dollars. Oh, another customer is here. I'll see you later. Thanks for helping. You know where to go, right?"

I nodded. "Mom gave me my assignments."

"It's a shame your sister-in-law couldn't make it. Your mother said she came down with the flu."

I smiled. Barbara was true to form.

Once Marcia departed, I strolled to the table with small kitchen appliances. That was where I was scheduled to work today.

Business wasn't great and by early afternoon the crowds dwindled. Marcia decided to call it a day. I wandered to where my mother sat.

"I thought Paul would be here," I said.

"He had business in the city."

"He's still coming to the house to pick you up for dinner tonight, right?"

My mother shook her head. "Change of plans. He's afraid he'll be delayed in Manhattan, so to save time, I'm meeting him at his hotel."

That would mess up everything. I hated lying to my mother, but for my plan to work, I needed Paul at my house tonight.

"Paul needs to pick you up at home. I have champagne and an engagement gift for the two of you," I lied.

"Kristy, how sweet. But can't we do it some other time?"

"No. I'll be busy all day Sunday at the aquarium's art and antique auction. Since you told me you're getting your engagement ring on Monday, and you're leaving Tuesday with Paul for Florida, there's not enough time."

"Well, I guess I can ask him. But I hate to be a pest—"

"Be a pest. Tell him we'll be crushed if we don't have the opportunity to celebrate your engagement."

My mother reluctantly agreed.

* * * * *

That evening, my mom headed upstairs to finish getting ready for her date. Matt and I stayed in the kitchen with Abby and a fake Jason.

Neither my mother nor Paul had met Abby's boyfriend, and neither had any idea of what he looked like. The fake Jason had fooled my mom earlier tonight, and I hoped he would also fool Paul.

About thirty minutes later, just as the doorbell rang, my mother came downstairs. Paul stepped into the house, looking dapper as ever in a camel sports jacket, dark brown pants, and a mocha colored turtleneck.

"So glad you could come," I said to Paul. "I wanted to see you before you left on Tuesday." I introduced him to the fake Jason.

"Isn't my granddaughter's boyfriend adorable?" my mother said.

Ignoring her comment, Paul faced my mother. "There's been a change in plans. I've got a little more business to finish, so I'm leaving for Philadelphia tomorrow. I'll be back on Wednesday. We'll get your ring on Thursday and leave for Florida on Friday."

My mother's wide smile turned downward. Her face was a picture of disappointment. "Oh, okay."

"Let's all go into the living room and have champagne," I suggested.

"We've dinner reservations at eight-thirty. Plus, I have allergies, so we can't stay here long." Paul seemed anxious to leave.

"I promise we'll be quick. We do want to celebrate your impending engagement."

"You must be a good basketball player, Jason," my mother said as we headed into the living room.

"What do you mean?" Fake Jason looked at me. I shrugged.

"Abby told me last year that you played basketball in college. You're pretty short, so you must be good to make up for your lack of height."

"Oh, yes. I'm a good jumper."

I hoped there wasn't much else that Abby had said about her boyfriend.

Once we were seated with our drinks, Matt made a toast. I noticed Paul swallowing quickly, almost gulping down his champagne. I realized there was no time for small talk.

"Marcia Silver didn't make a lot of money at her garage sale, but I understand, Paul, that you sold quite a number of items for her privately," I said.

"Yes." He glanced at his watch.

"You received four hundred dollars for her doll collection?"

He nodded.

"Well, someone made a killing since that collection included a Kachina doll worth more than $10,000."

Paul smiled weakly. "I don't think so."

"Oh, yes," I insisted. "When I was helping Marcia sort through the merchandise for the garage sale, I took a photo of the doll from Marcia's album, then researched it thoroughly. It's an antique Hopi warrior princess. Quite valuable."

"Paul, did you know that?" my mother asked.

Paul shook his head. "Of course not. I'm so sorry if I made a stupid mistake. I'm familiar with many types of antiques and collectibles, but not dolls. I should have performed more due diligence. I should have—"

"I think you did extensive research," I interrupted. "You knew exactly what you were selling."

My mother looked at me, then at her fiancé. "What is she talking about Paul?"

The fake Jason rose from his chair. "She's talking about the fact that Paul is a con man with a history of scamming people."

Paul's face turned ashen. My mother frowned and opened her mouth but closed it quickly.

"Remember when I snapped a photo of you and my mother. I sent it to Jason. By the way, this isn't the real Jason," I said, pointing to the young man next to me. "His name is Salvatore Perini. Detective Salvatore Perini. He's assigned to the police department's fraud and bunco unit."

"The real Jason is working on a case for his law firm involving fraud and he deals with Detective Perini," Abby said to Paul. "My Jason told the detective what my mom suspected about you. Detective Perini agreed to come here tonight."

"Detective Perini, why don't you take it from here." I suggested.

He nodded. "I sent the photograph Mrs. Farrell gave me to other law enforcement agencies. It seems Paul Andre also goes under the names of Carter Banks, Joshua Rider, and Chip Nightingale. He's operated more than a dozen scams, almost all of them aimed at wealthy widows."

My mother gasped.

"Some of his scams involved taking money for non-existent

investment opportunities, such as his latest scheme involving health spas that were never meant to be. He'd take the money, disappear, then change his name."

"But he didn't pressure me," my mother interrupted. "He dropped the whole issue. He must love me."

Perini shook his head. "That's because more recently, Paul Andre has been involved in schemes of selling antiques belonging to elderly women who have no idea of the value of these items. Women like Marcia Silver."

"Paul," my mother yelled.

"This is not illegal," Paul fired back. "*Caveat emptor*. Let the buyer beware. It happens all the time. People make deals that benefit one party over the other."

"But this time it's different," I said. "You didn't buy merchandise from Marcia. You told her you would sell items privately and give her the proceeds. But you didn't. You only gave her four hundred dollars for the entire collection. You received much more. That means you stole from her."

"You have no way of knowing how much I made. You can't prove I didn't sell the dolls for only four hundred dollars."

"Actually, I can," Detective Perini said. "I work with many legitimate antique dealers and collectors. Through my contacts, I learned about a woman in Maryland who recently purchased a Kachina doll. We talked to her and she verified you as the seller. She admitted to giving you more than ten grand."

"This is preposterous. You have nothing on me." He rose to leave.

"Not so fast." Detective Perini blocked his exit. "You are under arrest for fraud."

"Wait," I called. "I have a question. I saw you in a hotel bar with a blonde woman and a man I know as Bradford Monroe. What is your connection to them?"

Paul turned to face my mother and sneered. "The blonde is my girlfriend."

My mother put her head in her hands. I maneuvered to a spot next to her and placed my hand on her shoulder, rubbing it gently.

"What about Bradford Monroe?" I asked Paul. "I saw you with him, too."

"I'm not saying anymore until I see my attorney."

As Perini escorted Paul Andre away in handcuffs, I couldn't help think how wonderful it was to deal with a bright committed law enforcement officer like him, as opposed to homicide detective Steve Wolfe. Then my thoughts turned. I glanced toward my mother and saw the tears.

"Mom, I'm so sorry."

"Me, too," said Abby as she hugged her grandmother.

"It's better you found out now," Matt added. "Before you two were married."

"He wouldn't have married me. That's why he changed our shopping day for the ring until Thursday. By that time he would have disappeared."

"You're right," I said. "He would have been in another state with another name."

"I was such a fool. I didn't see the signs. He only stopped pressuring me to invest in his health spa scam after he saw Marcia's belongings. He just switched one scam for another." My mother sighed. "I'm going to bed."

The good news: my mother would recover from this. She didn't lose her savings, and Paul Andre would soon be behind bars, unable to scam more victims. On the downside was whether Marcia would recoup the money from what Paul had sold. The Kachina doll was only one of more than a half dozen valuable items that he had taken from my mother's friend. Victims of scams rarely get their money back.

CHAPTER FIFTY-TWO

Despite the October breeze, I felt the perspiration under my blouse as I entered the backyard of what had been Katie Chandler's house. I exhaled. How would I prove what I knew?

The preview for the art and antique auction was crowded with prospective bidders who were taking the opportunity to get a close look at merchandise. Chairs had been set up in the middle of the lawn in front of a make-shift platform and podium. Surrounding the seating area, in a horseshoe arrangement, were long tables displaying the items for auction.

Security guards kept an eye on the merchandise. Two other guards stood by the entrance, checking invitations before admitting anyone to the preview.

I grabbed a catalog from a nearby table and began reading. More than one hundred items were being auctioned today. There was something for every taste and pocketbook, but it was the last ten items that caught my eye. The required opening bids for this high-end merchandise ranged from ten thousand dollars for an art deco diamond necklace to fifty thousand dollars for a painting by a famous local artist.

The more interaction I had with the aquarium's staff, the more I realized the acquisition of the twenty acres was not a pipe dream. The aquarium could very well reach their fund-raising goal. I needed to be careful that my actions today wouldn't ruin it for them.

I stuffed the catalog in my bag and began wandering. While I stopped to admire some of the antiques from Katie's home, most of which were in the lower or moderate price range, Commander West approached.

"You have magnificent merchandise for sale today," I said.

"Yes. I'm sure you saw some of these items on your unauthorized visit to Katie's home." He smiled. "Detective Wolfe told me about that. Don't worry. Despite his urging, I'm not pressing charges. But remember, freedom of the press doesn't mean you can break the law."

I nodded. "I'm sorry. I won't do it again."

"I'm in a good mood today. This event should be a huge success."

"I hope so. But I'm sad, too. The last time I was here, Katie was alive,"

There was an awkward silence before I spoke again. "Are the Mulgraves coming today?"

"I don't know."

"They told me they met you in town the evening of Katie's cocktail party."

"Yes. I had just purchased a bottle of cognac. I occasionally enjoy a sniffer of brandy at night." He looked to his right and left before saying in hushed tones, "By the way, I feel I should apologize. Last week, when you ran into me at the Tipsy Toad Tavern, I may have overindulged. I was upset about the problems facing the aquarium."

"I heard you're getting a rough time from the village."

"The permits for rebuilding the aquarium's administration wing seem to be entangled in red tape—more than usual for government. I know Lucien Moray is pulling out all the stops to see that we don't make our financial goals, and his tentacles seem to reach everywhere."

"Think he'll be successful?"

"It's a horse race. If it were only our four fundraising events, there would be no way we could raise the money needed. But Bradford's idea for exhibit sponsorships has taken off. Two more donors in addition to the Mulgraves gave us checks this week. We now have the Carol and Lawrence Mercer *Mysteries of the Amazon* and the Linda Esposito *Otter Wonderland.* Bradford has seven additional potential sponsors that he hopes to sew up in the next few weeks. Altogether that's one million. And we still have ten more exhibits that he intends to promote for more sponsorships. "

Commander West shook his head. "Brad can be annoying at times, but he is one excellent fundraiser. Now, if you'll excuse me, I need to greet more of our guests."

Seconds after he departed, Bradford Monroe approached. "See anything you like?" he asked.

"Yes." I smiled. "Unfortunately, little I can afford."

"But we do have significant merchandise with low figure minimum bids. A lot of those items are from Katie's house."

I nodded. "Heirlooms from her great-great-grandfather, like the captain's clock, the Italian tea cart, and the Samurai sword which, by the way, is not low-priced."

"True. That's one of the pricier items coming from her estate."

"Are you auctioning all of her possessions?"

Bradford shook his head. "No. Only items where we feel comfortable placing a minimum bid of two hundred dollars or more. Even that is incidental when you look at our goal, but every little bit helps. The lower priced items also serve as teasers and lead-in for our high-end merchandise. It's those last items listed in the catalog that will bring in nearly seventy percent of all money raised today. We refer to them as the *big ten*."

"How did you determine value for the minimum bids?" I asked. "Are you an expert on antiques?"

"I know a little, but I'm no expert. I hired an appraiser. She's well worth her fee. This way nothing is undervalued."

"What will you do with items that didn't make the two hundred dollar minimum bid cut-off?" I asked.

"Probably sell to a wholesale liquidator. But I'll address that at a later date."

"So, you haven't gotten rid of anything yet?"

"No. If it's not here, it's still in the house." He glanced at his watch. "The auction will begin in about thirty minutes. I better make sure everything is ready to go."

"Thanks for allowing me to bring a photographer. He should arrive near the end of the auction."

"Wonderful. Great publicity. After the auction, your photographer can snap a picture of one of the *big ten* items with its buyer."

* * * * *

Minutes before the auction began, I slid into a seat near the back. Bradford had hired a professional auctioneer who ran through the inexpensive and moderate valued merchandise. I never thought I'd consider a minimum bid of five thousand dollars moderate, but compared to the painting and jewelry on the block today, I guess it was.

Prior to the auction of the *big ten* items, Bradford took center stage. Grabbing the microphone from the auctioneer, he announced a champagne reception in the house at the conclusion of the auction. It was open to the press as well as anyone whose purchase exceeded ten thousand dollars.

As the last item was brought to the auction block, my photographer arrived. We made eye contact, and he maneuvered around the crowd, finally sliding into a seat behind me.

He leaned forward and whispered, "Are you sure your plan will work? I've been taking photos with my phone for the last five years. I hope I can handle this baby." He was referring to an expensive camera I had procured for him from the *Animal Advocate* office.

"Since this whole event is invitation only, I had to tell Commander West you were my photographer. There was no other way to get you here. Besides, Clara showed you how the camera operates. Don't worry. You won't blow your cover."

When the auction finished, my photographer escorted me to the house for the champagne reception. We were immediately greeted by Bradford Monroe who thanked me again for including the auction in my story.

"I can't decide," Bradford said, as Commander West hiked across the room to join us. "Should we take a picture of the antique diamond necklace or the painting? Both buyers are willing to be photographed. Maybe we should take two pictures."

I grabbed my pad and pen. "First, I want some facts for the story. How much did you raise?"

"More than half a million. The painting from the Long Island artist alone brought in ninety grand."

I exhaled, then made my statement. "Think how much you would have received if you included all the valuable merchandise from Katie's house."

Commander West frowned. "What are you talking about?"

"You would have more than tripled your profits if you auctioned the stamp."

"What stamp?" Commander West asked. Brad paled.

"The one on the invitation to the Governor's Ball in Mauritius. It was sitting atop the desk in the captain's study on the day of the cocktail party."

"I don't remember any invitation. I don't know what you're talking about," Bradford responded.

"I think I remember seeing it," Commander West said, a solemn expression on his face.

"The day I illegally searched Katie's home, I knew something was missing, but I couldn't place it," I said. "Two weeks later, while I was browsing in a museum gift shop, I came across a series of collectible stamps. That jogged my memory. I realized the invitation was no longer on the captain's desk."

"Well, maybe it was thrown out accidentally before the appraiser came," Brad suggested.

I shook my head. "Nothing else upstairs appeared to have been touched. That meant the invitation wasn't moved or misplaced. Someone took it. Since it was more than one hundred fifty years old, I had a feeling the stamp might be valuable, so I visited a shop in Greenwich Village specializing in philately."

"That's stamp collecting, right?" the commander asked.

"Yes. And my hunch was on the mark. The stamp on the invitation was worth big bucks."

"As far as I know, you, your daughter, and Sam Wong were the only unauthorized people in the house. Perhaps one of you walked off with it," Bradford accused.

I placed my hands on my hips. "If I stole it, I wouldn't be mentioning it now, would I?"

"Just how valuable is this stamp?" Commander West asked.

"The Mauritius 'Post Office' stamp is among the rarest in the world. A limited number were printed from a single plate and issued on September 21, 1847. The stamps sold before it was realized that the words printed on them should have been *Post Paid* not *Post Office*. Many of these stamps were sent out by the wife of the Governor of Mauritius for a ball she was holding. In 1993, two of the stamps sold for nearly four million dollars."

"Four million," Commander West said as he stared at Bradford.

"Listen," Bradford said, holding up his hands. "I've no record of any invitation or stamp. Someone else stole it. If it wasn't you, it could have been Sam Wong."

"You're right. I thought of him, too. But we checked it out."

"We?" Commander West said.

My photographer spoke up. "I'm not really a photographer. I'm Detective Salvatore Perini from the fraud and bunco unit. When Mrs. Farrell told me of her suspicions, I investigated. I discovered a Mauritius stamp had been sold to a Gary Guster in North Carolina. I called and sure enough. He identified you, Mr. Monroe."

"Anyone could use my name."

"Remember the picture I took of you the other day with the Mulgraves? The one by the turtle exhibit," I said. "I sent that to Detective Perini who in turn sent it to Gary Guster. Mr. Guster said he traveled up here to buy it from you. There's no mistake."

Detective Perini handed me his camera and grabbed his handcuffs from under his jacket. "Bradford Monroe, you are under arrest for—"

"Please," Commander West interrupted. "Not here. Not now. I need time to explain this to my donors. Can you walk him outside, and put the handcuffs on there?"

"Sorry. It's against regulation."

"He doesn't have a gun, and it's only a few feet from the door." I pleaded, sympathizing with Commander West's plight.

Detective Perini smiled. "Okay. I don't think he can get very far." Facing Bradford, he said, "Walk in front of me, and don't try anything funny."

Several guests were beginning to stare in our direction. Wanting to shield Commander West from inquiries before he knew the entire story," I said, "Let's go outside, and I'll explain everything, so you can tell your donors the truth and do damage control."

As we stepped outside, I glanced ahead and gasped. Bradford Monroe was running away from the house with Detective Perini on his tail.

"He's trying to escape," I yelled. Commander West and I ran toward them.

Perini overcame Bradford and tackled him to the ground.

"He thought he could outrun me." Perini handcuffed his prisoner.

"Of course," I said, remembering the awards on the walls in Bradford's office. "He was a track star."

"That's funny," said Perini as he pulled Bradford off the ground. "So was I."

"Will you also be able to charge him with murder?" I asked. "Is there enough evidence?"

"My God!" Commander West exclaimed. "Who did he murder?"

"Jack Patterson and Katie Chandler," Detective Perini answered. He turned, now facing me. "It's a small world. It seems that Bradford Monroe and your mother's ex-fiancé, Paul Andre, go back a long way. But I'll fill you in more on that later. Paul turned state's evidence. He was the go-between that arranged for Bradford to meet with Gary Guster."

"Paul knew about the murders?" I sucked in my breath.

"Paul asked Bradford how he acquired the stamp. Bradford bragged about committing the murders.

Commander West sighed. "Boasting has always been Bradford's downfall. You would think a scammer would avoid having his picture taken and not actively seek personal publicity."

Detective Perini shrugged. "It's ego. Scammers like Bradford think they are smarter than everyone else. They don't believe they will ever get caught.

"I understand why he killed Katie," the commander said. "But why Jack? What did he have to do with this?"

"Let me offer a theory," I said. "Jack Patterson and Bradford Monroe both worked together at the Throckbrush Academy—Jack as a teacher and Bradford as development officer. During Bradford's time there, the academy inherited the estate of a wealthy industrialist, which included a valuable coin collection. The disgruntled, disinherited brother of the industrialist claimed that a 1943 copper wheat penny, valued at nearly one hundred thousand dollars, was missing. Rumors were that a staff member at Throckbrush had grabbed it. The police narrowed it down to Bradford, but they didn't have enough evidence to charge him."

"That can't be." Commander West frowned. "I checked his references. There was no mention of this."

"There wouldn't be. Throckbrush Academy runs on their reputation. If they let it be known that a former staff member was possibly an embezzler, their ability to raise future funds would plummet. They might not even survive the scandal. The headmaster told Bradford to resign and gave him a positive review."

"Plus, since there wasn't any real proof, they would open themselves to a law suit," Detective Perini added.

"Did Jack Patterson know?" Commander West wiped the sweat off his brow.

"Yes. As a teacher at the school, he knew all about the suspicions and the investigation. Madge, the marine mammal attendant, told me that a few days before he was killed, Jack asked Katie who she had told about the invitation. I didn't know at the time what that meant. I originally thought it had to do with the invitation for the aquarium's cocktail party. Now, I realize it was the invitation to the Governor's Ball. Katie's grandmother always kept the study locked, so Jack hadn't seen the stamp until Katie showed it to him a few weeks ago. Since Jack had collected stamps as a kid, he probably suspected it might be valuable. I'm sure he researched it."

"Do you think Jack was suspicious that Bradford might steal the invitation?" Commander West asked.

"Yes. Oscar Mejas had overheard a phone conversation. Jack used the phrases, 'I knew him years ago' and 'up to his old tricks.' I can only surmise Jack was talking about Bradford Monroe."

"Paul Andre told us everything. Paul was Bradford's fence," Detective Perini said. "When Bradford confided that Jack was suspicious, Paul said there could be no deal as long as Jack was around. He couldn't take the risk. The next day Bradford contacted Paul and told him he killed Jack. Supposedly, Paul was horrified. He had expected Bradford to move onto another scam, not commit murder. For what it's worth, Paul was a scam artist, but he wasn't a killer."

A Crown Victoria careened up to the edge of the property.

"That's Detective Wolfe," Perini said. "Bradford will be charged with both fraud and murder. Since I'm with the fraud section, as a courtesy,

I called the homicide division. Wolfe and I will take Bradford Monroe into headquarters together for booking."

Wolfe emerged from his car and made his way to where we stood.

"Good work, Perini," he said, without looking at me.

"Thanks, but I have to admit, most of the legwork was done by this lady here."

Wolfe glared at me. He turned back to face Perini. "As I said, good work Detective Perini. Good police work."

Detective Perini and I exchanged glances. We both laughed.

CHAPTER FIFTY-THREE

"Wait! You can't go in there," Clara called as I made my way toward Olivia Johnson's office.

"Olivia texted she wants to see me immediately," I said.

"She's on a phone call with corporate management." Clara lowered her voice to a whisper. "It's the CEO."

It felt like tiny spiders crawling in my intestines. "This can't be good."

"Hold on. I think she's finished." Clara's intercom buzzed. "Kristy is right here. I'll send her in."

I stepped into my editor's office. Olivia rose from her chair and stood behind her desk. Her face was deadpan as usual.

"Two excellent articles, Kristy. The one on the land acquisition is especially good. The part devoted to Ruby Diamond and her drug connection really steps it up a notch."

Olivia smiled, something she rarely did. "The circulation for this issue should exceed our expectations. Corporate management is pleased."

"Pleased enough to stop the merger?" I asked.

Olivia shrugged. "It's all about the bottom line. By the way, your advertising idea is working. Our new advertising manager has contacted a local businesses. Several have expressed interest in appearing in *Animal Advocate*. One is the Mulgrave Auto Dealership. I understand the Mulgraves are big supporters to the aquarium."

Olivia smiled. "If we keep circulation up and the ads keep coming, we may be okay. But every time corporate management calls, I hold my breath."

Olivia abruptly changed subjects. "You remember Schuyler Adams, right?"

"Sure." I said, hoping she hadn't heard me groan at the mention of the name. How could I forget Schuyler? An Ivy League graduate, he had been my major competition for the feature writer position at *Animal Advocate*. He was now back at graduate school, but I'd been told he planned to intern with us.

"Schuyler will be starting his internship here in November, and I decided to assign him to you. The next issue will feature the Heathermore Wildlife Refuge. Some animals have disappeared, and a few have been found dead. That will be your story, but Schuyler could do your preliminary research, including interviews."

"Of course," I said, smiling weakly. I liked asking my own questions, but I knew Olivia had her mind set. I wasn't sure how this would work out.

"You can leave now. Be on time for Monday's staff meeting. And when you work with Schuyler, don't forget, his dad's company is one of our biggest advertisers."

* * * * *

Abby had texted that Jillian Patterson wanted to see me. On my way home, I stopped at the horse farm. When I entered the stable, Jillian was mucking the stalls.

"I wanted to thank you, Mrs. Farrell," Jillian said as soon as she spotted me. "You saved this place from bankruptcy."

"Me?"

"You and Abby. Your daughter put me in touch with a horse rescue group. They're going to be renting space here. I'm rearranging things, and their horses will have the entire east wing. They'll be taking most of my empty stalls." She paused. "I'm giving them a good deal, of course, but their monthly payment will help me cover my costs."

"Sounds like a win-win for everyone. But Abby did that. How did I help?"

"Remember when you gave me the contact information for your accountant, and you recommended that I speak with him?"

"Yes. Was he able to help you?"

"He found out about a tax abatement for horse farms." Jillian grinned.

231

"Between the tax savings and the horse rescue group, the Patterson Horse Farm should start running in the black."

* * * * *

"Is it true the aquarium will be able to buy the twenty acres?" Abby asked. We were in the den, drinking apple cider that Matt and I had bought earlier today at a local farm stand. The two dogs and our newest addition, Gus, the Maine coon cat, were curled up near the fireplace.

I nodded. "Any negative fallout resulting from the arrest of Brad Monroe is not affecting contributions. According to Commander West, all sponsors are honoring their commitments."

"How much money will the aquarium receive from Alicia Wilcox Chandler's will?" asked Matt.

"Only three million. Calvin is still refusing to honor Katie's wish of donating the six million." I smiled. "It's his last ditch effort to help Lucien Moray acquire the land, but it won't do any good."

"Why not?" asked Jason, who had entered the room from the kitchen, carrying a bowl of "trick or treat" candy. Halloween was tomorrow, and the bowl was half empty. My family loved sweets.

After making a mental reminder note to run out to the store early in the morning to replenish the candy supply, I answered Jason's question. "Because the aquarium doesn't need the extra money to reach their goal. The aquarium inherited Katie's estate which includes the Mauritius stamp. That's worth—"

"But the aquarium doesn't have the stamp," Abby interrupted. "Gary Guster bought it. He owns it now."

"No, he doesn't," her lawyer boyfriend said. "When Gary bought the stamp, he purchased stolen property. He has no legal right to it."

"Jason is correct, Abby. Detective Perini told me the stamp will be returned to the aquarium after it's used as evidence. Commander West has several potential buyers lined up."

"Even if the case drags on, the aquarium can get a loan with the stamp as collateral," Matt added as he threw extra logs on the fire. "Don't forget the sale of Katie's house. That will bring in more revenue."

"And the million Katie inherited from her grandmother goes to the aquarium, right? Abby asked.

"Absolutely. Katie left all she owned to the aquarium. If you add that to the sponsorships, which I understand are piling up, the aquarium will reach its goal." I smiled again. "Bradford may be a crook, but he was a great fund raiser."

Abby grabbed a mini chocolate bar from the candy bowl. She frowned while unwrapping it. "He's more than a crook, he's a murderer. Does anyone know how Paul Andre and Bradford Monroe hooked up?"

I nodded. "I spoke with Detective Perini today, and he told me the whole story. Bradford and Paul both lived in Philadelphia at the same time—"

"Jack Patterson was there, too, right?"

"Yes. Jack and Bradford both worked at the Throckbrush Academy. Paul was an art appraiser with an office in the city."

"He really was a legitimate art appraiser?" Abby shook her head in apparent disbelief.

"That part of his story is true. He was not, however, an ethical appraiser. He would underestimate merchandise, purchase it at far less than it was worth, and then sell at a huge mark-up."

"As an appraiser, he shouldn't be purchasing it for any amount," Jason said.

"You're so right. Anyway, when Throckbrush Academy inherited the coin collection, Bradford took it to Paul for an appraisal. Bradford had conducted research and had a general idea of what the collection was worth, but to sell it for Throckbrush, he needed a professional appraisal. He found Paul through an online advertisement and chose him because his appraisal rate was the lowest in town."

"Of course it was low." Jason scowled. "He wanted to lure in customers so he could swindle them."

"Exactly. Paul tried to pull a fast one with Bradford. He appraised the coins at way undervalue. Then he made an offer to buy."

"But Bradford didn't sell because he knew these coins were worth more, right Mom?"

"He confronted Paul. But instead of reporting the scam to the police, Bradford made a deal with the devil."

"I'm guessing that's when Bradford and Paul went into business together." Abby shook her head.

I nodded again. "A tag team con operation. Meanwhile, a wealthy Philadelphian, who had tremendous knowledge of coins, contacted Throckbrush's headmaster and expressed interest in examining the collection as a first step toward making a purchase. Since this potential buyer would have an approximate idea of the worth of each coin, Paul couldn't scam him. The coins had to be appraised correctly, so they had to figure another way to make money off the collection."

"What did they do?" Abby leaned down and scooped up Gus who was now rubbing against her leg.

"Before the wealthy Philadelphian had a chance to view the collection, Bradford stole the cooper wheat penny, the most valuable coin in the set. Paul sold it secretly. They shared the money."

"But how could Paul sell the coin without attracting attention and without leaving a visible trail?" My daughter looked puzzled.

"I'm sure he sold it to a private collector. No one would know. The coin is rare, but it's not one of a kind."

"He and Bradford assumed no one would miss it, right?"

"Yes. But that was a bad assumption. The estranged brother of the deceased remembered the penny from years ago. The police were positive Bradford was the thief because he was the only person who had been alone with the coins since the school inherited the collection. But no one could prove the penny was there in the first place. The police couldn't verify the coin hadn't been sold by Marshall Cunningham prior to his death—despite his brother's assurance that Marshall would never have broken up the collection."

Jason nodded. "A good defense attorney would have ripped apart the prosecutor's case."

"After this happened, I take it that Bradford and Paul continued their business relationship," Abby directed her question to me.

"Bradford was asked to leave Throckbrush. That's when he got the job as development officer for the aquarium. Soon after, Paul's appraisal schemes caught the attention of the Philadelphia District Attorney. Before the investigation concluded, Paul left Philly and headed to Florida where his goal was to scam wealthy widows. But he kept contact with Bradford. He realized that Bradford's work in fundraising involved socializing with people who had money—big money. When Bradford started working at the aquarium, he sent Paul a list of donors. Paul convinced the Mulgraves and other contributors to invest in his non-existent health spas. That's why Paul came to New York."

"I'm assuming Bradford got a cut of the Mulgrave's investment money?" Abby said.

"Detective Perini told me it was a fifty/fifty split."

"Did the Mulgraves and the others get their money back?"

"They did. Bradford was caught at the very beginning of the scam, before he had a chance to spend the money."

"How did Bradford come to realize the value of the Mauritius stamp?" Abby asked.

"When Katie gave Bradford a tour of her home, he saw the invitation. He realized it was from the nineteenth century, so he assumed the stamp might be worth something. He didn't know how much until he told Paul, who realized they hit the mother lode. Bradford killed Katie and stole the stamp. Again, no one would be suspicious because the only other person who realized the stamp's value was Jack Patterson."

"And he was dead." Abby sighed.

"How did Jack Patterson figure in all this?" Jason asked.

"Jack collected stamps as a kid. He'd heard about the Mauritius stamp. When Katie showed Jack the invitation, he knew the stamp was valuable. But I'm sure he didn't want to tell Katie until he researched and found out exactly what it might be worth."

"Did he eventually tell Katie?"

"I think he was killed before he had a chance. But Bradford had found out that Katie had shown the invitation to Jack—"

"And then Bradford realized he had to get rid of them both," Abby said, completing the thought.

I leaned back. "When Bradford was hired by the aquarium, Jack had confronted him and told him to stay on the straight and narrow path. Jack said since there was no definite proof of Bradford stealing the coin at Throckbrush, he wouldn't say anything to Commander West. But if anything suspicious happened concerning the aquarium, Jack would tell what he knew. Bradford realized that if the invitation went missing, Jack would accuse him of the crime. So, he killed Jack before murdering

Katie."

Matt furrowed his brow. "I find it hard to believe Katie had no idea how valuable the stamp was."

"I don't," Abby said. "I'm sure she realized a nineteenth century stamp could be worth something, but Katie was never interested in money. She wouldn't have spent time researching the stamp's value."

"I agree." My mind wandered back to the cocktail party, when Katie showed me the captain's study. "She had a room of treasures, but she only valued them as part of her heritage, not for their monetary worth."

Abby shook her head. "There's still a piece of the puzzle we haven't solved. What was the rumor that Katie heard about Jack that might explain his murder?"

I shrugged. "Katie may have heard about Jack's angry outburst. The one he had at the aquarium three days before his body was found. When he vented to Oscar. She may have made assumptions based on what happened. We'll never know."

I paused. "At least Paul Andre knew nothing about the murders until after they happened. I shudder to think that my mother dated this man."

"How's grandma?"

"I spoke with her last night. She's still upset, but she's doing better. She's planning a trip to Greece next summer to visit the village where grandpa's family is from. She's getting ready by taking a class in Greek language at the local college. Also, Marcia Silver plans to visit her this winter. Once Marcia sells her house, she's thinking of moving to Florida, perhaps in the same condo development as grandma."

"I'll bet grandma's happy at the thought of having her best friend live nearby." Abby smiled, but it quickly faded. "Will Mrs. Silver get her money back on the valuable items Paul sold?"

"It doesn't look like it. Most is gone. Paul spent the money as quickly as it came in. "Luckily, Marcia didn't lose too much. I understand some of his victims lost tens of thousands of dollars."

"What about Paul's condo? Isn't that an asset that could be sold and the proceeds distributed to his victims?" Abby asked.

"He doesn't own it. He rents a unit. I understand he's two months late on payment. And the convertible he drove in Florida is about to be repossessed."

"What about Sam Wong?" Jason asked. "What's his plan?"

"I talked to him yesterday," Abby answered as she grabbed another candy bar. I'd definitely need to replenish my "trick or treat" supply for tomorrow. "Sam's opening up a private practice, specializing in criminal law. After being falsely arrested, he wants to make sure other people's rights are protected."

"I hope he tells his clients not to allow a search without a warrant." I chuckled. "Abby, did you ever find out why he had Katie's diary?"

"He took it after her death. He wanted to read about her thoughts and feelings. I understand he took some other personal items, too—just to be close to her."

"I'm glad this is over. Let's hope things quiet down." Matt stretched out his arms and yawned. "I could use less excitement."

"But I've got exciting news," Abby grabbed her boyfriend's hand. "Jason and I are going shopping tomorrow."

I smiled. "That sounds like fun. But I don't know I'd classify that as exciting news."

Abby grinned broadly. "Oh, but it is. We're shopping for a diamond ring. Jason proposed to me last night. We're getting married."

ABOUT THE AUTHOR

A mystery fan since she read her first Nancy Drew novel, **Lois Schmitt** combines a love of mysteries with a love of animals in her series featuring wildlife reporter Kristy Farrell. She is a member of several wildlife conservation and humane organizations, as well Mystery Writers of America. Lois received 2nd Runner Up for the Killer Nashville Claymore Award for her second book in the Kristy Farrell series, entitled *Something Fishy*. Lois worked for many years as a freelance writer and is the author of *Smart Spending*, a consumer education book for young adults. She previously served as media spokesperson for a local consumer affairs agency and currently teaches at Nassau Community College on Long Island. Lois lives in Massapequa, New York, with her family, which includes a 120-pound Bernese Mountain Dog. This dog bears a striking resemblance to Archie, a dog of many breeds, featured in her Kristy Farrell Mystery Series. The third Kristy Farrell Mystery, *Playing Possum*, is coming from Encircle Publications in December, 2021.

If you enjoyed reading this book,
please consider writing your honest review
and sharing it with other readers.

Many of our Authors are happy to participate in
Book Club and Reader Group discussions.
For more information, contact us at info@encirclepub.com.

Thank you,
Encircle Publications

For news about more exciting new fiction, join us at:

Facebook: www.facebook.com/encirclepub

Twitter: twitter.com/encirclepub

Instagram: www.instagram.com/encirclepublications

Sign up for Encircle Publications newsletter and specials:
eepurl.com/cs8taP

CPSIA information can be obtained
at www.ICGtesting.com
Printed in the USA
JSHW021239111122
33016JS00001B/1